The hollow moaning came again and died into a soft whistle. Amber was sure it was the wind, but she didn't stop scanning the bush. The old cow and her companions plodded onward. There was more deadfall on the trail now. Both the cattle and Chip were repeatedly climbing over or dodging around downed logs.

Where were the others? Hadn't they noticed she was gone? "Mitch! Ben!" she called again, but only the wind answered.

Amber looked around wildly. She knew she was very close to panicking and running in circles. "Ben! Ben, help me!" she yelled and gulped for air, almost sobbing. She longed for the solid feel of him. If only his strong arms were around her now.

Chip whinnied loudly. Amber jumped and then held her breath. Another horse had answered. Another horse! Maybe there were people! Chip topped the hill in two huge lunges, scattering the cattle in front of him. They blasted out onto a level space. Amber reined him in, staring around wildly. There was a tiny log cabin and some broken-down corrals.

A door banged and suddenly Ben was running toward her on foot.

In one quick movement, Amber was off Chip and in his arms. Shaking and sobbing, she clung hard.

"It's okay." His hand stroked her hair, gently pushing it back from her forehead the way her mother used to do when she was very small. "I'm here now."

He bent toward her and the touch of his lips against her cheek sent a quiver straight to her core. With a little moan she turned her head so their lips met. That kiss, hot and sweet as honey, seemed to melt her insides.

A PALISADES CONTEMPORARY ROMANCE

Rustlers

Karen Rispin

PALISADES

PALISADES IS A DIVISION OF MULTNOMAH PUBLISHERS, INC.

This is a work of fiction. The characters, incidents, and dialogues are products of the author's imagination and are not to be construed as real. Any resemblance to actual events or persons, living or dead, is entirely coincidental.

RUSTLERS
published by Palisades
a division of Multnomah Publishers, Inc.

International Standard Book Number: 1–57673–292–4

Cover illustration by Daniel Mark Duffy/ArtWorks, Inc.
Design by Brenda McGee

Printed in the United States of America

For information:
MULTNOMAH PUBLISHERS, INC.
POST OFFICE BOX 1720
SISTERS, OREGON 97759

98 99 00 01 02 03 04 — 10 9 8 7 6 5 4 3 2 1

In loving memory of my grandfather,
Robert Nichols,
who taught me to ride a horse
and helped to disciple me.

Acknowledgments

Thanks to everyone who had a part in this book, especially Ralph Loosmore, who sold me Chip and took me on the Centennial Cattle Drive; Robbie Fyn, who told me how to "paint" a horse; Debby Lewis, who worked with me to train Chip; Lori Lawson, who helped with the manuscript; Karen Ball, who supplied opportunity and encouragement; and my family, who gave me their patience and support.

Where can I go from your Spirit?
Where can I flee from your presence?
If I go up to the heavens, you are there;
if I make my bed in the depths, you are there.
If I rise on the wings of the dawn,
if I settle on the far side of the sea,
even there your hand will guide me,
your right hand will hold me fast.

PSALM 139:7–10

Prologue

Amber fought to clear her head, but the bright lights of the emergency room still had haloes. To say she was tired was an enormous understatement, but she was needed. She would do what she must.

She scrubbed and donned her greens with quick, practiced movements. She'd barely gotten home and into bed after a thirty-hour shift when she'd been jerked from sleep by a general call-in. By the time she arrived the triage staff had finished sorting the victims of a huge expressway pileup. The area smelled of blood, vomit, and disinfectant. Those judged in imminent danger of death had already been rushed to surgery. Controlled mayhem prevailed as the staff tried to deal with the many less desperately injured victims.

Someone she didn't recognize behind their mask waved her toward a gurney. "Boy, broken leg with a gash above the knee."

Amber headed at a run in the direction in which she'd been pointed.

The boy, who looked to be five or six, blinked at her with huge blue eyes. Freckles stood out on his pale, sweating face. Tear tracks streaked his cheeks.

"I'm going to help you. Can you tell me your name?" Amber said, taking his hand.

"Danny," he whispered with obvious effort. His cold hand tightened on hers. "I want my mom."

"I know, honey." Amber had no idea if his mother was here as one of the injured or dead. Her heart went out to the child. Quickly she focused on her task. "Let's get you fixed up first, okay?" She readied a syringe with a local anesthetic. "This is going to sting for a second."

The little boy stiffened, then relaxed slightly as the pain from his leg lessened.

"That's a brave boy." Amber kept talking in a reassuring voice as she worked to set his leg, then stitch the long gash. As tired as she was, she funneled her consciousness into a tunnel of concentration. This beautiful child would not have a scar because of her work, not if she could help it.

The boy moved uneasily, making tiny moaning noises.

Amber glanced up at his face. Her eyes flew wide. "Danny! Danny, talk to me!"

The boy's eyes were rolled up, showing only whites. She checked his pulse and found it weak and thready. Moving quickly, she checked his mucous membranes. Almost white. Shouting for help, she reached for a blood pressure cuff.

"Danny! Don't do this to me. Danny!" The child's blood pressure was horribly low. He had to be bleeding internally. In seconds another doctor was with her, and together they ran the gurney into an OR room.

Danny died under their hands.

The words barely registered when the other doctor told Amber that Danny might not have been saved even if she had realized immediately what was happening. After scrubbing off his blood, she went home, moving like a badly oiled machine. By the time she walked into her apartment she was shaking so hard she nearly dropped her keys. She ran for the bathroom and was violently ill.

Then she began to cry. Not gentle tears, but gut-wrenching, soul-shattering sobs. She had killed that child. She had calmly stitched his leg while he bled to death inside. Feeling again his small, cold hand holding hers, her stomach heaved once more. His hand had been so cold. Why hadn't she paid attention?

Suddenly Capi, her roommate, was there with her arm around her. "Amber! You look terrible. What's wrong?"

Amber took a deep, shaky breath and said in a hoarse whisper, "Capi, I killed him."

Capi took a look into her face and then wrapped her arms around Amber's shoulders for a long moment. She murmured soothing words as she patted Amber's back. After a few minutes, she went into the kitchen to get a glass of water. She held Amber's hands around the glass.

Amber's teethed chattered against the side of the glass as she drank. Slowly, and stopping often to swallow tears, she told her friend what had happened. Capi held her tightly and listened without saying a word.

"I can't call myself a doctor!" Amber said finally. "I didn't see what was happening."

"You said the triage people already missed the fact he was bleeding inside."

Amber shook her head. "So what? I should have known. I should have looked more carefully, checked again. How can I be a doctor if I make mistakes? I can't!"

Capi tried to comfort her, but Amber refused to listen. Finally Capi left her alone, telling her to let her know if she needed anything.

For the rest of the day Amber lay curled into a ball on her bed and stared at the wall, unable to sleep. All she knew was that her dreams of medicine were gone forever. Snuffed out, just as Danny's life had been.

One

It was a blistering day in May. The old Chevy Impala that Amber Lacey was driving had no air-conditioning. Its engine was running hot from hauling a horse trailer, and gusts of heated air washed back over her arm. Her eyes blinked shut for an instant, then snapped wide open as she realized she'd almost been asleep at the wheel. She forced her body upright and concentrated on the road.

After two days of nearly nonstop travel, she felt as worn as the beater she was driving.

She glanced at the map held down by a half-full bottle of warm Coke. She was about an hour out of Calgary, Alberta, and two hours from the mountains. Almost there.

Amber ran her fingers through her hair, hit unfamiliar tangles, and wrinkled her nose in disgust. She couldn't ask for a job looking like this. The muscles in her jaw clenched. She had always tried to do things well—academics, competing at riding, anything that came to hand. Now she felt like a rag doll left out in the rain. Fatigue lay across her shoulders, an aching weight.

Broke or not, she had to find a place to rest and clean up. A provincial campground on the map looked about ten minutes south of the highway. Twice she'd been turned away from campgrounds because she had the horse with her. Maybe out here in ranch country…

"God, please let me stay there," Amber said, then shut her teeth with a snap. A wave of grief closed her throat and she struggled for breath. Tears blurred her vision. She swiped at them with the back of her hand. Why should God care where she stayed the night? He'd let her fail when it really mattered.

A Bible verse came sharply to mind: "My God will supply all your—"

Amber shook her head violently. It wasn't easy to get rid of a lifetime of learning. The hurt kept coming back. God had betrayed her.

Amber turned south toward the campground taking deep breaths, trying to relax the tightness in her chest. She wouldn't cry, not again. Amber had always had close friends, but she'd told none of them where she was going. Now she felt desperately alone. She couldn't call anyone. They'd try to make her go back. She lifted her chin and focused on the road ahead.

The turnoff for the campground was across a bridge. Amber took the corner slowly to make it easy for the horse in the trailer. Her hands tightened on the wheel as she approached the gate, but no one stopped her. She drove to the very end of the little winding road and parked in the most secluded spot she could find.

As she climbed out of the car, a light wind pushed her sweaty hair off her face. She took a deep breath and looked at the trees overhead. The leaves on the poplars had the translucent glow of spring. Sticky golden bud covers littered the ground. Amber stretched luxuriously.

Natural beauty had always been like a healing drug for her. She pulled one foot up behind her, then the other. She was used to her body being lithe and supple, but now her muscles felt like half-hardened play dough. What she needed was a shower, lots of sleep, and then a good workout.

Breathy nickering sounds came from inside the trailer. Chip was asking for food and attention. She went to the back of the trailer, then stopped and rubbed her face hard. She'd better be fully alert before she handled Chip. The three-year-old was a big, excitable horse.

Amber had wanted the colt ever since she'd seen him at Joe Wilton's place. Last summer Amber had befriended the old man, an eccentric who lived near her uncle. Chip had been what Joe called a 'catch colt.' A neighbor's thoroughbred stallion had gotten out and impregnated one of his Belgian mares. Joe had no use for the spooky colt but had taken a dislike to the neighbor who tried to get him to sell the animal. Instead Joe let the colt run in pasture. To Amber, Chip looked amazingly good for a random cross. He had the conformation and movement of a European sport horse. It had bothered her to see a good horse unappreciated and untrained. Joe tried to give Chip to her. As a medical resident, Amber hadn't had time for a young horse. The first thing she'd done when she'd quit medicine was to go and get Chip.

As she opened the trailer door, she could feel her heart pounding. For a few seconds she'd be at the big animal's mercy. She took a deep breath and slid in alongside talking softly to reassure him. Joe Wilton had given Chip almost no handling.

"Back, back up, boy." The white of fear showed around the young horse's eyes. If he spooked and leapt forward, Chip would knock her down under his hard and pounding hooves.

"Back up, come on, boy, you can do this."

This time the horse stepped backwards, shaking slightly as he felt for the drop to the ground. He was trusting Amber, but still very anxious. Outside, Chip's head went up. His nostrils flared as he snorted big blasts of air from this new place.

Working with the horse was good. It took total concentration. There was no time to think about anything else. Amber put up three metal panels, making a light, temporary corral on one side of the horse trailer, and released Chip into the enclosure. Her arms, stiff with driving, ached as she lifted half a bale of hay out of the storage compartment on the trailer. She hesitated, glancing into the compartment. The hay she held in her arms was the last, and she was out of money.

"So I didn't plan very well. I'm tired. I'm scared. So what? There is no way I'm going back." She would train this horse, and she would get work outside where the air was clean and didn't smell of death. In the upheaval of her life, Amber held on to Chip as if he were the key to her survival.

She tugged her tent out of the backseat of the car. The black plastic poles seemed to fight her as she put it up. After stuffing her sleeping bag into the tent, she ended up lying on top of the bag. Her entire body instantly relaxed like a deflated inner tube.

The next thing Amber knew it was pitch black out. She was aching with cold and completely disoriented. Even though it had been hot in the day, the temperature was below freezing now. It took her a few seconds to realize she must have slept for hours. Shivering violently, she managed to get out of her shoes and into the sleeping bag.

Almost instantly she was asleep again.

"Hello! Hello the camp!" A male voice jerked her out of sleep. Morning sun on the yellow tent lit it like a lightbulb. Amber squinted and tried to make sense of her surroundings.

"Hello! Your horse is out of his pen."

Amber thrashed wildly to get out of her sleeping bag. She could imagine Chip spooking, running through other people's camps and into the bush. The tent collapsed on top of her as she fought to escape.

"Hey! Take it easy."

She shot into the sunlight. Barefoot in the cold dirt, she swung to face the man who'd been speaking. "Where is he? Where's Chip?"

"If Chip is the horse, I just tied him to your trailer. Spooky character, isn't he?"

Amber turned to see Chip watching her. She swung back.

The man was in his twenties. A little more than six feet tall, he had amused brown eyes and sun-streaked, caramel-colored hair. Suddenly she was aware of how she must look, dirty, slept-in clothing and all. She tried to run her fingers through her hair and they stuck in the curly tangles. There she was, in front of her collapsed tent with her hand stuck to her head. The twinkle in the man's eyes intensified.

Suddenly the funny side of it hit her and she was giggling.

The man lost it entirely and doubled over laughing. He pointed helplessly at the tent and gasped, "You should have seen..."

His laughter was contagious. How the tent must have heaved and bumped as she thrashed to get out. Her laughter built until it was perilously close to hysteria or tears. The last couple of weeks had been too much. Through blurred eyes she could see that the man had stopped laughing and was watching her. She took a deep breath and tried to steady herself. After a few seconds she was able to speak.

"Thanks for catching my horse for me." The laughter had created an intimacy between them that Amber felt as a kind of pressure. They were both suddenly very sober.

"I saw the trailer and pen. Two of the panels were down." He was watching her with concerned eyes.

"I must have been too exhausted to put the panels together properly. Sorry about that. Did he spook and wreck anything?"

"No. I was unloading firewood and he turned up snorting at me from about ten feet away. I had to move slow and easy to catch him. I didn't know they let people keep horses in the campground."

"I don't know if they do." His eyes were too concerned. They seemed to look right into her. She turned away from him, wishing he would go now.

"Do you need help?" he asked.

Amber shook her head.

"Um, look, if you do need—"

"Thanks for catching my horse, but I'm okay, really." She could feel his eyes on her, but she wouldn't look at him.

"Okay, I'll go. Hope the rest of your day goes better." His footsteps crunched away.

She looked up to see him almost out of sight. "Thanks for your help," she called. His arm went up in a wave. She caught a last glimpse of his face and he was gone. Amber let out a shaky sigh and headed for a much needed shower.

An hour later Amber was packed and on the road. She was more than slightly hungry and her insides quivered with nerves. In Wranglers and a sweater, she'd done her best to look competent and confident. Involuntarily she found herself wishing the guy who'd helped her this morning could see her cleaned up. She shook her head as if she could shake that thought out of it. Attention from a man was not what she needed. What she did need was a job.

As she drove, she came into the foothills, rich grassland swathed with darker bands of pine and spruce. The leaves on the aspens were only as big as a squirrel's ear. Snow still lay in the shelter of trees. Gray willows lined clear trout streams. Behind it all, the jagged ice and stone of the Canadian Rockies dominated the western sky.

If she had to lose everything else she'd valued, at least this was the kind of place where she wanted to be. Looking at the mountains, she let the car slow down and pulled to a stop at the side of the road. The peaks lifted their heads against the clear blue sky. Their beauty was as clean and powerful as gleaming steel. She flung open the car door and stood, opening her arms to the mountains and the wind. She spun with her arms out, dizzy in the cool, bright air.

A pickup truck swept past her. She had a split-second impression of a man's face giving her a quizzical look. It looked like the guy at the campground. No way, that had to be her overactive imagination. She stared after the truck, biting her lower lip. Whoever it was had seen her spinning like a crazy thing. She took one last long look at the mountains and climbed back into the car. Checking her directions, she realized she was very near her destination.

Capi Cloud, Amber's roommate in Toronto, had told her about the Miller Ranch in Alberta. She'd said her brother had worked there and kept his own horse with him. Capi's directions to the ranch had given her an objective that let her shift her inner flight into physical movement. In her mind it became the ideal refuge, a place where she could work outside and train Chip.

The springs of the old Chevy thunked as it waddled through the spring potholes in the driveway to the Millers' ranch buildings. Amber's hands were clammy on the wheel. She didn't know the Millers, and they had no idea she was coming. She drove slowly, looking at the churned-up ground, dirty ice on the north sides of the buildings and muddy bawling cattle. This was no ideal destination, but the gritty reality of a working ranch. No matter how nervous she was, she needed this job. Amber lifted her chin and stopped next to the largest house.

A big man who looked to be in his fifties was beside a stack of square bales near a corral.

He glanced at her, nodded, and went on with what he was doing. A yellow cat sitting on top of the stack watched with interest while the man forked flakes of hay over the rails. Three muddy quarter horses squealed and kicked, each trying to be first. Deliberately he placed three piles of hay more than kicking distance apart. With the horses eating contentedly, he walked toward her.

"I'm Gordon Miller," he said, holding out a square callused hand. "Can I help you?"

"I hope so. Are you in charge here?"

"Was last time I looked. What can I do for you?"

"Um, I'm hoping you can give me a job. I'm Amber Lacey. A friend told me you always hire for the summer. Her brother worked and kept a horse here two summers ago."

Gordon Miller looked past her at the horse trailer and the old Chevy. "You've worked with horses?"

"I compete at eventing."

Gordon shook his head. "The work we have is hard, dirty work, long hours, mud, mucking out barns, not much riding fancy clean horses in arenas."

"I'm not afraid of hard work."

He was still shaking his head. "I feel bad that you've obviously driven a long way to hear something you didn't want to hear. I was just heading in for dinner. I'd be honored if you'd come and join us."

At the thought of food, Amber's mouth watered. "Are you sure? I wouldn't be imposing?"

Gordon Miller smiled as if she'd said something funny. "No, you're welcome. Hanna and I don't turn many away. Besides, I'm sure Hanna cooked more than double. Ben and Julie, our grown kids, are going to be home for dinner."

Amber looked back at the trailer. Gordon caught the look and jerked his elbow toward the stack of bales. "Help yourself if the beast you have in there needs feeding."

"Oh, thank you," Amber said, moving toward the bales.

Gordon stopped her, motioning at an empty corral. "Put the horse in there. I'll get some feed."

By the time Amber had Chip out of the trailer, Gordon was cutting the strings on another bale. Out in the open, the young horse hesitated with his head high. Seeing the other horses, he let out a whinny that shook his entire body.

"You okay?" Gordon Miller asked, watching the young horse prance, jerking on his lead shank as Amber fought for control. Amber nodded and made Chip travel in tight circles until he calmed down. After they'd left Chip with food and water, Amber watched Gordon for some reaction. If he liked the way she'd handled the horse, maybe he'd change his mind and hire her.

She was convinced that he could if he wanted to, but Gordon said nothing to her as they walked to the house.

"Hanna! Julie!" he called. "I brought company."

A tall woman with a pleasant face came out of the kitchen wiping her hands on a towel.

Following her was a slight girl about Amber's age.

"My wife, Hanna, my daughter, Julie. This is Amber Lacey. She came looking for a job."

Hanna stepped forward and shook Amber's hand warmly. Julie gave a little wave. She had very short, dark hair and bright interested eyes.

"A friend of mine, Capi Cloud, told me you hire extra people in the summer," Amber explained.

"Cloud?" Hanna said. "Your friend must be Shane Cloud's sister then. How is he doing? Has he finished his engineering degree?"

Hanna's voice was warm and interested. She was obviously the kind of woman who remembered people and cared about what happened to them. Amber's hopes rose. "Capi told me

Shane is working in Texas now with an oil company. He's doing well."

Hanna suddenly looked past Amber and held out both hands. Amber swung around.

With a start she recognized the man from the campground. For a split second she hoped he wouldn't recognize her, but the laughter in his eyes killed that hope.

"Ben," Hanna was saying, "I'd like you to meet Amber Lacey. Amber, this is our son, Ben."

Two

Amber felt the hot pressure of a blush creep up her neck. It *had* been the man from the campground in that pick-up truck that passed her. He'd been on his way here.

Ben gave her a wide grin. "We've already met. I liked your hair better this morning."

Amber realized her mouth was open, and shut it quickly.

"What are you talking about?" Julie asked, looking with alert eyes from her brother to Amber.

"Food's ready," Hanna said. "We can talk at the table. Amber, if you'd like to wash your hands, the bathroom is down the hall."

Amber fled. She stared at herself in the mirror as she tried to regain some poise. Her image looked normal: thick, curly strawberry blond hair around a thin, freckled face, light brows and lashes. People said she was pretty, but Amber could never see it. Her green eyes were always big, but now they looked huge. Why did Ben have to turn up here of all places? She took a deep breath, ran a brush through her hair, and rejoined the family.

Ben pulled out her chair with a flair. She was very aware of his nearness.

"We always say grace before meals," Gordon Miller said. "Ben, would you do the honors?"

Ben bowed his head and very simply thanked God for the food. Hearing Ben pray gave Amber a hollow feeling in the pit of her stomach. She envied him his calm confidence. To Amber's relief no one talked much as they ate. The tender roast beef and dark gravy filled the air with rich smells. Amber had to force herself to slow down. Her whole attention was still on the food when Gordon said, "Ben, where did you meet Amber?"

Amber steeled herself. It was one thing to laugh with someone and another thing entirely to be laughed at.

"Amber was at the Carsland campground. I was out at Sid Crane's place and he asked me to drop off a load of firewood at the campground for him. You could say her horse introduced us."

Amber waited. Ben looked at her with a teasing twinkle in his eyes, but he said nothing else. Julie laughed. "Come on, Ben, there's more to it than that. What was that bit about hair?"

"Julie, don't pry," Hanna said, and Amber let out her breath in relief. Anywhere else, she would have enjoyed the laugh of telling the story herself. Here, she stayed silent. Telling Gordon Miller that she'd been careless enough to let Chip get loose didn't seem like a good idea, not if she wanted a job.

"Dad said you're looking for work," Ben said, as if echoing her thoughts.

"Yes, I am. I need to find a place to work where I can keep my horse. Capi said Shane kept a horse here." She looked straight at Gordon Miller. "I'm not afraid of hard, dirty work."

Gordon shifted uncomfortably. "I can't hire you, Amber. We've already got our help. Sharon and Alvin Kinvig will be here all year. They've moved into the other house on the yard. Even without Ben and Julie, we're all set."

"I see." Amber kept her face blank to hide a rising feeling of panic.

Hanna had brought in dessert. She began to talk to bridge the awkward moment. "Julie is going to be working for a rock-climbing outfitter in the mountains this summer, and Ben's gone into partnership with Doc Watson, our local vet."

"Ben likes to pretend he's a vet." Gordon's weathered face had creased into a grin.

"Hey, any more talk like that and you can shoe your own horses this afternoon," Ben protested. "You don't even pay me for farrier work."

"But then you're not a farrier." Gordon helped himself to a piece of pie.

"Just a son who knows enough to shoe a horse and will do it to save his father's aged and aching back."

"Aged! I wrench my back and you call me aged?"

"Yes, sir, and I'll come take care of you in your dotage whenever you need me."

"Oh, please!" Julie said, rolling her eyes.

Listening to the obvious warmth between them, Amber felt very much the stranger. She missed her own warm Christian family. She was going to have to get in touch with her parents soon. What on earth would she tell them if she didn't even have a job? She put up her chin. "Do you know any other ranches that might be looking for hired help?"

There was a pause, and then Gordon said slowly, "There are not many that would take on an inexperienced woman. Besides, most people have their help for this summer, but Ryder Niven had a help-wanted sign up by the post office. His spread is straight north of us."

Ben set down his coffee cup so hard a bit sloshed over the edge. "I wouldn't recommend that."

"Ben, Sterling Niven was a good neighbor." Gordon's eyebrows were high. "His son Ryder is an excellent horseman. We all have our own peculiarities."

"If I got work there, do you think he'd let me keep my horse with me?" Amber asked.

Gordon shrugged. "I can't see why not."

"Dad, Ryder's spread is no place for a green girl! No one Ryder hires stays for long." Ben turned to face Amber, his eyes intent. "Are you by yourself out here? Don't you have anywhere you can go?"

The meal she'd eaten lay like a hot lump in her stomach. There was no way she could answer Ben. Amber stood up. "Thanks for feeding me and my horse. I've really enjoyed meeting you. I'd better be going now."

Again Hanna stepped into the breach. "We were glad to have you. Amber, listen, if you ever need a place to stay, you're welcome here."

Hanna's voice sounded as if she meant it. Amber looked away. She needed a job, not charity. "Thanks. Like I said, I'd better be going."

"I'll come help you load your horse." Ben shoved his chair back.

Outside the temperature had dropped. Wind swirled around the house blowing curly tendrils of hair into Amber's face. She shivered and walked rapidly toward Chip's corral. Ben stepped in front of her. The impact of his direct hazel eyes stopped her in her tracks. He reached a big hand toward her, then dropped it. "Look. I'm sorry I got in your face. I realize what you do should be none of my business. Still, I wish you wouldn't go to Ryder Niven's place."

Amber shoved her hair back impatiently. She was already scared enough. What was Ben trying to do? It bothered her that she was so aware of his physical presence. It bothered her even more that she felt a kind of connection with Ben. "What is it to you? For all you know I might be a divorced transvestite."

Ben laughed. "You're no transvestite. I don't know if you're divorced or not. Are you?"

She made a quick impatient gesture. "No, not married,

either. Now that you know all about me, will you move?"

Ben hesitated, and then moved out of her way. In the corral Chip dodged her, dashing around in a high springy trot with his mane and tail flying. Ben stepped into the corral. "Change in weather always makes a young horse goofy."

"And his owner look like a fool?" Amber asked.

"Hey, I didn't say that." Ben placed himself so that Chip hesitated against the fence and Amber was able to walk up to the horse. Ben stood still, holding Chip by his presence as Amber slid the halter slowly over the horse's ears.

"Thanks," she said. "Look, about Ryder Niven, I really do need a job. Your dad didn't seem all that worried. I'm going to go there and ask."

"Do you at least have a good jacket? This is northern high country. It's been known to snow every month of the year and today isn't looking good."

"I'll dig it out when I get there." She led Chip toward the trailer. Ben opened the door then moved behind the horse to encourage him to load without fuss.

"Uh, thanks again for your help," Amber said as she climbed into the Chevy.

"Any time."

As Amber pulled away, in her rearview mirror she could see Ben standing in the road looking after her.

Ben stood ignoring the cold until his father came up beside him. "Quite the woman," Gordon said. "She'd probably be reasonably useless as a ranch hand, but I almost wish I could hire her. It's that good to see you interested. You've been punishing yourself for too long."

Ben looked at his father. "That's what you thought? Dad, I

haven't been punishing myself, I've been getting things straight, learning to walk with God."

Gordon shook his head. "Then you've got a monastic streak in you a mile wide."

"Maybe it just takes time to heal. The night Trevor Birch died was a wake-up call, but man, it hurt." Ben hunched his shoulders and half turned his back. "I haven't talked much about it, but it still hurts. I was such an idiot, drinking, then getting myself beat up over a woman who didn't care beans about me."

"Don't be too hard on yourself. That girl was playing you like a trophy fish, had you doing things you never would have done."

"What I did was my choice." Ben's voice was rough. "Then Trevor Birch, drunk as he was, tried to give me a ride home, rolled the truck, and was killed. Me, I just ended up in the hospital. I'm no better than Trevor. I don't know why God let me live that night."

Gordon put a warm hand on his son's shoulder. "I'm glad he did, Ben. I'm not sorry this Amber Lacey turned up here today, either. You wouldn't be finding some excuse to go over to the Nivens' in the next few days just to see if she is there?"

"Maybe, but don't you start on me. Mom is bad enough." Ben's voice changed to mimic his mother's. "Ben, you need to get out more, spend some time with people your own age. When you're on the big cattle drive, make sure you meet people, have fun—"

"Your mother worries about the people she loves. You know how she is."

"Gordon." Hanna was heading toward the men with her arms full. "If Ben is shoeing the horses, he should wear this brace. I don't want him hurting his back too. Here are your jackets. Weather's coming."

"Perfect illustration." Gordon was chuckling.

"Of what?" Hanna asked, hands on her hips.

"Of how you worry in silence for your family," Gordon said.

"Hey, that's her job, isn't it?" Julie said. "Let her do it." She had followed her mother and was leaning on one of the porch posts.

Hanna stuck out her tongue at her husband and daughter, then turned to her son. "I'd feel better if you went over to Ryder's place this week. I'd like to know if Amber does get a job there. It will be better if they know someone is looking out for that girl."

Julie walked over. "How come you and Ben are so uptight about the Nivens? I mean, so Mitch is a party animal and Ryder hates people, but it's not like they're dangerous or anything. I know I've been away at school. Is something going on I don't know about?"

"Not that I know of." Gordon Miller had finished buttoning his worn fleece-lined denim jacket. "If we're going to get these horses shod, we'd better get to work."

"I've been working," Julie said. "Mom and I finished the dishes and cleaned the whole kitchen. I've got to get into Calgary to pick up some stuff. See you later." She ran for her car.

"See you!" Ben called, then turned to open the big machine-shed doors. Stinging rain had begun to fall, so they'd work in shelter. As his father caught the horses, Ben drove the huge Massy tractor out. Then he sorted through the dusty horse-shoes, choosing the sizes to fit their riding horses.

Why hadn't he spoken to his father about the Nivens earlier? Still, there was no way he could have known what would hap-pen today. He shook his head, still surprised at his strong reac-tion to Amber Lacey. If he had spoken earlier, maybe she wouldn't be on her way to the Nivens' place. Maybe he was wrong and there was nothing to worry about. Ben ran his thumb over the edge of the hoof knife, testing its sharpness.

"You still on call?" Gordon asked, leading a chestnut mare into the building.

"Calving season is over now, so it's not quite as bad. At least I got to eat dinner with you. What do you bet I don't get all three horses done?"

"Any you manage are that many less for me to do." Gordon took a good grip on Candy's halter shank. "This old girl can be a pig to shoe." Cold wind swirled through the open door as the first raindrops splattered onto the shed's metal roof.

"You know, Amber Lacey doesn't make sense to me," Gordon said slowly. "She talked about competing in eventing. Both that and the classy colt mean money, especially if she's from back east. But I think she was really hungry, and I don't think she has feed for that colt."

"Whoever she is, I wish you hadn't told her about the Nivens."

"She'd have heard that Ryder was hiring if she asked around at all. I don't think she'll get work though. Ryder is looking for a housekeeper and a ranch hand. I can't see him hiring a woman to work cattle, and I don't think she'll take the housekeeping job."

"She might if she's desperate enough."

"You might be right. I don't think she scares easily. She's not a bit afraid of that big colt of hers."

Candy tried to jerk her foot out of Ben's hand. "Stand still. You old boot!" Ben grunted and held on, pitting powerful muscles against the mare's jerks and lunges. In a few seconds the mare realized she wasn't going to get her foot loose and stood still.

Ben started to clean her hoof. Without looking around he said, "Larson had me vet three fancy paints he said he'd bought at auction down in Medicine Hat. He said Mitch Niven had brought them there to sell. The pigmentation on one of the geldings was really odd."

For a long moment there was only the sound of the rain and the scraping of Ben's hoof knife. "So, you think there's something wrong at the Niven place." Gordon's voice sounded tired. "I wondered why you were so emphatic at dinner. Did you say anything to Larson?"

"No, I'm not that certain. I've been wondering where they got the money for the new house the way beef prices are." Ben was now working his way around the mare's hoof, trimming it with a pair of plierlike nippers.

"It's all speculation then. I don't like the way you're thinking, Ben."

"I don't either, but I think Mom's worried too." The raspy sound of a file filled the silence as Ben smoothed the edges of the hoof.

Gordon took his time before he answered. "I'll ask her, but I doubt she's worried the way you're talking about. She's been praying over Ryder for years, Mitch too. She frets about them. I figure she's made them sicker in her mind than they are. There's hundreds no worse than Mitch. Ryder is odd, but he's been coping just fine. Now she's fretting about this Amber Lacey being there, same as you are. Maybe Amber will go home to wherever she came from."

"I hope so," Ben said, and was startled by the sudden empty feeling in his stomach.

Three

The heater on the Chevy didn't work. Amber rubbed her arms and looked at the Nivens' ranch gate. She'd been sitting there for almost half an hour trying to gather the courage to go through that gate. The ranch buildings in the distance looked harmless enough. If only she'd asked Ben what was wrong about working for Ryder Niven. Why didn't he want her here?

Amber twisted in her seat and looked back toward the way she'd come. She could drive away, look for another job where she could keep her horse, but she was out of feed and money now.

She didn't have much gas left, either. Amber swallowed hard and shoved the car into gear.

The Texas gate buzzed under the car then under the trailer. In the farmyard, a huge house looked west toward the mountains. It was so new that the earth around it was still torn up.

Amber looked further and her face brightened. Ten very flashy paint horses were watching her with perked ears. They were splattered with mud and a bit sweaty but looked in great shape.

Gordon had said one of the men was a horseman, hadn't he? Maybe Ryder Niven was breeding paints.

Encouraged, she climbed out of her car and dug out her winter jacket. The front door of the house was well off the ground and there were no front steps. Amber began to circle the building, trying to stay out of the worst of the mud. A high, harsh, man's voice overhead brought her to a stop. "A white horse! I ask you, what am I supposed to do with a white horse?" Amber looked up to see an open window.

"Forget the white horse. Mitch already said he got it as part of a batch. Your business is to keep those paints out of sight. I don't want them in this yard again for any reason, and I want them taken care of properly. Do you hear me, Bull Schwartz?" The voice was low and vibrating with rage.

"Hey, don't get your shirt tied in a knot, Ryder," a third man said. "I asked him to trail the paints down. There's no way I'm going to haul the trailer up there in this mud."

Whatever the argument was about, it was none of her business. Amber swallowed hard and went on. Someone had laid down a couple of planks, making a path to the back doorsteps across the worst of the mud. Amber started down it as sleety drops of rain stung her cheeks.

A huge man thudded through the door and down the steps. His head was down and he was swearing loudly. Amber turned to get out of the way, but as he stomped onto the end of the plank, his weight made it buck like a seesaw. She yelped and fought to keep her balance.

The big man's head came up. He grunted and stopped just inches from knocking her off the plank. Amber found herself looking way up into small eyes set in a face like a flat shovel. A wave of foul body odor made her gag. The man completely blocked her forward view. In the house, the deep voice called, "Bull, no matter how angry you are, don't you founder that good horse on me!"

The big man was apparently called Bull. She could see why. He swung around and took several menacing steps toward the house, making the board buck. "You're trying to teach me about horses?" Bull's voice squeaked and broke. "Oh, that's sweet. You get me the horses I need and—"

"Who is that?" the deep voice bellowed, cutting Bull off.

Amber found herself facing the palest yellow-brown eyes she'd ever seen. The man in the doorway was glaring at her with what seemed to be hatred.

"One of Mitch's doxies?" Bull suggested.

Amber lifted her chin. "I'm no one's doxy! I came because I heard that the Nivens were looking for hired help. Is one of you a Niven? I've worked with horses."

"I'm Ryder Niven." It was the man with the pale angry eyes. "I suppose you figure you can be a ranch hand. You've worked cattle, roping, branding, castrating?"

Amber shook her head negatively.

"How about vaccinating and artificial insemination? No? Then I don't suppose I could use you as a cowhand. Besides, I just hired Lyle Smith for that position. I've got no other job to do with horses."

It was raining harder now and Amber was getting wet through her jacket. Shivering, she turned slowly to leave.

"Hey, I didn't say I don't have a job for you," Ryder said. "Do you know how to cook and clean? We need a housekeeper."

Amber stopped. *A housekeeper?* A second ago she'd been afraid because she had no job, no way to feed herself and her horse. If she hadn't had Chip, she would have walked away from those hateful eyes in a moment. Slowly she turned to face Ryder.

"Yes, I can cook and clean."

"Make supper and we'll see." He spun on his heel.

"Wait! I have a horse. Unless I can keep him here with feed and board as part of my wage, there's no point in me cooking your supper. I need good quality feed and stabling and time to work with him."

"If you stay, the horse can too. We eat at five o'clock. It'll be me, my brother, and the cowhand." Amber wondered if Ryder sounded slightly less hostile or if that was her imagination. He turned and went into the house.

"Looks like you got yourself a job," Bull said. "We wouldn't want the little lady to get her feet dirty, would we?" To Amber's relief, he stepped off the board and out of her way.

"Thanks," she said and headed into the house.

Inside, Ryder motioned to a passageway on the far sade of a huge living area. "The kitchen is over there." He went the other way and slammed a door behind him.

When she turned, Amber found one of the most gorgeous men she'd ever seen watching her from across the room. He wasn't tall, about five foot eight, but his easy grace and sensuous face reminded her of Michelangelo's *David.* He grinned and moved toward her. "So the recluse hired you, did he?"

"Recluse?" Amber began to pull off her soaked jacket.

"The elder Niven, the Niven that owns this place, the Niven who wants to remain alone in his castle." He made the last phrase a good imitation of the narrator in an old horror movie.

Amber laughed. "In that case, who are you?"

"Me? You have the honor to be in the presence of Mitch Niven." He leaned back, thumbs hooked in his jeans pockets. "Bulldogger, bronc rider, and all-around party animal. For a good time, apply within."

Amber rolled her eyes at the obvious come-on. "Excuse me," she said, shoving her wet hair off her face. "I've got to get my suitcase out of my car and change into some dry clothes."

Outside the rain had turned to sleety snow. By the time Amber got back she was shivering violently. Mitch was still leaning against the wall, obviously waiting for her.

"Seems you're learning some things about mountain weather." His grin was engaging. "I'll show you your room and we'll see if you dry off as pretty as you look wet."

When she came back down, Mitch followed her to the kitchen, flirting audaciously. The kitchen was a greasy mess. Mitch didn't offer to help but leaned against the fridge and talked, teased, and told stories as Amber dug into the work. It didn't take a genius to figure out that Mitch wasn't someone you'd trust with your little sister. He wasn't the sort of person Amber would ever date seriously, but Mitch Niven was fun, and Amber could use a little light relief in her life. Was he the reason Ben didn't want her here? He seemed harmless enough. Maybe it was Ryder. He certainly seemed more odd than Mitch at first glance.

"So what is with your brother?" Amber asked. "You said he's a recluse."

Mitch shrugged. "He likes horses better than people."

Amber stuck the last pot into the sink and scrubbed it. "I can relate to that."

"Not like Ryder, you can't. I swear he'd turn me out in a second if he thought I'd harmed one of his animals. Besides, you're talking to me. Ryder never talks if he can help it. I doubt if you'll get more than a few sentences out of him the whole time you work here."

Amber stopped scrubbing. "So, what happened to him?"

"I don't know. He was always kind of a loner, then Mom left when he was in junior high. He's just kept getting worse."

"You run this place then?"

"Me run the ranch? Ryder'd rather die first. No, he's king here." Mitch's smile turned secretive. "At least he likes to think so."

At supper, the cowhand, Lyle Smith, turned out to be a thin, nervous person. Twice he started to say something, and both times Ryder snarled like a dog. Mitch didn't try to talk and neither did Amber. At the end of the meal, Ryder stood up abruptly. "Lyle, I put you out in the trailer for a reason. I don't want you in my house except for meals. Get outside now." He looked in Amber's direction. "Supper was okay. You stay. Wash dishes, then unload your horse and feed him."

Amber resisted the urge to throw her plate at him. Chip was hungry. Even if she left tomorrow morning, she could at least get him a bellyful of food. She stood and began clearing the table. Ryder left, his boot heels hitting the ground hard at every step.

"Mitch, your brother is a jerk." Lyle's muddy brown eyes were narrowed.

"Look. My brother isn't exactly the easiest man in the world. Just don't try to talk to him, and you'll be okay."

"I'm not taking that kind of abuse. I'll leave."

"Soft, are you?" Mitch banged both fists onto the table. "Hey Amber, you're sure prettier than Lyle. Are you tougher, or are you quitting too?"

"No, I'm not." She had no reason to trust Mitch Niven and didn't see why she should tell him she might leave as soon as she and Chip had a good feed. Amber took the first load of dishes into the kitchen and realized the door hadn't closed properly behind her.

"Look, Lyle, I got you this job." Mitch had lowered his voice, but it came through clearly. "I don't want you copping out on me. You were out of work and a total washout as a rodeo cowboy. You're not even taking any risk for the extra money you've got coming."

"Okay, okay," Lyle said in a whiny voice.

"So when Ryder is around, you shut up. Is that clear?"

"Hey, I said okay already."

Their voices receded as they left the dining room. Amber frowned. Was Mitch giving Lyle some kind of payoff or had she misunderstood? She shrugged. At least she'd get Chip fed and then see what happened after that.

That night Amber spent a long time staring at the ceiling. If the atmosphere in the house was horrible, at least Chip had landed in gravy. The corrals, shelters, and hay were all top-notch. There was even a round pen for training.

Amber turned over with a jerk. Gordon said that most ranches already had their hired help and weren't likely to hire a woman without experience.

She'd never find a job that paid enough to allow her to board Chip in the city. It wasn't like she had easily marketable skills, besides her medical training. She bit her lip. She was not going back to that.

Okay, so I'll stay here, at least for a while. I can put up with Ryder's rudeness, at least I think I can. It's better than McDonald's, and besides, training Chip at least gives me a goal, something useful to do.

Thinking of the big, glossy red-gold colt comfortable and fed made Amber feel better.

She really would have to get in touch with her parents soon. Amber's father was a diplomat, so she had lived in cities all over the world. At that moment her folks were in Kazakhstan. Regular mail was unreliable. Until now Amber had been keeping in touch by e-mail. With no computer, she couldn't do that anymore. Still, she could send a letter snail-mail and hope.

Right, I'll just say, "Dear Mom and Dad, I've left my residency and my medical career. I'm working as a cook on a ranch in Alberta. My boss has the eyes and manners of a malevolent lizard, and I'm getting paid minimum wage." Wouldn't that just make their day?

Amber turned over again, tangling herself in the sheets. She'd been lying awake for hours. The wind was whooshing and rattling around the house. She found herself thinking about Ben Miller, his smile and the way his hand had felt on her arm. She sat up with a jerk and reached to turn on the light. One-thirty in the morning; if she couldn't sleep, at least she could unpack.

Quietly she began to move jeans and sweaters from her suitcase to a set of drawers. She put up the poster print of Monet's haystacks on the wall and sat looking at the people working in the sunshine. The impressionist print had been part of her life for a long time, almost as long as she'd wanted to be a doctor. Amber shook her head. Without that goal she wasn't sure who she was, but at least the room looked more familiar. Back in bed, she fell asleep almost instantly.

The next day Amber tied her hair up and tackled the accumulated mess like it was her personal enemy. It was as if by making order in this house she could make some sort of order of her life. Outside she could see the sun shining. A strong wind shook the trees around the yard.

While she worked, she thought about calling the Millers to tell them she'd got a job.

It wasn't just that Ben was attractive, not only that anyway. It was the fact that the Millers' house felt kind of like home. The way Ben prayed, he sounded like a Christian. She shook her head and scrubbed the kitchen floor harder. When she was a teenager, she'd promised God that she'd never date a non-Christian. She'd stuck to that too. So maybe Ben was a Christian. What difference did that make now? She wasn't even sure she was a Christian anymore.

All morning she was very aware of the telephone. It seemed

to sit there like a toad, teasing her to call the Millers. She carefully walked wide of the thing each time she passed. She was working on the back hall when a sound brought her head up.

"Good girl," Ryder said as if she were an obedient dog. "I like a clean house."

Amber stifled a desire to stand, curtsey, and say, "Thank you, kind sir." Instead she managed a relatively civil thank-you. Obviously this kind of work didn't carry the status that she was used to.

"Ryder, I need to ask you about working hours. When will I be free to work with my horse?"

"I don't care what you do as long as this house is clean and the meals are on time." Already he was turning away.

It sounded as if she could choose her hours. If she worked hard there was no reason she couldn't be outside for half the day. "It's okay if I work with Chip in the afternoon then?" she asked, to double-check.

Ryder kept going. His voice rose. "I said I don't care!"

Amber went back to scrubbing with a will. She'd get all afternoon outdoors, working with a horse! She hadn't been able to do that for years.

An hour later she'd just finished vacuuming the living area when a sharp crack on the huge picture window caught her attention. She went over and looked out. Sunlight hadn't hit the west side of the house yet. The ground was shadowed and frosty. At first Amber saw nothing, then her eyes focused on a tiny brown bundle. A bird had hit the window and was lying there. Stunned on the cold ground, it could die of hypothermia.

Amber ran for the door. Gently she lifted the tiny creature and carried it to her room. She laid some paper towels in a cardboard box and shut the lid on the bird. If her luck was good, in the warm box the bird should come to and be just fine.

She hesitated, looking at the box. Her mom had called her a born healer. Everything was so tied together. She wasn't sure what pieces of herself she could keep in this new place.

Even if she was no longer officially a healer, she wasn't going to let that bird die for no reason, not if she could help it. She ran back downstairs to put the vacuum cleaner away.

Four

That afternoon Amber finished the lunch dishes, then hurried into outdoor clothes. In her room she could hear the bird fluttering in its box. Carefully she carried it outside and opened the box top. For a second the little chipping sparrow stayed huddled in the bottom, then it sprang into flight. Amber watched it disappear, then laughed and ran to Chip's corral.

"Hey boy, how you doing?"

Chip trotted over and poked his nose through the rails at her. She reached out to pat him, but he spun away, kicking and bucking with high spirits. In a few strides he settled into a floating canter. Amber grinned. What movement! This was a horse worth training.

She caught Chip and brushed him down. He was in the mood to spook just for the fun of it, but there was no meanness there. Amber left him tied and walked over to check out the round pen. She nodded in approval. Whoever built it had done a good job. The sides were more than six feet tall and solid, and it was on high ground that drained well. Amber led Chip to the pen and began to teach him to move on the lunge line.

Time flew by. Watching Chip react and trying to figure out how to make him learn left her no chance to feel lonely or astray. When she felt Chip had enough of the lunge line, Amber carried a bale of hay into the pen. Getting the young horse used to having her above and behind his head was the first step to riding.

She put the bale beside Chip and slowly stood up on it. He danced away. She moved the bale to him and tried again. On the fourth try he stayed put. With her hands, Amber rubbed his back and neck while Chip watched her, wide-eyed, turning his head one way then the other to keep her in view. His skin juddered under her touch as if he were trying to shake off flies.

Chip was finally beginning to relax when a voice just outside the corral said, "Hi, Amber." She jumped, lost her footing on the bale, and windmilled her arms. Chip lunged away and tore around the pen. Losing her balance, she fell off the bale. She scrambled up quickly and found herself facing Ben Miller.

"Watch out!" Ben said.

Amber jumped aside just in time to avoid being run over. Chip was galloping blind, panicked by the loose halter shank whipping him around the front legs. She climbed the side of the pen to get out of his way. She watched the horse. He was spooked but safe enough in the round pen. Amber climbed out of the pen and dropped down on the outside next to Ben.

"Sorry. I didn't realize you hadn't heard me." Ben's hands were out, his eyes wide and anxious. Amber found her reaction surprising. Instead of being mad, she was just plain glad to see Ben. Besides, he looked so sorry.

She laughed. "I guess this will get Chip used to loose ropes anyway." The horse tore past them; each plunging stride jerked the rope so that it slapped at his shoulders and knees. Amber knew that he would keep running until he realized the rope wasn't hurting him, but reassurance might help. She called him and kept talking calmly until he began to slow.

"If you leave him stand with the rope on, he'll get used to it faster," Ben said.

"Good idea." Amber kept her eyes on the horse. She mistrusted her positive reaction to Ben. "If you're looking for

Ryder, Ben, I have no idea where he is right now."

"Actually, I came to see if you'd gotten work here. I assume you have?"

She grimaced. "Not exactly what I was looking for. I'm Ryder Niven's cook and housekeeper."

"I didn't think he'd hire you to work with the cattle. Ryder obviously let you keep your horse here."

"I'll have afternoons to work with Chip, so it's not all bad." Chip was still trotting around the pen, but his eyes were much less frightened. Both of them watched him for a few minutes.

"He's a good-looking animal, bigger than I like, though. What are you going to do with him?" Ben asked.

"Dressage, maybe jumping."

Ben laughed. "Better you than me. I'd rather ride a bronc than go leaping walls on that tiny flat saddle."

"It's fun! How do you know if you've never tried?"

Ben just laughed. "Um, Amber, look, I was supposed to be preg-testing a bunch of Charolais cattle, but the owner canceled at the last minute. If you've got some time, I could show you a marsh hawk nest."

"A northern harrier's nest on the ground?"

"Hey, you know what it is. Not many people do. You a birder?"

"No, but my mom is," she laughed. "I don't even own binoculars, and I've never seen a hawk nest on the ground. It must be neat."

"Come on, let's go then." He hesitated. "I mean, if you want to and can get away."

Amber looked at Ben. Instead of answering she opened the gate of the round pen. Chip had stopped and watched her with pricked ears. She picked up the lead shank and rubbed Chip's arched neck. She wanted to go with Ben, but should she? Was it safe to think about getting close to someone when she had so much to hide?

She bit her lip. It wasn't as if she was pledging her life to the man. What harm could there be in spending an hour together?

"I'd love to, Ben, but I have to be back in time to make supper. Will that work?"

"I guess it will have to." Ben gestured at the horse. "There's not room for this big guy in my truck. Do you think we could maybe leave him behind, or does he always come with you?"

"Won't Chip fit in the backseat? In that case, I'll put him away and be right with you. He's had enough lesson for today." As she led the colt toward his corral, Amber couldn't stop smiling. Something about Ben Miller just made her happy.

Fifteen minutes later, Amber was bouncing down a rutted track across open grassland in Ben's truck. "Are we still on Ryder Niven's land?" she asked.

Ben answered so eagerly that Amber wondered if he hadn't been trying to think of something to say. "No, we're on Dad's land." He pointed to the north at a nearby ridge. "That's Thad's Hump. Old Thaddeus Niven's homestead is just behind it. There used to be a pretty good barn there. The border between our place and theirs is just this side of it."

"You must know the Nivens pretty well living this close."

"You could say that. My great-grandad moved to the area with Thad Niven, and our families have worked together, haying and moving cattle ever since."

Amber thought about asking Ben why he hadn't wanted her to work for the Nivens. She decided not to. It would only make things uncomfortable.

The vehicle swerved violently, throwing her against Ben. He fought the wheel, catching her in the head with his elbow.

"Dumb badger hole! Are you okay?"

She scrambled to sit up. He steadied her. Their eyes met for an intense second. Ben pulled back and grabbed the steering wheel with both hands. She could see the muscles of his throat move as he swallowed.

"I'm fine," Amber said, trying to keep her voice steady. Why was she responding to this man so strongly?

"Sorry. I should have seen that hole." Ben's knuckles were white on the steering wheel.

"I'm fine, really. Don't worry about it," Amber said.

"The harrier nest is in that hollow ahead of us. We'll have to hike a bit. I should have told you before." He brought the truck to a stop.

"I love hiking. Not that I've had many chances for a while."

"What have you been doing that's kept you from hiking?"

"Just too busy," Amber said quickly and climbed out of the truck. Ben Miller flustered her. She'd have to watch what she said. "How about you, Ben? How did you decide to be a vet?"

"I've always liked working with animals. I thought for a while about doing exotic veterinary medicine, maybe working with the park service." He hesitated. "Um, then some things changed for me and I decided that working around home was good. You're not going to find more beautiful country anywhere in the world. I know that God is present everywhere, but I feel especially close to him here. So I studied large animal medicine and came home."

His response had been so open, and she couldn't reciprocate. Amber shifted from one foot to the other. "So where's this hawk nest you were telling me about?"

"Come on. I'll show you. Yesterday one of the eggs hatched. That little hawk is covered in fluff and no bigger than a teacup."

Wind swept through the short spring grass, making patterns like waves roll across the slope. As they walked, Ben pointed out flowers: shooting star, lupine, yarrow, windflower, and bright yellow buffalo beans. The love of the wild country was warm in his voice. Ahead of them a slough wrinkled in the wind, its surface glittering like fish scales. Suddenly Amber was running, dashing for joy down the beautiful hillside.

"Hey, wait," Ben called. She could hear him thudding downhill behind her. She sped up. On the flat near the lake, long grass tripped her and she tumbled, laughing, onto the ground.

"You are one crazy lady." Ben reached out a hand to pull her to her feet. It was wide, strong, and warm, just the way a man's hand ought to be.

Something flashed across the sky and dove low over them screaming. Amber ducked. "What was that?"

"That's the male marsh hawk. We're almost there and he doesn't like us close to his nest."

The hawk circled against the blue sky, looking smooth and dapper in dove gray. There was a white band across its tail. The long wings, held slightly upward from horizontal, tilted skillfully on the wind. "He's beautiful! But I don't particularly want to get clawed."

Ben grinned. "It's more of a threat. He's not likely to actually hit us. Come on."

"Not likely? And you think I'm crazy?"

"Did I say that?" He was laughing. "We're almost there. We don't want to leave an obvious trail. Skunks and coyotes like hawk eggs and hatchlings for dinner." He took huge steps, careful not to flatten the thigh-high bushes, then reached back to help her over the thick spot. "Watch out. There's wild roses in with the buck brush."

Amber jumped as a bigger brown hawk flew up not six feet away. It dove at them, then retreated to sit with the male in a nearby tree. "That's the female?" Amber asked, stopping to watch the hawk. When she turned around, Ben had disappeared. "Ben?"

"Right here."

She pushed through the last bit of bush to find him crouched, looking at the ground. Two fluffy off-white hatchlings sat in a stick-lined hollow. She knelt beside Ben. Seeing these tiny hidden things, she felt like she'd been let into an intimate secret of the wild land.

"The second one probably hatched this morning. Look." Ben waved his hand above the nest. Both chicks flopped onto their backs. "Already they're hawks. Those little talons can do damage."

Amber's throat got tight as she looked at the tiny creatures waving absurdly huge feet in the air, ready to defend their lives. Why did God have to make everything so frail, so vulnerable to death? She turned her head away and stood up.

"You're right. It's better not to disturb them for long." He stepped away from the nest in a different direction than they'd come. They hiked back up the hill.

Near the truck, Ben turned to face her. "Amber, there's something I wanted to ask you. At dinner the other day, I thought you'd bowed your head to pray before Dad asked me to say grace. Are you a Christian?"

The words echoed in her mind, *a Christian, a Christ one, one of Christ's.*

"I guess so," she said slowly. "When I was small, I gave myself to God, asked Jesus to forgive my sins and all that. Until recently, it was a big part of my life." She looked at Ben, meeting warm hazel eyes. "I *was* bowing my head, but that was just habit. Lately it's been very hard to trust God, hard to think he's fair and loving."

Tears stung her eyes. She turned and walked away, fighting for composure. To her relief, Ben didn't follow. She stood facing the mountains taking deep breaths of cool air. In a few moments she was able to walk over to the truck where Ben was waiting.

"Sorry about that. I've got some things to work out."

Ben nodded and started the truck. Neither spoke on the way back. In Ryder Niven's farmyard, Amber thanked him.

Ben put his hand on hers. "Amber, I know things can be rough." She was shocked to see the amount of pain in his eyes. "I do know that. No matter what you've gone through, no matter how you feel, God is love, and he still loves you."

Amber gave his hand a quick squeeze and fled.

Five

Ben knew he'd have to push it or he'd be late to the Beetons'. Still, it had been worth it. He closed his right hand, gently touching his palm with his fingers. The feel of Amber's hand in his was strongly with him.

There was something special about Amber Lacey. Her delicate coloring, huge eyes, and slight frame were appealing enough, but it wasn't just that. Her soul shone through somehow.

The first time he'd seen her, she'd bolted from her tent like a startled pixie. Ben smiled. She had even been able to laugh at herself, obviously enjoying the joke. Later the same morning he'd passed her, spinning in the wind like a nature sprite, her hair flung out like a halo. He shook his head. It had seemed too good to be true when she'd turned up at his house.

The best thing was that she was a Christian. He was sure of it now. She was in some kind of trouble, that wasn't hard to figure. She was upset with God, she'd as much as said so, but Ben knew how that felt. She had strength and courage that appealed to him.

Traveling alone from job to job, Ben had formed the habit of praying aloud whenever the notion took him. "Father God, I don't know what's troubling Amber, but show her your love and forgiveness the way you did me. And God, thanks that she came here."

By the time he finished praying he was pulling into Larry Beeton's yard. He opened his truck door to the sound of more than a hundred cattle bawling. Several men on horseback were moving the last of the herd into the big holding pens.

"Just about ready for you, Ben," Larry Beeton called from atop a bay gelding.

Ben nodded, got out his gear, and headed for the chutes. He was there to do his part in the late spring checkup of a herd of grade beef cattle. Several neighbors had come over to help.

"Got a bunch of calves coming through, Grandpa," Jason Beeton's high voice yelled, just audible over the bawling of the cows and calves already separated.

Ben grinned, watching fourteen-year-old Ruthann Beeton scramble across the slick, mucky ground to swat wildly at a cow that was trying to turn back. Nothing like a family operation.

Larry Beeton stepped off his horse and, in a few deft movements, slacked the girth, removed the bridle, and tied the bay to a post. His wife, Kelly, came out of the house pulling on a pair of coveralls. Larry nodded at her. "Ready?"

"Roast is in the oven," she said. The whole group was walking over.

"Okay, John here will be branding; I'll handle the gate and ear tags; Ruthann, you figure you can do fly tags?" Ruthann nodded firmly. "Kelly, you'll do the recording. Bev will do one vaccine and Ben will do castrating and the other vaccine."

"How about that gunk you pour down their spines against lice?" Old Slim Beeton called.

"You want to do that, Dad? Or would you rather work with Jason, bringing them down to us?"

"I'll do delousing. Jason can bring them down."

"Figure you can handle that, Jason?" Larry asked.

"Da-ad," Jason said with twelve-year-old disgust.

Everyone moved to get set up for their particular task. Ben could hear Jason calling, "Come on, calfy, get in there, little calfy."

There was a compact line of calves in the run behind the

chute. The first calf hit the gate at the front of the chute. Larry slammed the bars shut behind its head with a clang, and everyone got to work.

Ben prided himself on working quickly and bloodlessly. Still, it was messy and strenuous work.

Everyone got a good laugh when one of the calves threw its head while Ruthann was clipping on the fly tag. A big gob of saliva hit her across the face. "Gross!" she yelled, dancing back and swiping at her face with a sleeve only to realize that a glob of manure had earlier flown up off some cow's hoof onto that same sleeve.

After the calves were done there was a pause to set up for the cows. Kelly and Bev, John's wife, headed into the house as fewer hands were needed for the adult cattle.

"Did you hear there were three horses stolen just outside Carbon from Greg Atkinson?" Larry asked.

"When?" Ben looked up.

"Sunday night last week," Larry said.

Ben's jaw tightened. Mitch had been rodeoing up there. The time fit. Boy, did he wish Amber was not working at Ryder Niven's place.

"Wasn't that just after the rodeo?" John asked.

Larry looked at him thoughtfully. "You figure that would be worth checking out?"

"If it is a rodeo cowboy, he'd better keep it quiet," Old Slim Beeton said. "If he don't, the Royal Canadian Mounted Police will have one battered rustler to pick up. Rodeo cowboys as a breed don't take rustling too calmly." He cackled delightedly, showing great gaps between his crooked teeth.

John looked up from his branding irons. "My brother Silas called this morning. He said a neighbor had two good working-cow horses stolen a couple of weeks ago."

Larry frowned. "No rodeo anywhere near Gull Lake that weekend."

Ben had been cleaning and putting away instruments. He hesitated. Hadn't Mitch been north of there? Gull Lake would have been on his way home.

"What's eating you, Ben?" Larry asked.

Ben suddenly realized he'd been standing staring into space with a scalpel in his hand. He turned quickly to put it away. Old Slim had come up behind him. Slim jumped back wildly and said, "Watch who you geld with that thing!"

Everyone laughed at Slim's antics, but Ben couldn't put Amber out of his head. Even while dealing with seventy-five cows and the six herd bulls, he kept praying for her. When the job was done, everyone headed in for the big roast beef dinner Kelly and Bev put on. Twice Ben didn't hear when someone asked him to pass food.

"So Ben, what heifer has you distracted? You're as brainless as a bull elk in rut." Old Slim burst out with his infectious cackle. Ben laughed and tried to keep his mind on what was happening around him.

The next week was a long one for Amber. When she'd moved in the past, making friends had been easy and fun. Now, even though she had her car and could have left the farmyard, she made no attempt to get out and meet people. To make friends she would have to be willing to be open. Training Chip became the only bright spot in her day. Not only had she isolated herself, she was almost always physically alone. Immediately after breakfast each day, Ryder and Lyle left the yard. She hadn't seen Mitch since that first day. At least she'd learned one useful fact: If she avoided eye contact with Ryder, she did better. It was almost as though being looked at enraged him.

Amber was just setting out soup and sandwiches one noon when Lyle walked in alone and leaned against the door frame. "So, how do you like working for Ryder Niven?"

She nearly dropped a plate. The man was actually speaking to her. He hadn't done that before, but then he'd always been with Ryder. Now Amber had the impression Lyle was trying to look cool. He only succeeded in looking awkward.

Amber hesitated, searching for a response that couldn't get her into trouble. "I don't know. How about you?"

"Oh, I'm not really working for Ryder. He doesn't know that though." There was an unpleasant grin on the man's dirty face. "Do you think I'd stay and work for that jerk? I didn't talk for a week and he didn't even notice. If it wasn't for Mitch, I would—"

The back door slammed. Lyle visibly shied from the sound. A second later Ryder stomped into the room. "What are you doing in here, Smith? The woman I've got to put up with. She cleans the place. You stay outside until I say it's mealtime. Then you come in."

Lyle narrowed his eyes. "But Ryder, there's no one to talk—"

"You come in when I say, not before." The power of rage in Ryder's voice was compounded by his menacing stance.

Lyle cringed away. "Okay already. I'll wait for you."

Ryder sat down and started to eat. Lyle sat, but didn't eat. Like the days when he'd refused to talk, Ryder appeared to notice nothing. Amber sighed and took her meal back to the kitchen. Trouble between Lyle, Mitch, and Ryder was just one more hassle to put up with. It had nothing to do with her, or so she thought.

Deliberately Amber refocused her mind on something positive. If all went well, today would be the big day, the day she mounted Chip for the first time. As she ate, Amber thought carefully to make sure she'd left out no steps. The first time she'd saddled Chip he'd bucked hard. It took ten minutes before he stood still. Since then she'd spent time lunging him with the saddle on, leaning in the stirrups, and standing on a bale to put part of her weight on his back.

Outside, Amber found that her hands were shaking as she saddled Chip. *Calm down. He'll be able to tell if you're scared.* She took a deep breath and started the training session, going through each stage again.

Finally, with her heart hammering, Amber mounted her horse for the first time. Chip stood stiffly. Amber could feel him shaking.

"Take it easy, boy. It's okay. See, it's just me." Moving as evenly as she could, Amber dismounted. She'd survived! He hadn't blown up and plowed her into the turf. Automatically she began to thank God and then stopped herself and turned her attention back to Chip. She was on her own now. If she couldn't trust God, she'd just have to be more careful. She'd spend a couple of days mounting and dismounting, getting Chip used to the idea, before she asked him to move. Amber had the sick feeling God was nagging at her, trying to get her to talk to him, trying to make her go back and face things. Setting her jaw, Amber turned back to the horse. She would train Chip, then when he knew enough, she'd show him. He was going to be one awesome horse.

Ryder came in to supper looking through a handful of mail. He hesitated, then flipped a letter at Amber. Startled, Amber caught it. How could she get a letter when no one knew where she was? She glanced at the return address. Ben Miller.

"Woman! Quit staring like a gaffed fish! I want my supper."

Amber jerked her head up to meet Ryder's cold yellow stare. Lyle snickered. She blushed and quickly put the food on the table. Then she retreated to the kitchen. The card had a picture of a woeful little person standing by a huge houseplant. On the inside it said, "Feeling blue? At least you don't have to walk your philodendron."

That was crazy, but it made her smile. On the bottom Ben had written, "Thanks for an interesting afternoon. When you get time, check out the end of the eighth chapter in Romans. Take care. Ben."

Amber stared at the wall. She knew the passage Ben was talking about. It used to be one of her favorites. She'd even memorized it. With a tremendous wave of homesickness, Amber remembered saying the verses aloud to her mother in their living room in Paris. The apostle Paul had written, "For I am convinced that neither death nor life, neither angels nor demons, neither the present nor the future, nor any powers, neither height nor depth, nor anything else in all creation, will be able to separate us from the love of God."

What if it was something God himself had let happen? If God turned his back, didn't that make nonsense of the whole passage? Ben didn't understand. With shaking hands Amber tore the card in half. It would definitely be safer not to see him again.

Ben called three times in the next couple of weeks. Each time her initial response to hearing his voice was pure joy. Still, she made excuses to avoid getting together. She thought about thanking him for the card, but what would she say? "I used to like those verses but now I know they're not true." Right. That would make him feel good. Instead she said as little as she could.

"Have I offended you in some way?" Ben asked when he called the third time.

"No Ben, don't think that. I just can't see you right now, really I can't." Amber hung up abruptly, then sat there for a long time staring at the phone.

At four-thirty in the morning a sound woke her. Vehicle lights swept across her room. The rattle of a diesel pickup truck got louder. Amber rolled over and shut her eyes. A loud whinny of one horse calling to another split the night. Her eyes jerked open. That sounded like Chip. There was a metallic bang, repeated thuds, then a man's voice swearing.

Amber got out of bed and went to the window. Already the sky was gray with early dawn light. Mitch's flashy red pickup truck with a large horse trailer behind was parked in the yard. There was more thudding of hooves on the metal trailer floor and a horse's rump appeared. It backed out, followed by Mitch Niven. Obviously Mitch had come home from the rodeo and brought his bulldogging horse with him. Last week he'd done that too, but just overnight. Amber sighed and went back to bed, but her mind refused to go back to sleep. It replayed Ben's words about God's love.

Abruptly Amber threw off the covers. If it was light out, there was no reason she shouldn't go and spend time with Chip. She pulled on jeans and a sweatshirt and headed out. She came around the corner of the house and stopped. There were two strange horses in Chip's corral. Neither of the two horses was Mitch's bulldogging horse. He was tied to the outside of the trailer.

Chip was standing, stiff-necked, sniffing noses with one of the new horses. His long, limber form towered over the smaller horse. That horse squealed suddenly and stamped a front foot. Chip spun and dashed around the corral. Amber walked closer looking the newcomers over. A mare and a gelding, they both faced her, ears forward, friendly and unafraid. They had the wide-jowled, short heads of foundation quarter horse stock. Chip trotted over, his tail flying like a banner. When the mare whirled to face Chip, Amber saw a star-shaped scar on her flank.

Chip stretched his neck toward Amber and whickered.

Amber laughed. "What's the matter? Aren't I allowed to look at other horses?"

She caught Chip and spent a peaceful half hour currying him from head to foot. She'd been on him nearly every day, standing then walking. Finally when she rode him, he responded so calmly that she moved him into a trot. His ears went back. White showed around his eyes at the strange feel of a new gait with a rider on his back. His movements were jerky and he wouldn't respond to the bit at all. It was nip and tuck whether he would explode into a buck. Gradually his gait got less tense and Amber was able to bring him to a halt.

Amber took a deep breath. "Whee! Good boy! I can't believe we actually trotted."

By the end of the session she had Chip trotting uneven figure eights. As she led him back into his pen, she couldn't keep the grin off her face. The other two horses watched with perked ears. The mare had a fine line of white hairs down her face that gave her a quizzical look. As she released Chip, the gelding squealed and kicked at him. Amber stood watching the animals skirmish, establishing dominance. Should she move Chip away from the others?

Amber glanced at her watch. There was no time for that now. She'd have to hurry to have breakfast on the table by seven. Ryder came through the kitchen without looking at her and jerked open the back door.

"Smith!"

Lyle came in. As usual he looked like he'd slept in his clothing. "Mitch is back," he said keeping his head down.

"When did he get in?"

Lyle shrugged, blinking rapidly. "Don't know. Must have been late. He brought something you'll be interested in."

"Keep your fool face shut."

Lyle ducked his head. Amber looked from one of them to the other. Were the new horses the something that Ryder was supposed to be interested in? If so, what was the big secret? Obviously they didn't know she'd been up early and already seen the horses.

After the men left for the day, Amber set about cleaning house. It gave her pleasure to create peaceful order. Dragging the long tube of the central vac, she opened each door as she came to it and vacuumed inside. Ryder's office was usually locked, but this time the door opened. She entered, vacuuming as she went.

"Just what do you think you're doing?" Ryder growled from the doorway.

Amber jumped and spun to face him. What was he doing in the house? The menace in his body was so strong that she wanted to run. Instead she put the power head of the vacuum cleaner between them. "Um, I'm vacuuming your office. The door was open."

"Get out! You are not to enter this room! Do you hear me?" Was it her imagination or did he sound afraid?

"I hear you." As Amber left, she heard the office door lock behind her. In the kitchen she sat down with a bump. She'd felt like Ryder was about to hit her. It was worse when he sounded scared, like a cornered cougar. She swallowed hard. Was Ryder afraid of people? Was that why he hated to be stared at? Would he actually strike out? Most people would say she was crazy to stay here. It might even be dangerous. Taking a deep breath, Amber stood up and got back to work. She had nowhere to go. She'd just have to be more careful to stay out of his way. Her new understanding gave her a kind of sympathy for Ryder. The healer in her wanted to make things better for the man, but she couldn't see how.

Six

That afternoon when Amber went outside, the two strange horses were gone. So were Mitch's truck and trailer. Chip was standing with his left side towards her. When she came around his right side, she stopped in her tracks. His whole foreleg was covered in blood. It ran down to his hoof in long, greasy streaks.

Amber grimaced, then stepped closer to look. There was a big triangular tear in the skin of his shoulder. The flap hung down, pale and bloody, but the smooth sheath over his shoulder muscles wasn't torn. Amber sighed with relief. It was big and messy but only superficial.

Okay, I'll get it clean and then suture—No, she couldn't do that. People would ask questions. Besides, she had no equipment. She reached toward the wound and Chip shivered his skin anxiously.

"I know, boy. That hurts." Amber said gently. "It's not so bad really. We'll get you sewn up."

It wasn't until she was walking toward the house that she realized it was Ben she would have to call. His mom had said he worked with another vet. Maybe it wouldn't be Ben who came. There was only one local vet listed. Amber dialed the number.

"Watson vet service, this is Esther Watson, can I help you?"

When Amber explained, the woman said, "My husband is out at MacEwan's, but Ben Miller is right in your neck of the woods. I'll give him a call, and he should be over in half an hour or so."

Suddenly the day seemed brighter. *Stop it. You can't get close to anyone no matter how much you want to. Keep to business.* Okay then. What would he need? Soap and hot water were a pretty safe bet, though Ben would likely have some sort of sterile lavage to wash out the wound.

It seemed like only moments later that Ben's truck pulled into the yard.

"Hey, Amber, Esther said your horse was hurt?" Ben's concerned eyes were on her, not on Chip.

"Mitch put a couple of strange horses in with Chip last night. One of them must have pushed him into something sharp. It's only superficial though. The fascia over the muscles hasn't been torn. There's been some hemorrhaging but nothing significant. The wound needs suturing." Amber led Chip towards Ben.

"Hey, boy. You got kicked around a bit, did you?" Ben moved to examine the wound, then looked up at Amber. "You're right, this will need stitches. I'm going to tranquilize him."

A few minutes later Chip was standing flop eared. Ben struggled to hold the wound shut and stitch at the same time. "Amber, would you mind helping me here? There's another pair of gloves. Just wash your hands first."

"Be with you in a second," Amber said hoping she didn't sound too eager. She found herself scrubbing in as a doctor would. She stopped and tried to do it clumsily, but that felt dishonest. She glanced at Ben. He didn't seem to be watching. It would be no good for her to pretend she didn't know what she was doing and end up contaminating the sterile gloves. She turned her back and pulled the gloves on with the precise movements that were second nature to any medical doctor.

As she held the wound together, Ben's arm brushed hers. She swallowed hard and tried to focus her attention on the sutures. Ben was doing a good job. Her concentration went all to pieces when he reached around her to get at the other side of the tear. Amber held perfectly still. She could feel the warmth of his body behind her.

As he finished more sutures, the hide began to stay in place. Amber started to step back, but Ben's arm came down, stopping her. Startled, she turned her head and looked into his eyes. Every tiny detail was clear: his long lashes, the green and gold streaks in his irises, the wide, dilated pupils, the strength of the arm behind her back. His breath was warm against her cheek.

He dropped his arm and moved away. "Sorry." He hesitated as if he wanted to say more, then shook his head. "There's a little drain there. Could you hand it to me?"

She reached for the small plastic cylinder and found her hands were shaking. For a second she had wondered if Ben Miller was going to kiss her. The trouble was, she had wanted him to. Ben reached backward for the drain as a surgeon would. Automatically, Amber slapped it into his hand. As soon as she let go, Amber realized what she'd done. Ben turned around and looked at her. "Amber, are you a nurse?"

"No, no, I'm not. I guess I've watched too many *M*A*S*H.* reruns." She tried for a laugh, but it didn't work very well. At least she hadn't had to lie.

Ben gave her a puzzled look, then turned to position the drain in the bottom of the wound. Amber wanted to run. Until now it hadn't occurred to her that she might have to be dishonest. Why couldn't starting over be simple? She didn't want to lie to anyone, least of all Ben.

"The tranquilizer is already wearing off," Ben said, removing his gloves. "Chip should be fine loose in this corral."

Amber burst into speech. If she didn't let Ben talk, he couldn't ask any questions. "Thank you very much for taking care of Chip for me. I'll pay you at the end of the month if that's all right. I've got to go make supper now." She edged away.

"So what's going on here?" Ryder's bellow spun Amber around. He was striding across the yard towards them. "What are you doing in my yard, Ben Miller? This will be the second time you've turned up here without looking for me."

Ben shrugged, palms out. "Hey, take it easy, man. Amber's horse got himself torn and I came over to stitch him up."

Ryder grunted, not much mollified. "I like to know when people are in my yard. Are you hearing me?"

"In that case, I'll need to ask your permission to come over in a couple of days and check the wound."

"Make sure that's all you're coming for."

Ben stood facing Ryder, his gaze straightforward. After a few seconds, Ryder made an irritated noise and turned on Amber.

"Now you look here, girlie." He jabbed a finger at her. "If you want to keep your job, you'd better have supper ready in ten minutes."

Ben shook his head, watching Ryder's retreat. "You know, I think he's getting worse."

"Worse?" Amber asked.

"Dad said he was shy and touchy even as a kid. After his mom left, he kind of closed himself off. He had this sympathy with horses and used to train them for people, but then he'd fight with the owners, so that stopped." Ben turned to look at Amber. "It would have been better for Ryder if he hadn't been a rancher. He would've had to be around people more and might have come out of it. As it is, he's just getting colder and more eccentric."

"He isn't exactly the easiest man to work for, but so far I'm surviving. How come Mitch is so different? He just seems to want a good time."

Ben frowned. "I wouldn't be so sure about that. In high school Mitch Niven would do absolutely anything to make himself look popular and successful. Amber, you can do better for yourself than working as a cook here. This place isn't healthy."

"Uh, thanks for caring, but I really do have to go in."

Ben caught her elbow. "You should leave here, Amber. I'm not kidding. I'm starting to think that there's more wrong here than Ryder's eccentricities."

"Look, Ben, you have no idea what is going on in my life." She pulled away from him. "Why don't you just let me be?"

Amber took one look at Ben's hurt eyes and ran for the house. Ben's warning, together with the odd secrecy about those horses Mitch had brought, was making her nervous, but what was she supposed to do? The last thing she needed was to lose this job. Just where was she supposed to go? She was *not* going to sell Chip and go back to medicine!

In the kitchen Amber cracked eggs into a bowl, racing to be on time. Grating cheese to make an omelet, she caught her knuckle on the grater. Amber winced and slowed down. She cringed as she remembered the funny look Ben had given her when she slapped that drain into his hand like an OR assistant. Starting over had seemed so simple. She'd have to make it happen somehow, but how was she supposed to really start over without any connections to other people? It hurt her to turn away from Ben.

Amber shook herself and began to make a caesar salad. The motions brought back a strong memory of doing the same job with her mother. A wave of homesickness made her breath catch in her throat. Her parents must be worried sick by now. Even if she didn't tell them much, at least she should let them know she was okay.

"Rabbit food," Ryder said scornfully as Amber put the salad on the table.

Amber put the omelets down in front of the two men. "Ryder, I'd like some time off to go into Calgary tomorrow. There are some things I need to do."

"Going to run off?" Ryder asked, his pale eyes narrowing.

"No, I'm not. If you could pay me tomorrow morning, I'd be back tomorrow evening in time to make supper."

"I want you here until Wednesday. Mitch is supposed to be back after the Sundre Rodeo. I'll pay you Thursday morning after breakfast."

For a second Amber was angry. Who did the man think he was, dictating her life like this? Then she shrugged. What was a few more days anyway?

Sunday came and went with nothing to mark it as different from any other day. Amber sat on her bed for a while holding her Bible. She didn't open it. She had never felt so isolated in her life. Ben didn't call, but then she had told him to leave her alone. The hours dragged by. She sighed and went outside to spend time with Chip. He was a great horse, but not all that much real company. Besides, with the healing cut, she couldn't ride him. There was nothing to take her mind off herself.

Mitch didn't turn up after the rodeo. When Amber looked at the place she'd set for Mitch at the table, Ryder swore violently. In the ensuing silence Lyle fiddled with his fork. Ryder swore again and told him to quit fidgeting like a flea-infested chicken.

"Don't take it out on me, man," Lyle whined. "I'm not the one who didn't get back on time. I don't see why you've got your shirt in such a knot anyway. It's not like Mitch hasn't done this before."

Ryder gave Lyle a murderous look. Lyle shrugged and went back to eating. Amber caught a canny gleam in the man's eye that made her hesitate midstride. Did Lyle know exactly where Mitch was? After all, he'd said he wasn't really working for Ryder, and she'd heard Mitch promising him extra money.

Amber turned and walked out of the room. Ryder was an extremely unpleasant person, but she didn't like the idea of Mitch conning him. It would only make Ryder worse. At least on Thursday she'd get a break from this place. Surely she'd be able to find a place in Calgary where she could get on the Internet and send a letter to her folks.

Seven

Thursday was one of those days when fat white clouds slid on a gusty wind across a deep blue sky. The sunlight turned on and off like a slow-motion strobe. Mitch wasn't back by breakfast. In spite of that, Ryder paid Amber, practically throwing the month's money at her. Undaunted, she ran upstairs to get ready to go. It was going to feel so good to get away, even if it was only for a few hours.

Ryder and Lyle were still eating. She'd clean the dishes when they were done. A commotion took her to the window. Mitch was driving onto the yard in his truck, hauling the big horse trailer. He beat a wild tattoo on the horn. Lyle ran out of the house. Both he and Mitch got into the truck and Mitch drove off the yard, still hauling the trailer. They turned onto one of the small tracks that threaded the Nivens' pastureland. A few seconds later Ryder got into his pickup and tore out of the yard after them.

They were back within twenty minutes. Amber had cleared away the half-eaten breakfast and saw the truck and trailer pull in as she was washing the dishes in the sink. Mitch burst into the kitchen, grabbed her from behind, and gave her a smacking kiss on the cheek. By the smell of him, he'd been drinking. Amber jumped and tried to twist free.

Mitch laughed. "Hey, you don't realize how lucky you are, woman. You've just been kissed by the champion saddle bronc rider of the Sundre Rodeo. It's party time! Let's celebrate." He grabbed her hands and spun her around in a circle. Mitch wasn't big, but Amber was shocked at his wiry strength.

"I think you've already been celebrating. Let go of me!"

Mitch grinned and stepped back. "So maybe I did celebrate. Maybe that's part of the reason why I was late getting home, but is that any excuse to stop? I mean, how often are you going to get a chance to party with an awesome cowboy like me?"

Amber raised one eyebrow. "I'm going to have to pass up this fantastic privilege. I'm heading for Calgary in about five minutes."

"So, let me take you. My truck has more class than that old beater of yours anyway. There are some good bars in Calgary."

Amber shook her head and went toward her car. Mitch tagged along, extolling his virtues and all the reasons why she should go with him. Amber couldn't help smiling at his antics, but she kept walking. She pitched her backpack into her old Chevy, climbed in, and shut the door.

"Hey!" Mitch leaned in the open window. "I can't let a beautiful girl who lives on my own brother's property get away without partying with me, can I?"

"Can't you?" Amber asked and turned the key.

Instead of the normal grinding of the old starter, there was a dull click. She tried again and was rewarded with the same dead clicking sound. Stubbornly she tried twice more, then turned to see Mitch's grinning face.

"Lady, I believe your battery is dead." He bowed and made a sweeping gesture with his arm. "May I offer you a ride in my most humble chariot?"

"Do you have booster cables in that chariot of yours?"

Mitch rolled his eyes. "I don't, but there are some in the farm truck Lyle drives." He leaned against the wall, grinning as Amber walked over and asked for Lyle's help. Lyle drove the three-quarter-ton farm truck over and got out the cables. The man seemed to be trying hard to boost her car. He had no success. Mitch sauntered over.

"Okay, already," Amber said. "I give up. I'll go with you."

"Maybe I don't want to go with you now." Mitch turned away his head petulantly.

She needed to get to the city even more now. She had no desire to be completely stranded on Ryder Niven's farmyard with no way to leave without help. If her old Impala needed a new battery, she intended to get one.

"Okay, party king," Amber said, "I offer my humble apology for refusing to leap at your offer the first time."

"All right!"

Amber held up her hand. "On one condition. You have to let me do the things I need to get done. Also, I think you'll find I'm not much of a party type. I told Ryder I'd be back to make supper."

"Right!" Mitch pulled open the Impala's door and yanked out Amber's backpack. As Amber reached inside for her purse, Ben drove onto the yard. Amber stood watching him get out of his truck. The shape of him, his broad shoulders, solid strength, and direct eyes, the things that were uniquely Ben, seemed to touch some hidden part of her. Why couldn't it have been Ben who offered her a ride? She shook her head. No! It would have been better if she'd gotten away before Ben came.

"Hi, Amber, Mitch," Ben said as he walked over. "How's Chip doing this morning?"

"Forget the horse," Mitch said. "Amber and I are going to party. I just won the saddle bronc buckle at the Sundre Rodeo."

"Say again?" Ben asked.

Mitch repeated what he had said slowly and loudly as if he were talking to a very deaf old man, then added, "You have a problem with that?"

Ben stared at Mitch. "Yeah, I do."

Amber stepped forward holding out her hands. "Look, my

car won't start so Mitch was going to give me a ride into Calgary. It's no big deal." She looked at Mitch. "Will you wait for me? I want to go with Ben while he checks Chip."

Mitch tipped his Stetson down over his eyes. "I'm ready when you are," he said with a wicked grin.

Ben squared off facing Mitch until Amber took his arm. "Come on. We have a horse to look at." He turned and strode ahead of her to Chip's corral. Amber hurried to catch the colt. Without saying a word, Ben examined the wound and removed the drain.

"It's healing well, isn't it?" Amber asked.

Ben gave a quick jerk of a nod, then turned to Amber. "There is just no way you should go to Calgary with Mitch!"

"Ben!" Amber was shocked at his quiet intensity.

"Yeah, I know," he said. "I have no idea what's going on with your life. Maybe you have no idea about some of the things happening here. You should leave now, today. You could go to my folks' place. Just ride Chip over there, you know the way. Whatever is bothering you, whatever the matter is, it's not too much for God."

Amber stared at Ben openmouthed. Leave today? For a second she desperately wanted to agree, to get away from Ryder and the others. Amber patted Chip's neck and released him. If she left here, she'd be completely adrift, no job, no way to keep Chip, no goals. She'd have to give up and sponge off people.

"Look, Ben, I really do need to get to Calgary today. I need to get in contact with my folks. If you feel I shouldn't go with Mitch, are you offering an alternative?"

"I can't. Doc Watson isn't around and there are animals that need attention. Listen to me, Amber. Mitch is a drinker. You shouldn't go with him."

Suddenly all the grief, frustration, and doubt that Amber

had gone through in the last couple of months focused itself in anger. She turned on Ben. "Shouldn't go with him?" she said furiously. "Ben Miller, you are way out of line. How dare you tell me what I can and cannot do? Mitch has offered me a ride to Calgary and I'm planning to take it."

A chuckle made them both look up. Mitch had sauntered over and was watching. "Hey, Ben. What's the matter? You jealous that she's coming with me? Last time I looked, I hadn't killed anyone. Not like some I could mention."

Ben stared at Mitch, gave Amber a look, then spun on his heel and strode off. Amber's gut tightened. She couldn't remember ever seeing that much pain in a man's face. What on earth was going on here?

She took a couple of steps after Ben, but Mitch caught her arm roughly. "Come on! Forget the Bible thumper. Let's get out of here."

Ben had already slammed his truck door. Amber watched him start down the long driveway, then she reluctantly got into Mitch's vehicle. Mitch shoved his pickup into gear throwing Amber back in her seat. He shot out of the yard so fast that the truck skidded sideways across the gravel. Amber grabbed for her seat belt and managed to get it done up just as Mitch leaned on the horn. They were coming up fast behind Ben's truck. Amber saw him glance back then pull way over. As they swerved past him, Mitch gave Ben the finger out his window, still leaning on the horn with his other hand.

"Mitch, this is stupid. Quit it!" Amber yelled.

Mitch gave her a grin and accelerated even more. Amber folded her hands in her lap. No way was she going to give Mitch the satisfaction of seeing her look scared.

"You want me to slow down?" Mitch asked.

Amber looked away from him and said nothing.

“Hey, okay already. That good little mommy’s boy isn’t likely to catch us now anyway.” Mitch brought the truck back down to ten miles an hour over the speed limit. “You just watch. I’ll be a model driver the whole way to Calgary.”

“Good.”

“Look, girlie, don’t you get on your high horse with me. Ben Miller is bad enough. I bet he called me a drunk.”

“No, a drinker.”

Mitch grunted. “I guess that’s true enough. I know how to have a good time. You know the precious Ben Miller was once almost human?”

Amber looked over her shoulder for Ben’s truck.

“Yeah, him. You’re not going to see him back there though. He turned off on the grid.” Mitch pouted. Even that looked good on him with his down-tilted dark eyes and sensual mouth. “Called me a drinker? Well, he should talk. Ben Miller isn’t the goody two-shoes he’d like you to think. He’s got some history, he does.”

Amber looked out the window. She didn’t put any credence in what Mitch was saying. She felt sorry for blowing up at Ben. The fact that she was upset and confused wasn’t his fault; besides, it looked like Ben had been right about Mitch. Amber wrapped her arms around her aching insides.

Ben ground his teeth with frustration as he watched Mitch’s truck disappear into the distance.

“You sure blew that one!” he said. Why couldn’t it have worked out the way he’d pictured? He’d intended to start by apologizing for sounding so pushy the other night. Instead he had to go and make it worse. He shook his head. He sure could have done without Mitch Niven.

Then there was the matter of the strange horses in with Chip. He'd intended to ask Amber about those horses after he'd finished stitching Chip, but then Ryder had turned up and he'd forgotten. Should he call the RCMP and ask if any horses had been stolen between here and Sundre? Ben shook his head. What if the whole thing was only his overheated imagination? He'd definitely have to ask Amber about those horses though, that is, if she'd even talk to him.

Please keep Amber safe while she's with Mitch. Keep her safe both on the road and while they're in Calgary.

Ben's cell phone rang. "Ben here," he said picking it up. "Right, on my way," he said a second later and turned his truck around. Esther Watson had told him that the Broerses' three-year-old mare had foaled. The colt was half a day old now and Ed Broers had said he didn't think it was nursing.

The next couple of hours were extremely sticky, but ultimately satisfying. It turned out that the young mare was so engorged that the colt couldn't latch on to her teats. Ben had to milk her out.

"Why bother trying to milk her into that container?" ten-year-old Justin Broers asked. "It would be easier not to try to catch the milk with her kicking at you."

"The first milk is different." Ben was doing a crouched goose step as he tried to keep milking and stay with the uneasy young mare. "It's called the colostrum and it'll help protect the colt from getting sick."

All whiskers and wobbly legs, the little guy kept staggering in to try to nurse. "His name is Colonel," Justin said, then giggled as the colt clonked into Ben's back.

"I've got her milked down a bit now, so let's see if we can get Colonel nursing." Ben handed Justin the container and looped his arm around the colt's neck. The soft baby hide slid under Ben's hands as he tried to guide the colt, tipping and tilting into the right position. Colonel took wild swipes at his mother's udder. Holding him in place with one arm, Ben tried to get milk into the impatient mouth. More than once he got bumped in the face by the colt's very sticky muzzle. By the time he left, the baby's belly was round and tight with warm milk and he was nursing easily.

On the way into Calgary, Mitch told Amber rodeo stories. Amber sighed and tried to pay attention. She was stuck with this guy for a couple of hours anyway. It couldn't hurt to be polite. It didn't seem to occur to Mitch that the way he'd acted earlier might prejudice her against him.

Confident and cocky, Mitch hesitated halfway through one story. "Hey, do you know how to become a bull rider?"

"No," Amber said cautiously.

"You fill up your mouth with marbles, then you spit them out one at a time. When you've lost all your marbles, then you're a bull rider."

His grin was infectious. In spite of the fact that she knew the man was an incorrigible flirt, Amber found herself laughing. He could make even a dumb joke funny.

"You know I've never seen a rodeo except on TV."

"Whooo girl, you don't know what you're missing. Even Ryder has been known to come out to watch rodeo." Mitch frowned. "Not for the last couple of years though, not since I started winning."

"People say Ryder is an excellent horseman."

Mitch nodded. "Yeah, he trained Blue, you know, my bulldogging horse."

"Is he still working with horses? I'd like to watch him work."

"Oh, he's still working with horses. Not in the yard though, and I don't exactly think he'd welcome an audience and for more reasons than he knows." Mitch laughed as if he'd said something very funny.

"Is he working with those paints I saw on the first day? Ryder said they were part of another operation."

"Keep your nose out of other people's business and you'll be a lot happier. I can guarantee you that!"

The sudden harshness in Mitch's voice shocked Amber. She began to revise her idea about just how harmless Mitch actually was. Then the charm was back, and Mitch was flirting as outrageously as ever.

In Calgary he was impatient with Amber's attempts to find a place where she could get on the Internet. "So why don't you just write your folks a letter?"

"Because it might never get there, and e-mail is so much quicker."

Mitch snorted. "Look," he said, "drop me off at the Lazy Eight bar. I got some buddies I can call to meet me there. You take the truck. When you're done, come back and meet us."

Amber nodded, glad to be on her own. After a bit more looking she found a place where she could get some time on the net. "Dear Mom and Dad," she wrote. Then she stopped. She'd intended on giving them some kind of explanation as to why she was out west. The words absolutely refused to come. She realized that she had no explanation she was ready to share. For that matter, she hadn't let herself think about things so she couldn't explain coming out here to herself. How could she explain it to anyone else? She shook her head. She was paying for the time by the minute so she'd better get this done.

"I'm fine," she wrote. "I've left my residency and am living on a ranch in Alberta. You know how I love horses. As I don't have a computer, I've no address where you can reach me by Internet, but I'll get back to you when I get a chance. Love, Amber."

She stared at the letter. It would probably start all kinds of alarms in their heads, but at least they knew she was alive. Back at the bar, she found Mitch with a bunch of other guys, all dressed in western gear. He waved her over. One of the guys gave a loud, appreciative wolf whistle.

"Hey, Mitch, where'd you find this one?" a round-faced man asked loudly.

Mitch introduced her. It wasn't hard to tell that the whole bunch of them were a little drunk. Amber shifted uncomfortably. Why had she agreed to meet Mitch at a bar? The men with him were polite, though inclined to grin at each other as if they were sharing a private joke.

"Mitch, I told Ryder I'd be back in time to make supper. You know how he is about wanting supper exactly at five."

Mitch snapped his fingers and swore. "That's what I think of my stuffed-shirt big brother. If I listened to him, I'd run around like a poodle dog on the end of a leash."

The other guys laughed at him. "You'd be a cute little poodle too, Mitch," cracked a towheaded cowboy who'd been quiet up until then. The rest of the guys called him "Blondie."

"Come on, Amber, you said you'd celebrate with me. Me and the guys, we'll take you to the Keg and Cleaver for supper, best steak in Alberta. Then I got us a room booked in the Ramada Inn." Mitch was grinning at the other guys, obviously showing off.

Amber looked from Mitch to the others. There was no way

she was going to talk Mitch into leaving, but there was no way she was going to stay, either. She still had Mitch's truck keys in her pocket. When the blond cowboy got up to head to the washroom, she waited a second and got up too. Standing just inside the women's door, she watched for Blondie to come out.

"Excuse me," she said catching up to him where they couldn't be seen by the others. "Could you do me a favor?"

"Sure, whatever."

"In about half an hour, could you tell Mitch that his truck will be waiting for him on his brother's farmyard?"

Blondie grinned. "You just going to take it right on back without him?"

Amber nodded.

Blondie laughed. "I'll tell him. It won't hurt Mitch none to have one pretty lady get away from him. Have a good trip."

"Thanks!" Amber said and quietly headed out the back door.

Eight

"Where's Mitch?" Ryder demanded at supper.

Amber had thought about how she was going to answer that question. If she kept her eyes down and stayed calm maybe Ryder would too. "He stayed in town."

"His truck is in the yard."

Amber put cauliflower and cheese sauce on the table. "That's right. I drove it home. Otherwise, I wouldn't have been here to make this meal."

"He let you drive his truck?" Lyle's voice was high and indignant. "He never lets me drive that truck!"

There was an uncomfortable silence. She could feel both men staring at her. It would have been so easy to lie, to say Mitch had told her to drive the truck back, but the words wouldn't come. Ben had been so right. She never should have gone with Mitch.

"You stole his truck!" Lyle leaned forward in his seat. "Ryder, she stole Mitch's truck!"

"And brought it back here? Good guess, Smith. I'd say Mitch acted like a bubble-brained moose as usual."

"I don't know why Mitch comes back here! He's way better than you."

Ryder jumped to his feet, knocking his chair over with a bang. "Because he's never held a responsible job in his life, that's why. Now get out of my house!"

Lyle scuttled to the door, then stopped. "Are you firing me?"

"I will if you don't leave the room right now!" As soon as Lyle was gone, Ryder sat and began shoveling food into his mouth. His movements were jerky, and he ate without a glance in Amber's direction. She went into the kitchen. All that rage was going to give Ryder ulcers for sure, if he didn't have them already. Amber looked at her meal with distaste. Much more of Ryder and she'd have ulcers, too.

About three the next afternoon, a strange pickup pulled into the yard. From where she was in the round pen with Chip, Amber had a quick glimpse of Blondie in the driver's seat. Mitch got out and the truck left the yard. Carrying a big, cone-shaped parcel, he came straight toward her.

Chip was already snorting at that parcel. "Your keys are in the truck," Amber called, hoping to divert Mitch. He kept coming. Amber sighed, tied Chip, and went to meet Mitch.

"Hey, I'm really sorry I didn't bring you back." He hung his head and fidgeted. "I feel bad that I acted like such a jerk when Ben Miller was here."

Amber stared at him. An apology was the last thing she'd expected from Mitch Niven. "Uh, don't worry about it," she said uncertainly.

"Thanks, Amber. You're one of the nicest women I've ever met and I'd like us to be friends. Here, I brought you a present." Mitch held out the rustling bundle.

This was so weird. Amber unwrapped the bundle. "Red roses?"

"From me to you." He gave her a huge wink. "I've got to get out of here before big brother turns up. Be seeing you then, Amber."

He ran toward his truck. Amber looked down at the roses in her arms. Just what was she supposed to do with them? She didn't want to spend days looking at roses from Mitch, but they were beautiful. She laid them gently on the ground and went back to Chip. She had been teaching him ground manners. Now she found it hard to concentrate, glancing repeatedly at Mitch as he hitched the big horse trailer and loaded Blue, his bulldogging horse. She had the distinct impression that Mitch had been acting. She'd even thought she caught a couple of sharp glances, as if he was checking out the effect he was having. It made no sense.

In the next couple of days Amber tried twice to call Ben without success. She wanted to apologize for losing her temper and tell him he'd been right about Mitch. On the third morning, Amber looked at the phone again. She turned away. Both Ben's mother and Mrs. Watson must have told Ben she'd called, but he hadn't called back. No wonder after the way she'd yelled at him.

It was a long, gray morning. Amber looked up from the lunch dishes at the steady curtain of rain. Wet or not, she wasn't going to stay inside. Chip's back and shoulders were dark with water. A streak of wet curved like a comma, following the downward lay of his hide a hand span in front of his back leg. Amber went outside and caught Chip and looked at his wound carefully. It was time to take the stitches out. She was tempted to do it herself. She sighed and decided she'd better not.

"Hey, boy," she said softly. "That looks about healed to me. It would do you good to go out for a walk. How about if we go and explore the countryside a bit? You figure you could handle going for your first real ride?"

Chip turned his head and blew a warm breath against Amber's arm. He seemed to be in a particularly calm mood. Amber rubbed his neck under the mane where his hide was warm and dry and he nodded his head up and down, enjoying the scratching. She gave him a chunk of carrot out of her pocket.

"Chip, Ben must know I tried to get in touch with him, but he hasn't called me back. It's probably better that way. What do you think?"

Chip nuzzled for another piece of carrot, which Amber supplied. "I wish he'd call back, but..." Amber bit her lip and began to rub Chip's back dry with an old towel. She shook her head and went for the saddle. What good could wishing do? Things for her were a mess, and that was just the way it was.

Chip stood calmly for the saddling. The fine mist of rain felt cool on Amber's face. Outside the farmyard, she rode along a cow path that ran up the north side of a creek. Dimpled with rain, the water purled smoothly over boulders. To her right was a rough grassy slope. Across the creek, the slope was wooded. Shining water drops beaded the tip of every spruce needle, making a fairyland of silver trees. Pine scent seemed to be magnified by the mist, and every sound was twice as loud as usual.

Vividly aware of her surroundings, Amber kept her eyes open for anything that might spook Chip. She concentrated on staying balanced and ready. Wet grass swished against Chip's knees. Four tiny, grey juncos flew up in a spiral, scolding in high sweet voices. The path they were following rose steeply. Amber could feel the horse's muscles bunch as he dug in and began to climb.

"Hey, Chip, if you're doing this well, what do you think? Could you handle a small show? Just to get used to things, not to win, not yet."

Chip's ears flicked back to listen to her voice, then quickly forward again as they came to the crest of a ridge. Amber drew her breath in wonder. The clouds had lifted and long, silver shafts of light came through the breaks. For a few seconds the ranch was lit by one of these shafts of light. It shone like a jewel in the green hills, not looking at all like the cold, unpleasant place she knew.

The big colt fidgeted. Tossing his head, he started straight downhill for home. There was no path that way and it was very steep. Amber checked him. He fought her, dancing sideways in the wet grass. Amber pulled him into a tight circle and kept him circling until he began to calm down. "Good boy, now take it easy."

Chip wanted to go back to the Nivens' yard, but Amber would rather have stayed away. Riding her horse in this wild country, everything was so simple and beautiful. Amber shook her head. Dreaming never did any good, and she had a supper to make. She turned the horse back the way they'd come. A few moments later Chip shied, swerving almost into the creek. Amber turned in the saddle to see what had spooked him. Something white caught her eye. Turning the colt, she made him face what had startled him.

"See, it's not going to hurt you—" She stopped and narrowed her eyes. What was it? Sensing her inattention, Chip spun away. Amber brought him back around. She wrinkled her nose as the smell hit her. *A dead horse!* No wonder Chip had shied. The skull, with tattered bits of white hide still attached, lay in a fold of the ground. Long, wispy white mane hair was caught in the base of the bush.

Her eyes widened. There was a round bullet hole through the forehead of that skull. The white horse had been shot. She frowned. The first day she was at the Nivens' place, that big ugly man, Bull Schwartz, had been complaining about a white horse. Surely they hadn't killed it? Chip snorted loudly, and when she let him turn away, he tried to bolt. Amber had her hands full as he danced and skidded on the slippery ground. Gradually he slowed, but the set of his ears was still tense.

So much for a peaceful and idyllic ride. Amber made a wry face. Why would they have shot that horse? How could a white horse be a problem? Even if they didn't want white in their breeding stock, or if they just didn't like white, they could sell it. Maybe it had hurt itself fatally and they'd had to shoot it. That happened sometimes. She shook her head. That's not what she'd overheard. Bull Schwartz had been angry and upset because the horse was white. She could hear his voice in her head demanding, "What am I supposed to do with a white horse?"

As soon as the farmyard came into view again, Amber saw Ben's truck in the yard. The sight drove the speculations about the dead horse completely out of her mind. She stopped Chip. Sensing his rider's tension, the colt stood stock-still, ears at the extreme alert. Amber looked behind her. She could turn Chip and get out of sight. Ben would leave in a few minutes.

Amber sighed. That was dumb. He'd probably just come to take the stitches out. Chip was his case after all. As he hadn't called back, Ben probably didn't intend to talk to her anymore than he could help. Well, she'd just have to keep it that way. She urged Chip forward. He went stiffly, jumpy with tension. Chip's spookiness gave Amber a welcome distraction from the wild roiling of her own emotions. Ben looked up as she came into the yard and their eyes met. Amber felt the impact clear down to her gut. She turned so the horse would be between them and dismounted. Chip snorted and swung around, leaving her exposed as Ben came toward them.

"Amber, I..." Ben reached out as if to reassure a frightened child.

Realizing how she must look, huddled by Chip's side, she stood up straighter and turned to fumble with the girth buckle. "I assume you've come to take out the stitches."

"No—I mean yes." Ben sounded upset. "Amber, please look at me. I didn't get the message that you'd called until noon today. I was away at an equine respiratory diseases seminar."

Amber felt a burst of relief. "Oh. Um, I just wanted to say sorry for blowing up at you. You were right about Mitch."

"He didn't hurt—"

"No, but I ended up taking the truck home and leaving him there. He made the mistake of giving me the keys."

Ben laughed. "Good for you."

Chip bumped Amber impatiently with his head, eager to get the bridle off. "Excuse me a second." Amber led the horse to the post where she'd left his halter.

Ben followed her. "Amber, I'd intended to apologize last time I came over for getting so pushy. Even if I was right about Mitch, I had no right to try to push you around. It's just that I care."

To Amber's chagrin, she found herself fighting tears. This was crazy! She couldn't afford to go breaking down. Forcing her voice to be steady she said, "Maybe you could take the stitches out while I put this tack away."

Inside the tack shed, Amber was shaking as she put the saddle on a peg and wiped it dry. The tack shed door wasn't quite shut. Amber could see Ben bent over the line of stitches on Chip's shoulder. Ben was such a good guy. If only she could go to him and tell him everything. Her knuckles tightened on the cloth. Things would change fast if she did that. Ben liked her now, but that wouldn't last long. Amber was sure Ben would only confirm her own self-loathing.

Half blinded with tears, Amber reached for the neat's-foot oil and began to oil her saddle. A couple of minutes later a shadow blocked the light from the door and Ben stepped into the shed.

"Amber?" Resolutely, Amber kept her eyes down. "Please

don't wall me out. At least say you accept my apology."

Amber's fingernails dug into her palm. The fact that she was in trouble was no excuse for her not to accept Ben's apology. She nodded jerkily. "I'm not mad at you, Ben."

"Will you come riding with me a week from Saturday?"

Her control was slipping. She had to get out of here or she'd be bawling. Agreeing seemed the quickest way to escape. "Sure, whatever." She said, then jumped blindly for the door and straight into Ben's chest.

He caught her, keeping her from falling. For a split second she clung there against his warmth and comforting solidity. Then she twisted away and ran for the house.

"We'll meet at nine o'clock, bottom of the Nivens' drive," Ben called after her.

Amber's throat was too tight to answer. Up in her room, Amber scrambled out of her damp clothes and into the shower. There she turned her face into the hot water and fought with her emotions. Why had she ever agreed to go with Ben?

The verses which Ben had reminded her of, about God's love, came into her head. *Neither death nor life...*She clenched her teeth. It just wasn't true. She faced into the hot water. With both hands she kneaded shampoo into her thick, curling hair, fingers rubbing her scalp hard as if she were trying to erase the thoughts inside. Why wouldn't God leave her alone? Why did he keep after her like this? She couldn't afford to think now. Supper had to be on the table in forty-five minutes.

"Ben Miller was in the yard again today," Ryder said as Amber brought the meal to the table. "I passed his truck in the driveway."

Amber was very tired of Ryder's perpetual rage. She sighed and said, "He came to take out stitches. Remember, he said he'd be treating Chip."

"I don't like it! I could have doctored your horse for you."

Startled, Amber made the mistake of staring at him. "You?"

"Yes, me. I don't like other people looking after my horses, and I don't want them looking after yours if he's on my yard. I haven't lost a horse except to old age for years." He was glaring at her as if daring her to challenge him.

"But the white horse..." Amber said without thinking.

"What?" Ryder was on his feet. Amber found herself backing away. "Don't stare at me like a freaked-out kitten! What white horse?"

Out of the corner of her eye, Amber saw Lyle get up from the table and slink toward the door. Ryder appeared not to notice. His yellow glare stayed on her. She swallowed hard. "There's a dead white horse up that cow track behind the round pen. I rode Chip there this afternoon."

Ryder shut his eyes and seemed to sway on his feet. Amber started forward to catch him, but his eyes snapped open and suddenly he was bellowing. "You stay off my land with that big fancy colt of yours. Ride him down the driveway and onto the roads if you have to go out. Get him broke to vehicles. I don't care what you do with him, just stay off my land!"

Abruptly Ryder got up and left the table, stalking out of the room. Amber was positive that the news of that dead white horse had shocked him profoundly. What was actually going on here? Why had Lyle snuck away like that?

Amber slowly began to clear the uneaten food. Working here had been weird right from the start, but she'd put that down to Ryder's neurosis. Now she wasn't so sure that was all of it. Ben had said something unhealthy was happening when he'd tried to get her to leave, but she hadn't paid much attention. Amber went to wipe off the table. A white horse had been shot and the Niven brothers were strange people. That hardly added up to crime.

Halfway through the night Amber woke up and couldn't get back to sleep. The suspicions she'd dismissed earlier wouldn't stay dismissed. Lying there in the dark, she kept remembering things: Mitch's reaction to her mention of the paint horses. Ryder saying, "Those are part of another operation." Lyle slinking out of the room when the white horse was mentioned. Lyle and Ryder's secrecy about the horses Mitch had brought in the night. It didn't make sense. What kind of illegal activity was there to which a white horse would be anathema? And if the white horse was shot because of something illegal, why was Ryder shocked?

Abruptly Amber flipped on the light and got out of bed. Even if she didn't understand what it was, something was definitely going on. Maybe she should get out as Ben had urged. Amber was suddenly full of fear. She'd bought a new battery for the Impala, but it wasn't installed yet. She was trapped here.

Things always seemed worse in the middle of the night. She was probably being irrational. But if it was bugging her so much, at least she could put the battery in and make sure the car worked. She pulled on jeans and a sweater and went outside. The chill dawn wind cut through her clothing. The yard light was on, so Amber could see well enough, but she'd never changed a battery before. Surely it couldn't be too complicated. All she'd have to do was look carefully as she took the old one out and copy the way it had been. She'd seen tools in one of the sheds. If she could take out an appendix, she ought to be smart enough to change a battery.

She did manage, but she had badly skinned knuckles before she finished the job. Those batteries were heavy! With shaking and filthy hands she tried the starter. It ground over a couple of times and then fired.

"Yes!" Amber yelled and flicked the engine off. Okay, so she wasn't trapped. What was she going to do about it? There was a streak of gray along the eastern horizon now. She climbed out of the car and stared at her battered old horse trailer. It would be so easy to load Chip and drive away, but where would she go?

It wasn't really the lack of transportation that trapped her here. She rubbed at her cold arms, huddling in on herself. She felt like God was chasing her. It was becoming more and more obvious that unless she was willing to face what had happened, she couldn't belong anywhere, not even out west. She couldn't tell her parents what she was going through. She couldn't talk to Ben. Her world was getting smaller and smaller, constricting her like an anaconda.

She set her jaw to stop her teeth chattering and went into Chip's corral. The big horse nickered at her and walked over. For a long time Amber leaned against Chip. Both her body and her spirit felt as cold as stone. The colt was the only warm thing in her world. He demanded no explanations. If she left here, it would be nearly impossible to keep him. Training him was the one project she had left, the one avenue she had to some kind of success. As the sky lightened to full dawn, Amber turned and slowly walked back into the house. The warmth of her room enveloped her, making her suddenly overwhelmingly sleepy as she dropped into bed.

Nine

Amber was late with breakfast the next morning, which amplified Ryder's normal state of rage. Silently Amber put up with his haranguing. As soon as the men left, Amber headed for the telephone. If she was going to put up with this kind of grief so that she could keep and train Chip, she'd better get her act in order. She called directory assistance to get the number, and a few minutes later was talking to a woman at the Alberta Equestrian Federation.

"I've got a green horse, a three-year-old, that I'd like to give some exposure in small shows. I'd also like the schedule of shows for the rest of this year."

They talked for a few moments, then the woman said, "You know, if you're looking for small shows, why don't you try one of the high point shows different riding clubs run? There's one nearly every weekend. Brooks and Glenmore are the weekends coming up." She gave Amber the numbers of the people in charge.

Amber thanked her and hung up. It was too late for this weekend, but maybe the Glenmore show would work. Within ten minutes Amber had herself and Chip signed up for the English equitation and pleasure classes. It felt good to be planning positively again. It wasn't until she was well into the morning's housework that Amber realized the show was the same day she said she'd go riding with Ben.

She'd been making cinnamon buns. Now she stared blankly at the dough. That ride with Ben had been worrying her. How could she be with him for hours without falling apart? But the thought of canceling was worse. It was like the sun had suddenly gone behind a cloud. Absently Amber finished rolling out the dough and began to spread butter and cinnamon sugar. She ought to cancel with Ben and go to the show. Amber finished forming the buns, left them to rise, and slowly went back to the phone.

She called Ben at work. She'd leave a message with Mrs. Watson and not have to talk to him. To her surprise, Ben was actually there. "Just a second, I'll get him for you," Mrs. Watson said. "I know he'll want to speak to you."

There were soft bumping noises as Mrs. Watson put a hand over the receiver. Her voice came through muffled, but still clear as she called, "George, get Ben quick. It's that girl at the Nivens' place he's been mooning about."

Amber felt a little spike of joy. Ben did care about her. Smiling at the older woman's words, Amber tried to compose herself to talk to Ben.

"Amber!" Ben said warmly as he picked up the phone. "Are you okay? Can I help you with something?"

"I'm fine, Ben, thanks. It's just that I'm going to have to cancel for Saturday after next. I'm taking Chip to a high point show at Glenmore that day."

There was a little silence, then Ben said, "Would you like a ride? Your car isn't the most reliable thing in the world. Most of the high point shows start at nine, so why don't I come over with a truck and trailer and pick you up at seven?"

Amber felt as if the sun had suddenly come out again. She steeled herself and said, "Thanks, Ben." She searched for the words to tell him she couldn't accept his help, but Ben didn't give her time.

"Good, I'll be there. How about we get together some evening before that? Even if I'm on call, we could go for a walk or something."

"No, Ben, I can't," Amber said unsteadily and hung up without saying good-bye. Why hadn't she had the guts to tell him she'd rather go by herself? Amber wrinkled her nose. Because it wasn't true, that's why. She looked at the phone. She could call him back and tell him not to come, but that would sound insane. If she was going to say anything, she should have said it immediately.

She went to put the cinnamon buns in the oven and stopped with the oven door open. What if Ryder wouldn't let her go? At least that would solve the problem with Ben. She asked at lunch and, to her surprise, Ryder agreed without much fuss.

"At least you like horses, not like some of the other bird-brains that have worked here. They didn't stay long."

I bet they didn't. She wouldn't have been here long either, not without other reasons.

Over the next week and a half, Amber thought more than once about calling Ben and canceling. The trouble was, she did want to see him. She spent a lot of time getting Chip ready for the show. He was learning fast. In spite of herself she was looking forward to showing Ben what she and Chip could do.

The Saturday morning of the event she got up very early. Buttermilk clouds streaked the sky and the mountains shone pink in the west. A light wind stirred the cool air, darting around the edges of buildings and toying with Chip's mane. Amber had put her thick hair into a braid so she could put her riding hat on top. Curly wisps which refused to stay braided blew around her face.

She set to work on Chip, trimming his ears, whiskers, and fetlocks, wrapping his tail. The young horse danced, sensing

Amber's excitement and tension. "You going to settle down and do a good job today?" Amber stripped a few last hairs to even out his mane. "Will you listen to me and not be silly?"

Chip pranced sideways. "Hey, careful. You've got to be good. Ben is coming. I'm pretty mixed up about that, both afraid and happy. Just for one day do you think we could focus on the happy and forget the fear? Do you think we could have fun no matter what?"

Chip nudged her nearly knocking her off her feet. She laughed. "Okay, it's a deal. Now I've got to get changed."

Ben whistled appreciatively as Amber walked toward his rig leading Chip. The pants she had on weren't what he would call jodhpurs. They were more like thick, soft creme tights that outlined her sleek form beautifully. With the tall boots and jacket, she looked elegant, competent, and stunningly beautiful. For a second he felt intimidated, then she smiled.

"Hey Ben, it's an awesome day!" she motioned toward the mountains. They'd lost their pink tinge now and were gleaming white against a deep blue sky. Ben stepped toward her holding out his hands. She took them and they looked into each other's eyes. He watched the joy cloud over in Amber's eyes.

"Ben, can we just keep this light? Not talk about anything heavy, nothing harsh? Can't we have one day that's just fun?"

Ben squeezed her hands and let go. "If that's the way you want it? Sure."

He'd wanted a chance to tell her how God had helped him through the mess he'd gotten himself into a couple of years ago. Not that talking about something that had hurt so much would be easy, but somehow he wanted to explain himself to

Amber Lacey. He wanted her understanding and approval more than he cared to admit. He'd also been hoping that hearing him speak about those horrible days after Trevor Birch's death might encourage her to open up about whatever was troubling her.

Remembering the pain and confusion he'd been through made it easier for Ben to give Amber the space she wanted. He could only keep hoping and praying that she'd open up to God's love, and maybe to his.

In Glenmore they pulled into a line of trailers behind a small grandstand. Girls in English gear and their fathers in western clothing were unloading horses. Several people were already on horseback. Ben caught Amber looking with puzzled eyes at some contraptions along one side of the arena.

"Bucking chutes," he said. "It's a rodeo arena."

Amber laughed. "I hope I don't end up putting on that kind of show."

"I don't know. I think you could do pretty much whatever you put your mind to."

Amber shrugged, her fine-boned face suddenly unhappy. "I'm going to go register." Ben walked with her. It was obvious that his compliment had upset her somehow. As he watched, her eyes locked on to something across the parking area and widened in a look that approached terror. She hesitated and almost fell.

Ben caught her and turned to see what had alarmed her. Two perfectly harmless-looking women were walking away through the trucks and trailers. He could feel the tension in her slight body. "Amber, are you okay?"

Her face had gone white, making the sprinkle of freckles across her nose stand out. "Sorry, I thought I saw…" She visibly took control of herself and stepped away from his arm. "Yeah,

I'm fine. Thanks. Um, Ben, would you go unload Chip for me while I register? I'd really appreciate that."

"Sure, if that's what you want." He turned away thinking hard. Was he being foolish in paying attention to Amber Lacey? He was sure she'd seen someone she recognized and it had frightened her badly. Could Amber be running from a crime of some sort? He shook his head. He couldn't conceive of her as a criminal.

As soon as Ben was gone Amber ducked through the vehicles until she could see without being seen. The feel of Ben's supporting arm around her back was still strong in her mind, but she couldn't think about that now. Not if she was right about who she'd seen. She cut through the trucks until she found a better vantage point. It was Ruth Davis! An older English woman from Ontario, Ruth had competed with Amber many times. They were casual acquaintances, but Amber was positive Ruth knew she had been in medicine.

Amber stood there for a long time after Ruth was out of sight. If she recognized Amber, Ruth would probably come over to talk. What were the chances she'd mention something to do with medicine when Ben was there? So what was Amber supposed to do, just leave? That would be worse. Ben would want to know why.

Amber lifted her chin. She wasn't going to be defeated that easily. If she stayed far away from Ruth Davis, there was a good chance she wouldn't be recognized. Ruth wasn't expecting to see her here. Amber pulled her jacket hood up, hiding her abundant red-blond hair. Even in a braid it would gleam in the sun, drawing attention. She'd have to make sure she got all of it under the hat when she was competing.

They didn't ask for ID at the registration booth. On a sudden impulse Amber gave her name as Alice Tracy. She walked slowly back to the truck. This was turning into a nightmare. Lying, hiding her name...she walked more slowly. What if Ben asked why she went tearing off like that? As Amber got close to the vehicle, she saw with relief that he was talking to some people.

"Amber, these are the Burlingames, Art and his daughter Laura. They ranch south of us. Laura is going to be competing in the junior English classes."

The man was stocky with a red, seamed face and graying blond hair. His daughter was an awkward fifteen-year-old with clumsily applied makeup. It wasn't hard to tell that both of them liked Ben and thought well of him. The loudspeaker announced the first of the events and they joined the general movement into the stands. Art had asked Ben some technical question about worming horses. Laura sat by Amber and immediately started talking.

"Ben said you're from back east," the girl babbled. "There's another lady here from Ontario, Ruth Davis, but she's not competing. She moved out here with three great horses. I mean, the horses were totally awesome at jumping and stuff."

"So why isn't she competing?" Amber asked, smiling at Laura's eagerness to talk about horses. Part of Amber's attention was still on what was happening in the arena. It was a halter class, mostly quarter horses. Laura was right about Ruth Davis's horses. Back east Amber had seen her compete on two of her horses many times. She'd heard the talk when Ruth bought the third horse, a beautiful young Trakehner.

"Didn't you know?" Laura said, her eyes wide. "They got stolen a couple of weeks ago, all three of them. She, like, put up posters, pictures of them, all over the place. I saw them.

There was a white one and two bays."

Remembering the dead white horse in the coulee, Amber lost all interest in the arena. Laura kept on babbling about a horse-stealing ring. Amber felt sick. There had been those strange horses that Mitch brought. Could the Nivens be involved in stealing horses? Then she frowned. If they were stealing horses, why should Bull Schwartz be so upset about a white horse? Why had the news of a dead horse shocked Ryder? Nothing made sense.

Amber realized that Laura had asked her a question and she didn't have any idea what she'd said. "Sorry, I guess I was day-dreaming."

"Your horse is beautiful. I just wanted to know where you got him. Dad said maybe if I do a good job with Lightning, that's what I named my horse, he's just a grade quarter horse, then Dad might get me a warm-blood. Yours is a warm-blood, isn't he? What's his name?"

Amber smiled. "His name is Chip. He's not from one of the European warm-blood breeds, but technically I guess he is a warm-blood. He's a heavy horse, thoroughbred cross. Still there's no reason a sound quarter horse shouldn't do well."

Laura's dad cut in. "Your classes are coming up. You'd both better get ready."

It was fun to slip back into show mode, especially with Ben helping. By the time she had her hair thoroughly hidden under her hat, Ben had unwrapped and brushed out Chip's tail. Together they put the final grooming touches on the young horse and saddled him.

Amber watched Ben's big, gentle hands as he slipped the bridle over the horse's ears. Ben looked up and met her eyes. She had such a strong impression of his compassion for her that she quickly looked away.

He stepped around the colt and linked his hands, ready to give her a leg up. That was a normal courtesy. The stirrups were not long on an English saddle, and mounting a tall horse could be quite awkward. But these were Ben's hands. Amber swallowed hard. To do anything but accept his offer of a leg up would look very silly. She stepped up beside Chip, collected the reins, and bent one knee. Effortlessly he lifted her into the saddle. The feeling of Ben's warmth and strength stayed with her.

Chip pranced excitedly, bringing her back to reality. She settled herself and began to concentrate. She would have liked to ride Chip through the vehicles and close to the arena to give him a good look at everything so it wouldn't startle him later. The only trouble with that was that it might also give Ruth Davis a good look at her.

Amber turned Chip to the far side of the arena. Walking and trotting the colt, she concentrated on getting him relaxed and ready to pay attention. It seemed only a few minutes had passed before she heard the loudspeakers announce her class.

Amber trotted Chip toward the gate to the arena. Around the sides of the arena were advertisements and flags. Chip, as far as she knew, had never seen a flag. So far he hadn't noticed them since there was no wind and the flags hung limply. Chip bobbed his head, dancing sideways. As they entered the arena, she was the third of six people. Totally focused on the task at hand, she didn't hear Ben call, "Go Amber!" She'd even forgotten the possibility that Ruth Davis might be watching.

Following instructions, she tightened her reins slightly and moved the colt into a trot. He responded beautifully, flexing his neck and taking long, rhythmic strides. She could feel that Chip was enjoying himself, giving back everything he'd learned as a kind of glad offering. Around and around they went. At each gait, Chip obeyed instantly. It seemed too good to be true.

A touch of wind on her cheek brought Amber to full alert. It *was* too good to be true. She was ready when Chip spooked at the flags so she didn't lose control. Chip was still listening to her, but white showed around the edges of his eyes as he watched the strange things flapping. His movements were rough and uneven. She and Chip placed fourth in the class.

As Amber left the arena, she caught sight of Ruth Davis watching. She turned Chip to put him between her and Ruth, dismounted, and trotted him away from the arena. Ben came to meet her. "Bad luck about that wind coming up just then."

"He still needs to get used to flags." She glanced over her shoulder and relaxed. Ruth was out of sight. "Ben, did you see him at the beginning, before the wind? He is going to be one awesome horse!"

"I figure he had one awesome rider, too. Did you realize they got your name wrong when they announced you?"

"Um, I'd like to get Chip out of here. I think he's had enough."

Ben looked at her thoughtfully. For a second she thought he was going to demand an explanation. Instead he gave a little nod and walked with her toward their truck and trailer. Amber gave Ben the lead shank and began to unsaddle Chip. She was standing between the tall colt and Ben's truck.

"Hello!" a voice called in an English accent. "Do you have a minute?"

Amber's heart seemed to stick in her throat. She glanced under Chip's neck. Ruth Davis was coming over!

"Sure," Ben was saying.

Amber pulled off Chip's saddle and practically ran to the far side of the horse trailer, leaving Chip with Ben. There were two tack compartments in the trailer, on either side just behind the trailer hitch. Taking the saddle to the far side gave her an excuse to keep out of Ruth's sight. To Amber's horror, Ruth was following her around the trailer.

"I didn't catch your name," the woman was saying, "but I wanted to ask you if you'd be interested in selling me your horse?"

Amber let out her breath in relief and stuck her head and shoulders into the tack compartment. Ruth hadn't recognized her, at least not yet. "Sorry," she said with her head still inside. "Chip is not for sale. Thanks for your interest though."

There was a small silence as Ruth Davis apparently waited for Amber to take her head out of the tack compartment. Instead, Amber started to arrange things, picking up and dropping the hoof pick several times for good effect.

"Thanks anyway," Ruth finally said. "Maybe I'll see you again at another meet."

"Good-bye," Amber called hollowly. She stopped clanking things around and listened carefully. She could hear Ben and Ruth's voices briefly on the far side of the trailer, and then silence. Slowly she pulled her head and shoulders out of the tack compartment and looked up.

Ben had led Chip around and was watching her with a barely suppressed twinkle in his eyes. Amber shook her head and suddenly they were both laughing.

"Do you often keep dignified women talking to your backside while you hide your head?"

"Don't ask. I've never done it before and I hope I won't have to ever again."

"She said you remind her of someone she knew back east," Ben said. His eyes were definitely speculative.

"Come on, let's get going. Do you know anywhere good to eat on the way back? I'm starving."

Ben shrugged. "If that's how you want it. Look, Amber, whenever you want to talk with me, I'm ready to listen. Otherwise I'll leave you be."

"Oh, Ben, thanks. I don't mean to be weird but—"

"There are just some things you've got to work out," Ben finished with one of the nicest smiles that Amber had ever seen.

Ten

"On the way home from that meet yesterday, I asked Amber to come to church with us," Ben told his folks at Sunday dinner the next day. "She said no, but I've never seen anyone look so sad in my entire life."

"Is Amber a Christian?" Gordon paused with a fork full of roast beef halfway to his mouth.

"I asked her that once. She said that she was, but that something had happened to her that made trusting God very hard."

Julie was home for the weekend. She looked at Ben with narrowed eyes. "Are you sure she's not in some kind of trouble with the law or something?"

"Ben, there are obviously things you know nothing about in Amber Lacey's life," his mom said. "We want a healthy, sound Christian woman for you, not someone who is crippled emotionally. Trying to rescue someone is not the way to find a spouse."

"I don't think she is crippled!" Ben looked at Julie. "Besides, it's not the fact that she's troubled that attracts me to her. It's who she is. She's smart, brave, and determined."

"And good-looking?" Gordon said, eyes twinkling.

"That too. I think she has some medical training, and she's very gentle with animals. From what I've seen of her, there is no way Amber Lacey could be a criminal."

Julie raised one eyebrow. "And you're a completely neutral observer?"

"Julie is right," Hanna said. "You should be careful getting close to someone who is as troubled as Amber seems to be."

"Get close to her! If only she would let me. Watching her

reminds me so much of the way I've felt the last couple of years. You've been patient with me. I'd like you to cut Amber some slack, too. I can't believe she's been involved in any real crime, but she certainly is hiding." Ben laughed. "You should have seen her at the meet on Saturday. A woman came over to try to buy her horse. I think Amber must have known her back east. Anyway, Amber kept her head in the tack compartment on her trailer the whole time the woman was there."

"If she's so innocent, why don't you just ask her what she's afraid of?" Julie asked.

"She'll tell me when she's ready. At least I hope so."

"Well, your father and I will certainly pray for her," Hanna said. "No matter what's troubling her, I would be happier if she wasn't at the Nivens' place."

Ben nodded. "That makes two of us. Burlingame and his daughter Laura were at the show. We ended up sitting with them. Anyway, Laura told us that some woman's horses had been stolen and described them. Amber went sheet white and very quiet. I think she may know something."

Gordon pushed back his plate. "We're moving cattle with the Nivens next week. I just wish old Sterling was alive. He'd straighten out those boys of his in no time."

Hanna frowned. "Gordon, you know better than that. Sterling never cared about Mitch or Ryder, and his wife was drunk half the time before she left them."

"Ryder has been getting more and more antagonistic and reclusive, but I can't see him putting up with..." Gordon paused, apparently unwilling to voice his suspicions.

"With what, Dad?" Ben asked. "Why don't we just say it? The Nivens might be involved in horse rustling. You are so wary about me spending time with Amber, yet you keep right on working with the Nivens."

Gordon chuckled. "I'm not thinking of marrying Ryder or Mitch. Besides, we really know nothing tangible. The Millers and Nivens have been helping each other out off and on for almost eighty years. I'm not one to end that on suspicion. The way Ryder cares about horses, I can't see him stealing them."

"Not unless he thought he was doing the horse a favor," his wife said. "He certainly wouldn't worry about the owners."

"Even so," Gordon said, "the Bible never said anything about being good only to those who are good to you. In fact it says even the heathen do that. We're supposed to go the extra mile, give our shirt when someone takes our coat. When I know for sure crime is happening, that's when I'll deal with it. Speaking of that, didn't you say you were going to check with the RCMP?"

Ben put down his fork. "I asked, but no horses were reported stolen in the days just before Amber said there'd been two strange horses with Chip. There were some reported the day after, a couple of stock horses, a mare and a gelding. The trouble is, the police said the owner didn't know exactly when they'd gone missing. They were out in pasture and he hadn't checked on them in a couple of days."

"So we're none the wiser. I will not base my behavior on hints and speculation. I don't see how helping move cattle to summer pasture makes us accomplices in horse stealing."

Hanna put her hand on her husband's arm, "You're right, Gordon, but I still wish Amber wasn't working for Ryder and Mitch. What do you say to Ben inviting her to come here?"

"Good idea!" Gordon set down his empty coffee cup for emphasis.

Julie was nodding. "Maybe she'd talk to me or Mom when she wouldn't talk to a great lout like you."

Ben rubbed both his hands over his face. "I'm glad you said

that Amber is welcome here, because I kind of tried to invite her already. She acted as if she hadn't heard me."

"So, maybe she didn't, or she didn't think your father and I wanted her. I'm going to call right now and try again." Hanna got up and reached for the phone.

Amber was washing dishes and worrying. Even her chance to compete with Chip was ruined if Ruth Davis was going to turn up at all the meets. Unless she was willing to let people know her background, she was going to end up a hermit. Was God doing it on purpose? Shutting doors on her to make her quit running? Was that why she'd landed in a place where it was so hard to stay? Her mouth was dry as she fought a feeling close to panic.

When the phone rang, Amber didn't move to answer it because Ryder was in the house. When he bellowed from his office for her to pick up the phone, she was suddenly afraid that Ruth Davis had tracked her down. Hearing an older woman on the other end didn't reassure her. Amber's voice was shaking as she confirmed that yes, she was Amber Lacey.

"This is Hanna Miller. I called to—"

"Hanna Miller, Ben's mom?" Even to Amber the relief in her voice was obvious. They were going to think she was a total lunatic.

Hanna chuckled. "It's good to talk to you too, Amber. Actually, I'm calling to confirm Ben's invitation. If you need to leave the Nivens, both you and your horse are welcome here until you can sort things out."

"But you don't even know me!"

"Only enough to hold out a hand. God's been good to us over the years and we like to pass that on."

Tears choked Amber's throat. How could she keep her defenses up against someone as kind as Hanna Miller? She swallowed hard to force the tightness away so that she could speak.

"Thank you very much, but I can't accept."

"Remember there's an open door for you here if you need it. Just a second, Ben wants to talk to you."

Amber was shaking her head no, but Ben was already on the phone. "Amber, Mom meant what she said. Please come."

"I can't," Amber said desperately. "Ben, please leave me alone." As soon as the words were out, she wished she hadn't said them, but she wasn't going to take them back.

There was a long pause. "Dad and I are going to be over there weekend after next to help move the Nivens' cattle to summer pasture, so I'll have to be there that day. Please, before I leave you alone, I'd like to tell you about some things that happened in my life."

"So tell me about it then," Amber said, trying to keep her voice steady in spite of her tears. She hung up the phone without saying good-bye. Holding everything in was getting harder and harder. She squeezed her eyes shut tightly, feeling two tears slide down her face. After a long moment of fighting for composure, Amber succeeded. She took a deep breath and went back to washing dishes.

That week it poured for days. On the fourth day of rain, Amber had enough of sitting inside. Outside, the wind whipped her raincoat, spooking Chip and making mounting very difficult. In the arena, his feet kept skidding in the mud. Twice he nearly fell. Amber licked the rain off her top lip and decided to try the gravel driveway. The footing there was better, so she started down the road. Rain poured off the plastic cover on her riding helmet and down her neck in cold rivulets.

Every time the wind lifted the edge of Amber's slicker, Chip shied. In spite of all the water, Amber's mouth was dry. She concentrated on staying balanced and in control. She moved Chip into a trot, hoping that would settle him down.

As she turned the young horse at the end of the half-mile-long driveway, she didn't see Mitch's truck and trailer coming fast. The plastic on her hat was so noisy with the rain that she didn't hear them either until Mitch leaned on the horn, grinning and waving at her.

Chip leapt sideways, away from the scary noise of the horn. Amber kept her balance. She had just begun to think that she might be okay when the trailer's back wheels hit a big puddle. She and the horse were hit with a fountain of cold, muddy water.

That was too much for Chip and he exploded into a full buck. The world snapped and jarred around Amber as she rode out the first leap and kick. Chip tried to twist away from the road on the second jump. His feet shot out from under him in the mud. Amber was catapulted clear as the horse landed hard on his side.

For Amber, the spinning and jerking were suddenly ended by a numbing thud. Winded, she lay flat and took stock of herself. At the same time she realized she was probably all right, she also realized that one side of her face was in cold water. She sat up spluttering to see Chip heading for home at high speed. Mitch's truck had stopped and he was walking back toward her. Amber had been pitched into the ditch and was sitting in what amounted to a small creek.

Mitch was grinning. "You might get a reride since the horse fell. Good effort though. What are you still doing on the ground?"

Amber got shakily to her feet. Cold water ran down her body, finding new places to trickle. Mitch hadn't even asked her if she was okay. As if he'd read her thoughts, he hesitated and suddenly became the picture of compassion, or tried to.

"Hey, I'm sorry you got dumped. You're not hurt, are you? Come on, I'll give you a ride back."

He reached for her gingerly. Amber had the distinct impression that he was trying to keep his fancy western clothes clean. In spite of everything, that made her want to laugh.

At the truck door he paused. The inside of Mitch's truck was gorgeous, slate gray leather seats, big stereo. Mitch looked into the truck, and then at Amber's dripping muddy form. Her teeth chattered. She desperately wanted to get back to the yard, see that Chip was okay, and get warm. She reached for the truck door.

"Hey, wait," Mitch said. "I can't let you in the truck like that." He reached in past her and pulled a blanket off the wide back bench seat. He pushed it at Amber. "Come on, I don't want mud all over my truck. Strip off that wet stuff and wrap in this."

"No, I'll walk if you don't want to get your truck dirty."

Mitch frowned, obviously struggling with himself, then he flung open the truck door with a flourish. "What the heck. I'll even sacrifice my truck for a damsel in distress."

Still, he didn't let her in right away. Amber stood shivering, watching Mitch cover the seat with his slicker and two blankets that he pulled out of the truck's spacious backseat. It wasn't hard to guess why he kept them there, or why he'd bought a crew cab. As they drove into the yard, Amber saw Chip standing outside his corral watching them with stiffly pricked ears. One whole side of the colt's body was covered in mud, but he looked okay. She could afford to leave him for a few minutes while she got into dry clothes.

The touch of a finger running along the line of her chin jerked Amber's attention back to Mitch. "You look great soaking wet. If you're cold, I could warm you up."

Amber turned away from him and reached for her door. "Uh, thanks for the offer but I'll try a shower and some dry clothes."

"Hey, I'll catch the horse for you, then come make us some hot cocoa. Sound good?"

"Thanks." She wasn't sure Mitch could handle Chip safely, but she wasn't going to stand and argue as wet and cold as she was. She shot into the house to take one of the fastest showers of her life.

As she came downstairs, Mitch was in the kitchen stirring packets of instant hot chocolate into mugs. "Horse is in the corral, saddle and bridle are wiped off and hanging up." He grinned at her. "Not bad, eh?"

"You really did all that? Thanks, Mitch," Amber said. She kept going toward the door. "I'm just going to go check on him."

Mitch grabbed her elbows and led her to the kitchen window. She could see Chip in the corral. "See. The animal is fine." He turned her around so she was facing him. "Come on, loosen up. Sit down and have some hot cocoa with me."

"Okay," Amber said, relenting. Instead of letting her go, Mitch tried to bring her into an embrace. Amber twisted quickly and stepped away. "The cocoa is in the kitchen I assume?"

He followed her there and pointed toward the table. "Look. I brought you a present. Open it." Beside her cocoa cup there was a big, fat envelope. Across it in big block type were the words Western Stockgrowers Association Centennial Cattle Drive.

"Come on, open it."

Amber hesitated, not wanting any more presents from Mitch. Before she could say anything, the sound of the back door opening brought their heads around. Mitch rolled his eyes as Ryder walked in.

"Mitch, I want to talk to you." Ryder jerked his chin toward his office door.

Mitch gave Amber an apologetic shrug and followed his brother. As they left the room she could hear Mitch saying, "Hey, don't worry, brother. In spite of the mud that shipment is already delivered to the painter."

Ryder snapped at Mitch, telling him to shut his big mouth. Amber frowned. To the painter? What on earth did he mean? She shrugged and shoved the packet Mitch had given her into a little-used drawer in the huge new cupboards. Then she worked fast to get meatloaf and potatoes in the oven and ran out to check on Chip.

As she went past Ryder's office, she heard Mitch's voice raised. Almost against her will she stopped to listen. "Sure I shot that white horse. The fool thing broke its leg when we were unloading it. I knew that would make you mad so I didn't say anything."

Ryder growled something unintelligible and Mitch protested, "Would I steal when you gave me money to buy horses at auction? You want receipts, I'll get you receipts."

Amber shook her head and went outside. The more she was around the Nivens the less sense they made. Amber's bruises were beginning to stiffen. Her body ached as she bent to run her hands down Chip's legs. She found no hot or swollen places.

He nudged her with his nose, getting her clean shirt dirty. She started to dodge, laughed, and stood still. "There's no way I'm going to be as fussy as beautiful Mitch Niven trying to keep his classy clothes and truck clean. I wish I knew what he was doing. It's like he puts on this act around me."

She rubbed Chip's forehead. "I also wish I knew what those two were talking about. If Ryder isn't in on the horse stealing, why is he so secretive, and what's the painter thing? Ryder knew about that, whatever it was."

Amber looked at the colt. "You know, you're a complete mess. Still, I'd better get on and make sure you're left with a good memory of being ridden instead of a scary one."

She had just dismounted after a gentle ride around the corral when Mitch came up. "See, I told you he was okay. I do know a bit about horses." With one smooth gymnastic motion he swung himself over the corral fence. "I came to tell you I've got to go, but I talked Ryder into saying you can come when we move the cattle to summer pasture Saturday. It will be good training for Chip, too. What do you say?"

Amber looked at him warily. Still, a chance to help move a herd of cattle across this beautiful country sounded too good to miss. Besides, Ben and his dad were going to be there, and Mitch was right, it would be good for Chip. Slowly Amber nodded. "Yes, I'd like that."

"Good. I bet you liked the present I gave you too." Mitch reached to pat her behind. She dodged, but Mitch just laughed and headed off. "See you later, beautiful!" he called over his shoulder.

Eleven

Amber was up before her alarm went off at quarter to five the Saturday morning they were to move cattle. Ben was coming! Ryder had told her to have a big breakfast ready at five-thirty. Quickly she dressed, wearing layers that would be easy to shed later in the warmth of midday. She watched the men down pancakes, eggs, and coffee. How could anyone eat this early?

Outdoors, there was frost on the grass. Ground fog lay in the hollows of the land, but the sky was a clear, brilliant blue. The mountain's rock and snow reflected the morning sun, gleaming pink gold above the fog. As she was tightening the girth of her saddle, Ryder, Mitch, and Lyle came out of the house.

Ryder stopped behind her and grunted in disgust. "There is no way you're going to come along with that little pancake of an English saddle."

"It's the only saddle I've got. I don't have a western saddle."

"So put the colt away. He doesn't know enough to be any help and neither do you. Get back in the house where you belong." The low sunlight came under the brim of Ryder's Stetson and caught his eyes, making their strange yellow irises glow like a cat's eyes. He looked completely unbalanced. Amber began to back up.

"How about if I give her Dad's saddle?" Mitch said. Amber jumped as if a hypnotic trance had been broken.

"If you do that and bring the woman," Ryder said, turning the pale glare on his brother, "be it on your head. If she or that colt spooks the cattle, I'll take it out of your hide."

Amber let out her breath in relief when Ryder turned away. "Thanks, Mitch. You do have your good moments."

He grinned and winked. "Come on, I'll get you Dad's saddle."

That snapped her back to reality. Chip was going to be hard enough to handle without the added complications of a saddle strange to them both. "Are you sure I can't use mine? I'd much rather."

Mitch rolled his eyes. "You heard Ryder; besides, where are you planning to tie your slicker? I don't see saddle strings on that thing. How about lunch? How about your lariat?"

"Lariat?" Lunch and somewhere to tie extra clothing made sense but…"You want me to carry a lariat?"

"So if you can't use it, someone else may need it," Mitch said and headed into the tack shed. A few seconds later he came out carrying a heavy western saddle. Without ceremony he slapped a blanket onto Chip's back and threw the saddle up. His movements were confident and economical, but he wasn't gentle. The heavy stirrup and cinch thudded against Chip's ribs and he shied, dancing sideways. Mitch swore and jerked down on the lead shank. Staying with the horse, he quickly ran his hand under the blanket and tightened the cinch. "There you go. I've got to get my horse."

Amber looked at Chip standing white eyed and shaking and felt much less grateful to Mitch. Talking to reassure her horse, she struggled to adjust the stirrups to a length that fit her. The heavy sliding metal sleeve-and-pin contraption looked like it hadn't been moved for years. Chip would not stand still. The butterflies in Amber's stomach seemed to be growing into oversize bats.

Mitch came over on Blue. "Listen, Amber, I'm in deep you-know-what if you mess up this drive. Stay at the back and do nothing, like absolutely nothing, unless I say." He moved off, putting Blue into a showy collected canter.

"Are you as impressed as I am, Chip?" Amber said. "If I could just make this thing…there." The metal sleeve was back where it belonged. One stirrup was right. Amber walked around Chip to work on the other. "At least Mitch made it so you and I can come along. I suppose I should be grateful. What do you think?" The horse pawed the ground impatiently. "Okay, I'll get on with it."

As she was fighting to adjust the other stirrup, the Millers' rig pulled into the yard. Past Chip's shoulder, Amber could see Ben and his dad unloading saddled horses. Ben caught her eye and waved, but they didn't get a chance to speak. Just seeing Ben made her feel better.

Amber found the first few minutes in the saddle nerve-wracking. Chip was excited and difficult to control. The western saddle complicated matters, forcing her legs farther forward than she liked for balance.

Ben came up beside her. "Looking good."

"Don't I wish!" She was trying to calm Chip, who was not in a mood to stand still.

Mitch forced his horse between her and Ben. "Your dad wants you, Benny boy."

"You'll do fine, Amber, don't worry," Ben said and moved off.

Mitch moved in and said something that Amber didn't catch. The whole group had started walking their horses out of the yard. This was good as it gave Chip direction. He began to calm down and Amber could pay more attention to what was going on around her.

"I said, did you like the present I gave you?" Mitch repeated. He sounded none too pleased at being ignored the first time.

Amber was puzzled for a second before she remembered the envelope he'd left on the table last week. "Um, actually

Mitch, I didn't get a chance to look at it."

"Hey, it's something you're really going to like. Used most of my rodeo winnings for it too, just about eight hundred bucks."

"Eight hundred bucks!" Amber said, her attention full on Mitch now. "What on earth?"

Mitch grinned. "I signed you up for the Centennial Cattle Drive. That was your registration packet. It's going to be an awesome time. You'll see."

Centennial Cattle Drive? What was he talking about?

Mitch laughed. "You know, even when you're confused, you're beautiful, Amber Lacey."

"Thanks, Mitch," Amber said absentmindedly. Eight hundred dollars! Mitch's brilliant blue, thick-lashed eyes were on her. He winked. Amber looked away. This was nuts. Why would Mitch spend that much money on her? He'd been coming on to her in a way that seemed artificial, not sincere. Now this.

"Hey, Mitch!" Ryder yelled from ten yards away. "You, Ben, and Lyle get out there and do the sweep around the south end of the Moor place. We'll come in from the east and do the gather that way. We'll bring them all out through the gate by the old cottonwood."

Lyle, who'd been with Ryder, was already moving fast. Mitch swore, but he nudged his buckskin into a canter. Chip jumped forward, wanting to run with the other horses. She couldn't stop him, but she did manage to turn him. Ben waited until he was well past her before letting his gray flatten out in a run. Chip popped off his front legs, fighting to turn and run with the others.

"Easy, fellow." Gordon Miller moved his horse in close and stopped.

Seeing another horse next to him, Chip began to relax. "Thanks," Amber gasped.

"Thought you were going to eat some dirt?" Gordon asked, chuckling. "Working all day will be good for that big fella."

Amber nodded. "I hope so." She patted the sweating colt's neck and turned him back around to walk with Gordon Miller. "Mitch just said something to me about some Centennial Cattle Drive. Was he talking about today?"

"Today? Not likely. The Centennial Cattle Drive is happening in a couple of days. It's to celebrate one hundred years of the Western Stock Growers Association. There's supposed to be fourteen hundred riders along."

"Fourteen hundred!" Amber said, eyebrows high. "To move cattle?"

Gordon laughed. "It's more of a party than a cattle drive, but there'll be a couple thousand cattle along. We'll be moving them across the British Block. That's about seventy miles of open shortgrass prairie."

"We?"

"Ben and I are going. It should be fun and it's about time Ben did something just for fun."

Amber gave Gordon a puzzled look. What did he mean about Ben? She shifted in the saddle and went back to her immediate problem. "This Centennial Cattle Drive, how much does it cost?"

"Just about eight hundred bucks or the donation of a steer for the drive, but I think they're all booked up anyway. Did you want to go along?"

Amber shook her head negatively. Eight hundred dollars. That was the amount Mitch had mentioned. What was he doing spending that much money to impress her? Nothing at the Nivens' place made sense! She could see Ryder about twenty yards ahead. He'd kept his distance from everyone, but that wasn't surprising. One brother feared and seemed to almost hate people, and the other was behaving in a fashion she couldn't understand at all.

They crested a ridge. Amber drew in her breath. They were on the edge of a wide green bowl. Cattle dotted the grassy expanse. She could see Mitch, Lyle, and Ben spread out around the far side of the herd. They weren't moving toward the cattle, but seemed to be searching along a fence line.

"Looking for calves lying down in the draws," Gordon explained.

Ryder had come back toward them. At Gordon's words, he snorted. "We're not running a tour outfit for dudes. You've done this more times than I have. Go and make sure the cattle don't cut back east at the creek."

"No need to be rude," Gordon said mildly.

Ryder looked at Amber and swore. "That's what you think. What am I supposed to do with this one? Getting one green hand is like losing five good ones. I should have sent her with Mitch. He's the fool who wanted her along."

"Leave her with me," Gordon said. Ryder nodded and cantered off.

"Thanks," Amber said with feeling.

"Don't worry. I've been working this drive for a lot of years. If he lets you stay with me, I figure I can keep us out of trouble. If he sends you somewhere else, though, you go. These are the Nivens' cattle so Ryder is cow boss. Main thing is, never hurry a cow. To start with, stay behind me and well away from the cattle. We move them slow and easy."

Gordon set off at a trot southeast. Amber didn't have any idea how Chip would react to hundreds of cattle. He was already eyeing them with suspicion. She didn't want to look bad in front of Ben. If she scattered these cattle, her name would be mud to every one of the men here. Still, Amber wouldn't have missed this for the world. It was like being part of an old western.

There were two well-worn cattle tracks that cut back east along the creek. Gordon put her and Chip on the northerly one. "You figure you can keep your horse standing there? Just seeing you should turn any that come this far, but I figure they won't." He gave her a reassuring nod and trotted off.

Chip gave a loud, anxious whinny. "Easy boy, I'm here," Amber said, patting his neck. The herd was moving closer. Amber could now see individual cattle. Most were reddish with white faces and muddy legs. There was a continuous bawling, like a fat man sitting on the middle register of an out-of-tune pipe organ. Chip stood, ears stiffly pricked, watching the first animals come by. Gordon had his horse a hundred yards to the left, turned at an angle that deflected the cattle. Two cows with their calves tried to dodge behind him. Gordon swung his horse, efficiently turning them back into the main herd.

Ben and the other two men were getting closer, bringing up the rear of the herd. Both Lyle and Mitch were doing a lot of yelling. Ben was quieter. The cows didn't seem to want to get close to a horse and Ben was using his horse's body position to keep the cows moving where he wanted them. Amber watched Ben with a feeling of warm pleasure.

As they got closer, Mitch began to show off, cantering his horse back and forth along the edge of the herd, yelling and swinging his lariat with a big loop in it. He yanked back, jabbing Blue in the mouth with the bit. The horse threw its head up and kicked in the air. Startled, a calf dodged and ran out of the herd. In two leaps, Ben had it turned and heading back. Amber grinned at how he'd shown Mitch up so easily.

The sudden realization that the commotion had started a lot of cattle trotting in her direction wiped the smile off her face.

Gordon turned most of them, but a knot of ten kept coming. She could see their down-turned horns and slimy noses. Chip snorted loudly, making the alarm sound of wild horses. Legs and reins tight, Amber held him on the path. The cattle came to an abrupt halt about ten feet away, fuzzy ears forward, big stupid eyes startled. There was a brief standoff as Amber and Chip stared at the cattle and the cattle stared back. Amber thought about yelling but wasn't sure if it would turn the cattle or spook Chip.

She heard a thud and skidding sounds behind her and suddenly Gordon was with her. He'd brought his horse around behind her and down the steep bank beside the path. "Good job!" he said, trotting past at an angle that turned the cattle back into the herd. As the back of the herd was now passing, he motioned for Amber to follow. Chip's ears were pricked with interest and Amber realized that the young horse had enjoyed stopping those cows.

Mitch forced Blue to a hard, sliding stop. "You stay with me! Ryder said we're to ride drag."

"Drag?" Amber asked.

"Tail-end Charlie. Bring up the rear. Stay in the back. Get the picture?"

Amber looked for Ben, only to find him cantering around the far side of the herd. Mitch followed her glance. "Forget the good little boy. Ryder sent him to open gates. Hey, you're a lucky girl, you're with me." He tipped his hat, grinning.

"God's gift to women?" Amber asked.

"Dang right I am," Mitch answered. "Better 'n Ben, that's for sure."

If Ben and his father were doing what Ryder wanted, she'd better do the same. Amber reined in beside Mitch. She'd meant to tell Mitch she wasn't going on the Centennial Cattle Drive, but the gritty physical reality of hundreds of moving cattle made her forget all about it.

Once they were through the gate, Ben got into position to turn the cattle west. Slowly the big herd moved through the gate. Amber and Mitch trailed along at the back.

It was obvious that Ben and his father had helped do this before. Ben had said that the Nivens and the Millers had worked together forever. The Millers knew something was happening at Ryder's place, or Ben did anyway. A sudden sick feeling made Amber swallow hard. Could it be Ben hadn't done anything because his father was involved, too?

Mitch laughed, bringing Amber back to the moment. He was pointing at Ben. "He looks like a great cowhand, turning the herd, but those old cows don't need him. About all we have to do is keep them moving. They've gone this way every year since they were born. We could go home now and most of the herd would be on summer pasture by dusk."

Amber didn't answer. The idea that Gordon Miller was involved with the Nivens made her stomach hurt. Trying to get rid of that thought, Amber focused on the cattle moving in front of her, a bawling mass of packed-together backs, dirty tails, and hairy ears. Walking, they brought their back legs forward under their bellies with a ludicrously dainty jerk. She had to keep turning Chip to make the slower animals stay with the bunch.

One of the cows just in front of her seemed to be stiff. It lagged behind and had to be continuously nudged back into the herd. Another, a big Hereford bull, was lame on one back foot. After Chip accepted the slower pace, the young horse seemed to be interested in the job at hand. With very little guidance he would slide behind a dawdling cow. Once he used his head to nudge a calf back into the herd.

Mitch laughed. "Maybe that giraffe of yours has some cow sense after all."

"You think so?"

"Yeah, he's doing okay. Watch me and you'll see how it's done." He launched into a story about how he had heroically stopped a stampede on this drive last year.

Mitch stayed at her side, flirting and showing off. After a bit she tuned out his crowing as so much background noise.

Grassland merged into forest. The cattle moved through clumps of spruce and poplar, following braided tracks that split apart and came together around the trees. Mitch kept talking for a while, but he finally quit. Maybe he'd gotten the hint that she just wasn't interested.

Both the slow cow and the lame bull were in the group in front of her. Amber concentrated on keeping the slower cattle moving. It was fun learning a new skill. At least for the moment her life had a doable goal and she wanted to do it well.

The trees were small, most less than a foot in diameter, and packed closely together. Amber followed 'her' cattle down one arm of a split. She could hear other animals in the bush and Mitch yelling at them. That noise gradually faded. Surely in a few minutes they'd come out into the open and she'd be able to see the others. She tried to hurry the cattle in front of her. Time went on, there were no breaks in the trees, and Amber began to worry.

Stopping Chip, Amber yelled, "Mitch?" Only silence answered. She called again, "Ben? Mitch? Anyone?" There was no answer. Chip lifted his head and whinnied anxiously. Knowing that the whinny would carry further than her voice, Amber listened. No other horse answered.

Twelve

"Ben! Gordon! Anyone?" Amber called. The woods seemed to swallow the sound of her voice and throw it back at her. She dropped the reins onto Chip's neck. Maybe he knew where the others were.

Chip started forward at a trot whinnying anxiously. He hesitated, ears flicking, called again and stood listening intently. Several times he did much the same thing, but he never went in the same direction twice. She could feel him trembling. It wasn't hard to tell that Chip was as lost as she was. If he'd been out here before, he'd at least have been able to take her home.

Amber picked up the reins with shaking hands. Her mouth was very dry and she could feel her pulse right down to her fingertips. She'd been out in the wild before, but always on hiking trails, and always with other people. These woods looked to her as if they'd never seen a human being before. *Don't be silly, all the others know their way. They've been here before.*

But they weren't with her. "Ben!" Amber yelled again. One of the cows bawled just in front of her. Several of the other cattle had stopped and were grazing, but the old stiff cow had kept moving. With a start Amber realized that the old cow was almost out of sight. If Mitch was right and the cattle knew their way, that old cow must know it very well. At least she was going somewhere purposefully, which was better than Amber could say for herself. It wasn't hard to tell that most of Mitch's stories were embroidered. Amber fervently hoped that he hadn't made up the story about cattle knowing their way.

What choice did she have anyway? Amber started to trot

Chip past the other animals that were grazing, and hesitated. The whole point of this exercise was to bring all the cows to a new pasture. It would be humiliating to turn up behind one old cow having lost the others. She checked Chip and swung him wide behind the grazing cattle.

"Get up, cow! Ha! Ha!" Amber yelled, imitating the men. She rode Chip at a dawdling cow and calf. The animals threw up their heads and broke into a shambling trot. "No, don't pass the old cow," Amber yelled. "She knows the way. At least I hope so."

She kept her little bunch moving. Amber wanted in the worst way to hurry, to get back to the others. The trouble was, if she hurried the other cattle, they would pass the old cow. Gritting her teeth, Amber checked Chip and stayed just close enough to keep the animals together and moving.

A harsh croaking overhead made Amber jump. She looked up to see the big black shape of a raven flying over. As they went on, the air got colder and the spruce trees began to have long strands of pale green moss hanging off each branch. The wind picked up, making the timber clack and groan. It was like part of a nightmare.

A hollow moaning sound jerked her head around. There were wolves here, weren't there? She'd heard a guy on the radio complaining he'd lost a colt to wolves. Amber swallowed hard and peered through the tree trunks expecting to see ghostly, gray forms at any moment. She'd read that wolves don't attack people, but somehow that thought wasn't very convincing at the moment.

The hollow moaning came again and died into a soft whistle. She was sure it was the wind, but she didn't stop scanning the bush. The old cow and her companions plodded onward. There was more deadfall on the trail now. Both the cattle and

Chip were repeatedly climbing over or dodging around downed logs.

Where were the others? Hadn't they noticed she was gone? Mitch must have. He'd been right at the back with her. "Mitch! Ben!" she called again, but only the wind answered.

Time stretched past. Amber had forgotten to put on her watch in the excitement of the morning. Now it seemed she'd been following these cattle for an eternity. She'd always loved Tolkien's and C. S. Lewis's books, stories full of haunted magical woods. This place looked the part, hanging lichens, ravens, and all. Amber's teeth clenched. *Don't be a total idiot. That's fantasy, not fact. You are not trapped in a time warp. You're just lost.*

*Lost...lost...lost...*The words echoed in her head. She was warm enough now, but she knew the dangers of hypothermia, every doctor did. Alone out here at night without gear, she could die.

The old cow turned steeply downhill. Chip's hooves slid as he followed the cattle, skidding and scrambling down a steep bank into a small creek. They were halfway across when Amber checked Chip suddenly. She stared at the muddy bank. There weren't enough tracks. The herd had not come this way. The old cow wasn't following the others.

Amber looked around wildly. She knew she was very close to panicking and running in circles. "Ben! Ben, help me!" she yelled and gulped for air, almost sobbing. She longed for the solid feel of him. If only his strong arms were around her now. Lost people were supposed to stay put and wait to be found. She'd been taught that in Scouts, but she'd already disobeyed that dictum. What was she supposed to do?

Chip settled the matter by starting after the cattle. Apparently as far as he was concerned, any four-legged company was better than none. Amber swallowed convulsively. At least the old cow seemed to be sure of where she was going.

"God, I don't know if you care about me at all. It doesn't seem like you do. Please help me find other people. Help me be okay."

Amber suddenly felt less afraid. It was as if there was a warm loving presence around her. The things that had seemed creepy, like the noise of the wind in the trees and the swaying moss, began to seem hauntingly beautiful.

Amber puzzled over the love she could feel around her. How could God still love her after what she'd done? How could she love a God that would let something so rotten happen? It didn't make sense, and yet she wasn't quite so frightened.

Already the day seemed to have lasted several weeks. The big western saddle creaked under her, and trees clanked in the wind. As time crawled slowly by, Amber's fears grew again. She sucked in her breath. Didn't God kill rebellious Christians sometimes? She was sure she'd heard that. Maybe that's what he was going to do to her.

"Ben! Ben, I need you!" It was only a whisper this time. She knew she was being irrational, but the fear only grew. Chip was climbing hard behind the cattle now. Amber could feel the heaving of his powerful muscles as he clawed for footing on the steep mossy hillside. Then Chip's ears snapped to full attention.

"What is it, Chip?" Amber's voice came out as a hoarse croak.

Chip whinnied loudly. Amber jumped and then held her breath. Another horse had answered. Another horse! Maybe there were people! Chip topped the hill in two huge lunges, scattering the cattle in front of him. They blasted out onto a level space. Amber reined him in, staring around wildly. There was a tiny log cabin and some broken-down corrals, but no people, no horses, nothing.

"Ben? Anybody?"

A door banged open and suddenly Ben was running toward her on foot.

In one quick movement, Amber was off Chip and in his arms. Shaking and sobbing, she clung hard.

"Thank you, Father!" Ben's voice whispered into her hair. His arms were around her in a tight hug. For a long moment he held her as she gradually controlled her sobbing. Nothing had ever felt as good as that powerful, secure embrace.

"Ben, I was so scared! I called you, I kept calling you..." She gulped and buried her face in his chest.

"It's okay." His hand stroked her hair, gently pushing it back from her forehead the way her mom used to do when she was very small. "I'm here now."

He bent toward her and the touch of his lips against her cheek sent a quiver straight to her core. With a little moan she turned her head so their lips met. That kiss, hot and sweet as honey, seemed to melt her insides.

"No." The sound of her voice was just a breath, but Ben stepped back. She swayed on her feet and his arm came back around her. Her knees felt as if they were going to buckle. Kissing Ben had felt like coming home after a long, lonely trip. It had felt like everything warm, safe, and secure. Yet at the same time she'd been torn by a deep excitement. She tried to gather her scattered wits. There was some reason she shouldn't stay in Ben's arms, but she was having trouble thinking.

Suddenly a loud whinny nearly deafened her and she was jerked backward. Amber had Chip's reins looped around her arm, and he'd thrown his head, nearly knocking her down. Chip had had enough. He wanted to go to the other horse he'd heard.

Ben's hand on her elbow steadied her. He took Chip's reins with the other hand, looked past her, and laughed. "Looks like we've got an audience."

Amber followed his eyes and couldn't stop herself from giggling. The cattle had come up the hill and were standing in a half circle, staring at them with wide, stupid eyes. The old cow lifted her muzzle and bawled a body-shaking moo at them.

"Go on, you old boot," Ben waved his hat. The others jumped back, but the old cow merely lowered her head as if she were trying to see over a pair of reading glasses. Amber giggled again but sobered instantly at the touch of Ben's hand on her chin. He lifted it gently until she was looking straight into his eyes.

"Amber, I'm sorry that happened." He shook his head. "No, that's a lie. What I'm trying to say is that I care about you, but I'll leave you be. I'll be waiting for the time, if and when you're ready and things can be right before God."

Ben's eyes seemed to be mostly pupil, a deep well she could fall into. "Ben, I don't know..." She wasn't ready for this. Amber changed the subject. "Where are we anyway? How did you find me?"

"I thought that old crock of a cow might bring you here."

"Why here? Where are the others?"

"Ryder used to bring the cattle here until a couple of years ago. Last two years he's taken them on into the forestry lease through another gate. It's only a mile or so over. The others have probably been there for a bit now. I dropped back to check on you, and when you weren't there..." Ben's brows came down and she could see the muscles in his jaw bunch. "Mitch admitted he hadn't seen you for a while, said you'd been trailing the old cow and lame bull. I backtracked far enough to know you weren't following, and then I thought the old cow would have headed here."

"How'd you know I'd stick with those cows and not run in circles?"

Ben smiled. "I figured you had too much sense, and besides, I was praying."

"I almost did panic, Ben. I was terrified for a while." Amber ducked her head. Her hair had come out of the braid and veiled her face.

"For a while?" Ben asked gently.

"I prayed too, and..." Amber shook her head. "It was probably you God answered, not me."

"Amber, God loves you. I'm sure he answered—"

"Shouldn't we be getting back to the others?" Amber cut in nervously.

"Yeah, we should, but..." Ben's big hands clenched into fists. He bowed his head for a few seconds and then looked up with a rueful smile. "Okay, I won't talk at you. It's only a bit more than a mile to the others. Think you can handle that?"

"Do I have any choice?"

Ben grinned. "I could carry you across the front of my saddle."

"No way!" She took Chip's reins from Ben and, refusing his help, climbed slowly into the saddle. She ached in places she hadn't even known about.

The cattle were grazing around the cabin and were in no hurry to leave. Amber watched Ben move his gray around behind them. She brought Chip around the other side. The old cow trotted away from Ben and tried to dodge around Chip. Amber pushed Chip forward and swung him to face the cow.

"Good for you!" Ben called when the old cow turned. "You and that colt are doing okay." Ben's praise made Amber feel good right down to her toes. It even made her muscles ache less.

"Thanks, Ben. I might survive this day yet if we don't get lost again."

Ben laughed. "I'd say that isn't too likely. I've been here a couple of times before."

"How long have you been doing this?"

"Here, with the Nivens? Since Dad would let me come along. I must have been about nine. Dad has worked hard to keep the two families on good terms. The Millers and Nivens were business partners from way back. Dad runs the ranch so I'm not much involved yet. We don't see things exactly the same."

Business partners? This had to be a bad dream.

A squirrel chattered at her from just overhead, sounding like a cheap windup alarm clock. It pitched a pinecone down that hit Ben on the hat.

"Hey!" he said, looking up. The squirrel yelled again and they both laughed. Ben was such a great guy. There was no way he'd be involved with the Nivens himself, was there? She looked over and caught him watching her.

"Amber, remember I said there was something I wanted to tell you about?" Chip suddenly pricked his ears and whinnied. Another horse answered some distance off.

"Ben! Is that you?" It was Gordon Miller's voice.

"Right here, Dad!" He turned to Amber, talking quickly. "If I don't get a chance to talk to you alone today, come with me to church tomorrow. I'll come by around nine in the morning."

Amber looked away. It hurt her not to answer Ben, but she wasn't ready for church, wasn't sure she ever would be again.

Ahead of the cattle, movement caught Amber's eye. Patches of pale hide, then a hat. Gordon Miller had gone well off the path to let the cattle past. His horse stepped carefully over deadfall. "Good! You found her. Mitch said you'd gone looking.

It's quite the experience you're having, Amber."

"She even kept the cattle with her."

"Excellent!" Gordon sounded really pleased, but his next words didn't make Amber feel so good. "Ben, that roughneck Bull Schwartz turned up at the camp. Ryder's been yelling at him and Mitch is drinking. Both are touchier than grasshoppers on a hot griddle. Don't you go asking questions."

Amber turned her head in time to see Ben give his dad a hard look, and then nod. The old cow suddenly began to hurry, breaking into a limping trot. Gordon laughed. "She knows where she's going now, don't you, old girl?"

"A good thing too!" Ben dropped back beside Amber. "We're in the forestry lease now, so Ryder has just let them scatter. The horse trailers are right over here by another little cabin."

"We don't have to ride back?" Amber asked with incredulous relief.

"You a little sore?" Gordon asked, chuckling. "You're in luck this time. Hanna brought our trailer up this morning and I think Lyle Smith must have brought Mitch's trailer up yesterday."

They were riding into a clearing with several horses tied to trees. Amber dismounted beside a paint horse and began to tie Chip. She glanced over at the paint horse and stopped halfway through the knot. Slowly she finished tying and stepped closer. The paint watched her with friendly interest. A line of white hairs, a wide quarter horse face. Amber glanced under the animal. A mare. If this animal hadn't been a paint, she could have sworn it was the same mare she'd seen the morning Chip got cut. She frowned. That mare had a star-shaped scar on her right flank. Amber stepped around the paint. The scar was there. Amber stood with her heart pounding. What was happening here? That mare had been a chestnut and this one was a flashy paint. The background color was the chestnut though.

Amber reached to touch the big white patches with the goofy idea that they might have been drawn on somehow. No, the hair was really white. She looked again. The mare's skin under the white patch was rough and peeling, like she'd been sunburned.

Amber stepped back. She felt like Alice in Wonderland, when one thing kept turning into another. There was no way to actually turn a horse into a paint, was there? She sucked in her breath. Hadn't Mitch said something once about delivering a shipment to the painter, and Ryder had told him to shut up? *If they catch me looking at this horse…*

Quickly she moved back to her own horse. Ben was already there, easily lifting the heavy western saddle from Chip's back.

"Hey!" Ryder's voice suddenly bellowed. Amber looked up to see him nearly running toward them from the porch. "Move your horses away from there. That paint is a kicker. She'll nail you good."

Amber looked at the paint, who was standing flop eared, looking as lazy and relaxed as a horse could look.

"I said move them!" Ryder bellowed.

"Better do it," Ben said under his breath, putting down the saddle and going toward his gray.

As they tied the horses again to different trees, Gordon said, "When you get the horses settled, come on in. There are drinks and sandwiches. Hanna packed enough for everyone."

Thirteen

"Bringing women along to move the cattle now, are you?" Bull's question met Amber as she walked into the tiny cabin. She recoiled as the huge man got to his feet.

Ben stepped in front of her, holding out his hand. "She did all right, Bull. How are you—"

"Just where exactly were you, Ben Miller?" Mitch was nearly yelling. Amber clutched the door frame. "My brother is cattle boss here, and he set you to ride flank. What did you think you were doing leaving the cattle and taking off after a piece of skirt?"

"You're drunk, Mitch," Ben said, his voice even.

"What is it to you?" Mitch grabbed Ben's shirt with both hands. "I told you she was with me. Did you get a feel of the cold princess here while you were out chasing her?"

Ben growled and pushed Mitch away. Mitch stumbled, sending the table and coffee cups crashing across the floor. He scrambled up out of the debris and leapt at Ben. The two hit the ground twisting like wildcats. The rough wood of the door frame bit into Amber's hands. This was like a nightmare. Someone bumped into her. Amber barely registered that it was Lyle Smith pushing his way outside. Her attention was locked on Ben. He came over on top of Mitch. One of his legs flew wide, digging for purchase, and nearly toppled Ryder.

"Bull!" Ryder bellowed. Amber had a vague impression of Gordon Miller yelling something, then Bull Schwartz surged forward like an angry elephant. He seized the two combatants, holding each at the end of one loglike arm. Ben stood still, but Mitch thrashed and swore until Bull shook him, snapping

Mitch's handsome head back and forth as if he were a rag doll.

"Ryder, why'd you let him drink while you were moving cattle?" Bull asked. Mitch hung limply now, as if the sense had been temporarily shaken out of him.

"Let go of my son," Gordon Miller said in a quiet voice.

Bull let go of Ben and turned back to Ryder. "What do you want done with Mitch?" He tried to stand him on his feet, but it didn't work very well as Mitch's knees buckled.

"Pitch him out!" Ryder said.

"Hey, man, he's your brother." Bull tried again to stand Mitch up, this time with more success.

Mitch shook his head and looked at Ryder. "Don't do this. It was her fault." Scrambling backward he pointed at Amber. "She owed me, and she was treating me like a—"

Ryder grabbed Mitch by the elbow and pushed him toward the door. Amber jumped outside to get out of the way. Propelled from behind, Mitch stumbled through the opening and fell into the dirt. "Get on your feet and get out of here!" Ryder yelled at him. "I don't want to see you around here again! I'm finished with your nonsense! Do you hear me?"

"Fine!" Mitch said, staggering upright. "So what are you going to do? Go out into the wide, wild world and conduct your own business? I don't think so, big brother. After years of hiding like a hermit in a cave, you'll actually go on the Centennial Cattle Drive?"

There was an instant of silence so intense that Amber could hear her heart beating. In spite of herself, at that moment she felt pity for Ryder. Then Ryder growled, "If I have to, I will. Now get out!"

Mitch pointed at Amber. He was nearly screaming now. "This is your fault, Amber Lacey. You humiliated me in front of my friends, got me into some crazy bet, and now this! I won't forget!" He spat on the ground, spun, and ran staggering toward his horse.

Amber stood frozen, staring as Mitch hauled himself onto the animal's back and cantered into the trees. Humiliated? A bet with his friends? Was that what the roses and the eight-hundred-dollar registration for the cattle drive was all about? She grimaced. She was not even going to think about what that bet must have been.

"Smith!" Amber jumped as Ryder bellowed. "Get back here."

Lyle was caught halfway through mounting his horse. He hesitated. "I was just going to make sure Mitch gets back okay."

"Leave him!"

Lyle made a protesting motion. When Ryder ran toward him, he got off rapidly and stood with his head hanging while Ryder harangued him.

Ben spoke just behind Amber. "Is Mitch going to be all right, Dad? Should I go after him?"

Amber turned and her eyes widened. Ben's lip was split and there was blood on his chin. Marked with dirt and violence, he'd come out of the cabin and was standing protectively close behind her. She could feel the heat of his sweat. Yet this powerful male was offering to help the man who'd just attacked him.

Gordon Miller chuckled. "I don't think Mitch would value your help much right now, Ben."

Ryder came back toward them frowning furiously. "Bull, you close up here. I'll be talking to you tomorrow."

"I told you, my cell phone don't work," Bull said. "Mitch told me you'd be moving cattle today so I come up here."

"I said I'd be talking to you tomorrow!" Ryder walked toward his horse. "Let's get these animals loaded and get out of here."

"Ryder, we'll give Amber a ride back with us," Ben called after him.

"Not if she wants to still be working for me at the end of the day, you won't!"

Ben looked at Amber and raised one eyebrow questioningly. Amber looked away. If she went with the Millers now, she'd still be sponging. There'd be questions to answer. Again she had the horrible feeling that God was cornering her, pushing her into a situation that would force her to quit running and face things.

The metal floor of the trailer boomed as Ryder's horse jumped in. Ryder climbed back out. "Smith, load Amber's horse! I'll get the tack."

Ben's voice was deep and gentle, close to her. "Amber, after what Mitch said, I don't think you—"

"I know what you think, Ben." Looking at the tenderness and concern in Ben's eyes, Amber had never felt so torn. Gently she reached to touch his cut lip. "You should put some ice on that."

"Amber."

The anguish in his voice was too much for her. She turned and ran to Chip, getting there just ahead of Lyle. She untied the horse and headed for the Nivens' trailer. Inside, she leaned against the big colt's shoulder.

"Get in the truck, woman!" Ryder called.

Amber climbed out of the trailer and found Ben beside her. He opened the door of the truck for her and looked across to Ryder and Lyle. "Listen, I want Amber treated decently. She matters to me."

Ryder's eyes narrowed. "Hey, the woman can leave anytime if she doesn't like the way we treat her." He shoved the truck into gear.

Pushing herself against the truck door, Amber stayed as far away from Lyle and Ryder as she could. She felt sick inside. Could Ben's father really be involved with the Nivens? He seemed like such a good man, yet he had warned Ben not to ask questions. More than that, the look in Ben's eyes haunted her. She had wanted to go with him, but she couldn't. She just wasn't ready to face some things. Why couldn't God leave her alone? Why did things have to be so complicated? She closed her eyes and withdrew, feigning sleep.

Ryder and Lyle must have thought she really was asleep because after a bit they began to talk softly. At first, Amber let their words flow by without listening. Then she began to hear what they were saying.

"You figure Mitch is going to make trouble?" Lyle asked as if he was fishing for information.

Ryder snorted. "He's making himself trouble. I can do without him, the fool."

"You think so?"

"Yes, I dang well do think so! You start siding with Mitch against me and you'll be out of here so fast your feet will be smoking."

"I never said anything against you," Lyle said, in a defensive, whining voice. "I know some stuff. I could help you."

"You know some stuff, do you?" Ryder's voice was oddly flat. Amber caught the menace, but apparently Lyle didn't because he babbled on eagerly.

"Mitch told me you were saving horses, auction horses, young ones that weren't broke and weren't flashy. Horses that would have gone for meat without you. Look, Bull said those two big bay horses are healed up. We could take them to the auction at Innisfil and skip taking them on that Centennial Cattle Drive."

"If Mitch had bought them at auction."

"He said he'd show you the receipts," Lyle protested. "I could call him and I bet he'd meet us at Innisfil tomorrow."

"You do that."

"Okay, I will!" Lyle said loudly.

Ryder hissed a harsh warning sound. "You'll wake the girl."

There was a short silence and Amber could feel the men's eyes on her. She tried to keep her body limp and her breathing deep. The last thing she wanted was to have them know she'd overheard. Lyle had said the horses were healed. Healed from what? Her stomach ached. What were these people doing?

In the yard Ryder brusquely went about his own business, and Lyle followed, trying to get his approval like a submissive dog. Amber climbed out of the truck. Stiff and aching, she put Chip back into his corral. No matter what was going on, she was too tired to deal with it tonight. In the house she opened cans of stew to feed the two men, but she didn't eat any herself. As soon as they were done, she dragged herself into a hot bath, and then to bed.

Around two in the morning, Amber rolled over and came awake with a groan. Her muscles hurt! Headlights flashed across the ceiling of her bedroom. Amber watched them blearily and then got up to go to the washroom. Glancing out the window on the way back, she could see truck and trailer lights disappearing in the distance.

Back in bed, Amber couldn't sleep. Memories tumbled over one another: Mitch fighting Ben, the aching terror of being lost, a raven croaking above the evergreen trees, the old stiff cow mooing, that strange paint horse. Of all the images, Ben's kiss was by far the most disturbing. Just thinking of the feel of his mouth on hers made her heart pound.

She turned over onto her back with a jerk, making stiff muscles protest. No matter how much it seemed Ben cared about her, it wasn't real and she may as well not pretend differently. Ben didn't know who she really was. If he did, he would surely turn away. She swallowed hard. Ben had said God loved her and…it wasn't fair! Tears tracked in warm trickles into her ears.

Amber got to her feet. She threw the window open and let the cool night air caress her face. The moon was full, bathing the farmyard in flat silver light. Did Chip feel as stiff from the long day's work as she did?

She looked for her horse, frowned, and looked again. In the bright moonlight she should have been able to see the big animal clearly. Carefully she searched the striped shadows along the corral fence and the dark area in the shelter shed. Nothing.

Mitch wouldn't steal a horse out of his own yard, would he? Amber whipped around and, still in her pajamas, ran out of her room and down the stairs. Forgetting her sore muscles, she vaulted the corral fence. She called Chip's name but there was no answering whicker. The cold ground made her bare feet ache as she searched through the corral. It was empty. The gate stood open. Had she failed to shut it last night when she put him away? Outside the gate Amber could see a muddle of tracks in the moonlight, but nothing was clear.

A violent shiver shook her. She needed warmer clothes and a flashlight. She ran for the house. Trying to move silently, she pulled on clothes and grabbed her jacket and a flashlight.

Back outside she crouched, playing the flashlight over the ground by the gate. She was no tracker, but she was intelligent and persistent. Slowly she puzzled out what she could see.

The cold night had laid a thin layer of delicate frost on the soft ground. She backed up and could see her feet destroying the delicate filigree. Her bare footprints from a few minutes ago had no frost on top either. All the other prints did, except…

She bent to look closer and slowly began to follow darker unfrosted marks. These went through a lower muddy spot and she could clearly see the open half circles of Chip's prints, plus a set of boot tracks. They ended in between tire tracks. Mitch *had* taken Chip.

Amber stood up and stared into the dark. God knew that Chip was one of the reasons she didn't want to go back. She hadn't wanted to give him up. Now Chip was gone. If God thought he could force her! Amber set her jaw. No matter what weird game Mitch and Ryder were playing, she'd finally had enough. She was done with the Nivens. But she was going to find Chip, and she was not going back.

For a split second, Amber wished with all her heart for Ben's strong, comforting presence. She steeled herself against her emotions. If she was going to stay tough, she didn't dare get anywhere near Ben Miller.

She rehearsed the words she'd say to the RCMP as she walked toward the house. There had been the strange horses in the yard, then the paint horse that looked burnt. She was not going to let them mutilate Chip.

She reached for the phone. It was dead, no dial tone, nothing. She bumped the disconnect button a few times; nothing changed. Amber clenched her fists. She wasn't going to be stopped that easily. She ran for her car.

Shoving the keys into the ignition, she pumped the gas and turned the starter. Nothing, not even a click. Shaking with fear and anger, Amber jumped out to open the hood and shine her flashlight inside. Torn wires dangled like spaghetti.

Amber stood still, trying to calm herself enough to think clearly. Mitch had said he was going to get even. He was spoiled, ruthless, and angry. She was sure he'd taken Chip. It was likely the dead phone and her damaged car were Mitch's doing as well.

She frowned. She'd seen truck and trailer lights when she first woke up. She'd actually seen Mitch leave and those lights hadn't gone down the driveway. They'd gone west on one of the little ranch roads. Amber had an immediate urge to go after Chip. It just wouldn't work. The Niven ranch was huge. Her chances of finding Chip in the dark were abysmally small.

Amber looked south, toward Ben's place. Should she try to cover the ten miles to Ben's? Would Ben help her in spite of what his father might be doing? The image of the white horse's torn head flashed into her head. If Mitch thought Chip might get him in trouble, Amber was suddenly certain he'd kill the horse without compunction. If there was even a chance Gordon Miller was involved, she didn't want to risk asking Ben's help.

She clenched her jaw to stop her teeth from chattering. If she acted ignorant, maybe Chip had a chance at living until she could somehow rescue him. Mitch wasn't likely to tell Ryder what he'd done, not after today. Ben had said he would come to take her to church. That would give her a chance to get off the Niven place. Surely there'd be a chance for her to get away from the Millers as well and call the police. She took a deep, steadying breath. For now she'd just have to play stupid.

Trying to move silently, Amber went upstairs and climbed into bed. In spite of her fears she dropped into a troubled sleep, barely waking in time to make breakfast. She'd half expected Lyle to be gone this morning, but he walked in with

Ryder. Keeping her eyes down, she burst into speech.

"I was outside. Chip is out. He's not around the yard, either."

Ryder stopped dead in the doorway. "Your horse is gone?"

Amber nodded, finding it easy to look anxious. "The gate was open. I was tired last night when I put him into his corral and it's easy to be careless with gates when you're tired." Lyle looked completely uninterested. He seemed too stupid to act that well, so he probably didn't know what Mitch had done, either. Amber gathered her courage. "Can I take one of your horses or the truck after breakfast and look for Chip if he's not around the yard by then?"

She was certain that they wouldn't let her do that, but it was the obvious question.

"No!" Ryder said explosively. "I told you I don't want you to be riding out of the yard. Lyle and I will go search for him."

Lyle gave Ryder a startled look. "Last night you said we were going to check out the Innisfil auction. I called Mitch on the cell phone this morning and he's going to meet us there. If you want to skip it, Mitch won't mind."

"I bet," Ryder said and swore. "Go drive the rest of the horses out of the yard and pull the battery out of the farm truck. It needs a new one."

He turned to Amber. "With the other horses out, Chip will tag in with them. If he doesn't, we'll look for him tomorrow. Don't you try to take that old bomb of yours on the ranch roads, either. You'll just tear the suspension out. If he's loose, Chip will be okay. There's a cattle gate so he can't get off the place."

He'd sounded almost kind. Besides, if Chip had really been loose, what Ryder was saying would have been okay. For one wild second Amber thought about telling him the truth and asking for help. She made the mistake of looking at him as she tried to make up her mind.

He shoved back his chair. "Go on! Get out of here. You must have work to do, woman."

Amber fled and sat in the kitchen watching the clock. She wanted the men gone before Ben turned up. She stared at the wall. It seemed pretty obvious that Ryder had told Mitch to buy horses at auction, and he'd been stealing them instead. They brought the horses somewhere on the ranch close enough that Ryder was afraid she would find them if she wandered on his land, and then they…

They did what? Made them into paints? Why would Ryder have that done to a horse he'd bought legally? If they were stolen horses, at least that made some sense. They'd certainly be very difficult to identify again.

At the sound of the men shoving back chairs and leaving the house, Amber let out her breath in relief. She didn't care whether Ryder caught Mitch out at Innisfil or not. She just wanted the time to rescue Chip. The memory of that dead white horse kept haunting her. What if Mitch had already shot Chip? No, he had to be alive!

A sound outside the window made her look up. Ryder was yelling at the top of his voice as he slammed the driver's door of his truck and strode forward to jerk open the hood. Amber turned away, half grinning. Mitch had obviously disabled the other vehicles in the yard too.

A thought wiped the grin off her face. What if Ryder and Lyle couldn't leave? She didn't want them around to mess up her chances to get off the yard with Ben. Ryder jerked open the hood of the farm truck. He shook his head in disgust, slammed the hood, and walked away.

With the truck disabled, he'd obviously decided it wasn't

worth his time to pull the battery out. Amber watched him stomp back over to his truck. Lyle trotted up with some tools and they both bent forward under the hood. It didn't take them long to fix whatever Mitch had messed up. In fifteen minutes they were on their way out of the yard.

Fourteen

After the men left, Amber still had time before Ben had said he'd come. As she began to clean the kitchen, she looked outside at Chip's empty corral and bit her lip. It was a bright, still morning with the promise of coming heat. A perfect day, but not for Amber. She started to scrub the counter furiously. Halfway through the job she suddenly froze. Leaving the dishcloth where it was, she ran for the stairs. Ben was going to expect her to be dressed for church.

Amber pulled open her closet and hesitated. If she hobbled herself with a skirt and heels she wouldn't be able to run if she needed to. She probably should stick to jeans and tennis shoes. Amber found herself choosing dress pants, sandals, and a soft blouse. In front of the mirror, she twisted her hair into a knot, a style people had told her looked good.

She wrinkled her nose at her image. "You're being dumb, you know. This whole thing with Ben is going nowhere."

A horn beeped outside. Amber whirled and ran down the stairs. She wanted to be out of the yard before Ben noticed Chip was gone. She burst out the door and straight into Ben. He caught her and she felt the solid, clean strength of him. She wanted to cling to that strength and blurt out that Chip was stolen. She needed help. Fighting that impulse rendered her completely mute for a few seconds.

Ben set her gently on her feet. "What's the matter?"

"I saw your truck and—"

"You came out to meet me?" Ben's eyes crinkled into a good smile. "You know, you look fantastic."

Ben was so pleased she'd come and she was just using him

to get off the place. She ached inside. Nothing was right. Fighting with God was hurting more all the time.

As soon as she walked into the building, Amber realized that being in church again was going to be harder than she thought. People in good clothes were visiting in the foyer. An organ was playing. Everything about this particular church was strange to her, yet as a church it was painfully familiar.

Hanna Miller came over and took her hand. "I've been praying for you, Amber. I'm so glad you've come."

Ben began to introduce her to others and she was immediately surrounded by a group of welcoming people. Hands and smiles walled her in. Amber pasted a smile on her own face, trying to hide her growing panic. She'd come so she could call the police about Chip. She wasn't ready to deal with all this. People kept looking at her and smiling at Ben, obviously happy that he'd brought a woman friend. She broke away muttering something about finding the washroom.

Hanna Miller came with her. "I'll show you. It's just down the hall." Hanna talked all the way about how well Gordon had said Amber had done at moving cattle, and how sorry she was that Amber had gotten lost. Amber had intended to get away and look for a phone, but she couldn't get rid of Ben's mother.

When they came out of the washroom, the first hymn had started. It would have looked odd to do anything but follow Hanna into the sanctuary. She ended up next to Ben who was singing in a comfortable, glad baritone. Amber started off confidently enough, her clear alto blending nicely with Ben's baritone. The second song was "What a Friend We Have in Jesus." After the first line, Amber found she couldn't sing at all. Ben glanced at her. She turned her head away, but she couldn't shut out the words of the song.

She was trapped beside Ben and his family in church. She

couldn't walk away from the Bible, or just refuse to think about God as she'd been doing. The hymn rolled relentlessly on. "Have we trials and temptations? Is there trouble anywhere? We should never be discouraged. Take it to the Lord in prayer."

The words still echoed in her mind as they sat back down. *What a friend we have in Jesus, all our sins and griefs to bear...*

Sins, Amber thought. All her life she'd been taught that Jesus forgave sins, but she'd never really thought about it. She'd never before felt terribly sinful. She did well in school, didn't drink or sleep around. Sure, there were some things she'd done that she shouldn't have, but she didn't figure they were any big deal. Asking for Christ's forgiveness had merely been the right thing to do. Something you just kind of did if you wanted to be a Christian.

Amber heard nothing of the announcements. She stood up for the next group of hymns without singing or even really hearing what other people sang. *Sin?* Was that the problem? Was she just too proud to face up to her errors? Too proud to ask for help? Could Christ's forgiveness cover something that terrible? If she couldn't stand herself, how could God want her? Was she even interested in a God who could put up with evil?

If the words of a hymn had touched a raw nerve, the sermon was worse. The pastor, a big man with a bald head, spoke on Isaiah 53. Amber tried to block out the voice. She thought about getting up and simply walking out. The trouble was, this church stood beside a tiny cemetery on a gravel road miles from any town.

For a wild second, Amber thought of stealing Ben's truck. He'd put the keys in his pocket. He had on black Wranglers and a western shirt. She looked at him as he sat calmly listening to the pastor. There was no way she'd ever get the keys out of his jeans pocket without him knowing. Feeling her eyes on him, he glanced over. She quickly looked away.

The pastor's voice went on. "No, God does not condone sin. It is horrible to him, but he loved us enough to carry our filth on himself."

Those words sank into Amber's mind and stayed there like a terrible taste one can't get rid of. *Carry my filth on himself?* Amber almost gagged. The pastor was reading from Isaiah now. The words filled the room and beat at her. "'Surely he took up our infirmities and carried our sorrows, yet we considered him stricken by God, smitten by him, and afflicted. But he was pierced for our transgressions, he was crushed for our iniquities; the punishment that brought us peace was upon him, and by his wounds we are healed. We all, like sheep, have gone astray, each of us has turned to his own way; and the LORD has laid on him the iniquity of us all.'"

It was too much. The realization that the things she'd been hearing all her life meant this! That Christ had died to rescue her from her own horrible errors. What if it was God's love, not just her own failure, that she'd been running from? She felt as if a huge dam built up inside her was about to burst. There was no way Amber wanted to deal with this, not here in front of all these people.

Desperately she looked for escape. If she ran from the building, she couldn't get away, not out here. People would follow her and pray for her. It would be unbearable. Amber took a deep breath. This was stupid. Her horse was missing and she didn't even know if she could turn to Ben or trust his family. There was no way she could fall apart now.

Amber retreated into herself like a turtle retreating into its shell. She sat on the bench, a woman carved of wood, and forced her mind to concentrate on plans to rescue Chip. Whatever was going on wasn't the horse's fault. There was no way she was going to let him be shot or burned or whatever. Not if she could help it. So what if she was using Chip as a shield against the horrible pressure of God's love? Shields were useful.

As soon as the service was over, Amber asked Ben, "Is there a phone here I could use?"

"I don't know. Dad, did they get a phone installed out here or is the church phone number still at the pastor's house?"

"It's still at the pastor's house," Gordon said.

When Hanna invited Amber over for Sunday dinner, Amber accepted. Anything was better than being dropped off back at the Nivens' yard without any chance of help. If she asked careful questions at the Millers' place maybe she'd be able to tell by their answers if she dared trust them. Even if she couldn't, maybe she'd get a chance to use their phone unobserved.

Six miles southwest of the Nivens' main ranch yard, Bull Schwartz was getting ready to paint a horse. He was in the barn at old Thaddeus Niven's homestead. Ben had been right when he told Amber the isolated old barn was still in good shape. Sunlight through the barn door made a bright stripe, highlighting the dusty barn air.

Bull's little eyes narrowed. Mitch had brought in two horses last week, and then last night another one, a tall young horse. Bull looked across the barn at the stall where he'd tied that horse. Mitch had been more than a little drunk. Bull was pretty sure most of the horses he'd painted lately had been stolen. Mitch had been ready enough to slip him a little extra cash to cover any brands. But Mitch's manner in handling this one had been odd. Bull wished he was well rid of it. Not only because he had a strong suspicion Mitch had done something stupid, but because the horse was big, powerful, and spooky. He was going to be a real pain to handle. Not at all like the quiet quarter horse Bull had tied in the barn alley.

Bull's hands were fat and blunt like flippers. His fingernails were filthy, ridged with black grime. But his movements were surprisingly delicate as he picked up a wide black marker and began to draw on the rounded back end of the quarter horse. Bull Schwartz considered himself an artist. He stood back to admire the pattern he'd drawn and grunted in satisfaction. This little gelding was going to make one classy Appaloosa.

A loud pounding brought Bull's head up. The little mare he'd painted a couple of hours ago was starting to hurt now. She was tied with two ropes, one to each side of the stall. Her head was held forward in a crib, a corsetlike brace that kept her from bending her neck. Bull was pretty sure she couldn't bite at the painful spots, hurt herself, and damage his artistry. He took a couple of steps down the alley to double-check. The mare rolled her eyes at him and whickered anxiously.

"It'll get better, girl. Just you hang in there and you'll be real pretty." Bull stepped closer. The area he'd burnt was blistering nicely. In a week or so the dead skin would shed and the new hair would begin to grow in white. In seven or eight weeks the mare would be good as new. Bull's sausagelike lips parted in a smile. Not good as new, better than new, with lots of fancy markings—chrome, as a horseman would say.

When he'd first started this business, he'd made mistakes. In trying to put socks on one gelding, he'd gotten impatient with painting the leg and simply stuck the horse's foot into the liquid nitrogen. He'd left it too long and the burn had deformed the horse's foot so badly he'd had to destroy that animal. Bull frowned; every great artist had occasional failures.

He'd learned to burn them just right so there was no dent around the white area and no badly burnt areas where the hair didn't grow back properly. The horses weren't hurt permanently at all.

When Ryder had approached him, Bull had been able to assure him that he could paint a horse in a way that would double its value. There were fads in horse coloring and for the last several years, flashy paints had been bringing big bucks. That was starting to change now and Bull had been turning more horses into Appaloosas.

He walked back to the tied quarter horse and began to meticulously shave the entire area that he intended to turn white. That job done, he picked up a large container of Vaseline and applied it thickly to the surrounding area. The grimy creases in Bull's neck folded as he nodded his wedge-shaped head. This one would be a good one. The Vaseline would keep the liquid nitrogen confined, leaving clear, sharp edges to the blanket Appaloosa pattern.

Looking into the Vaseline container, he frowned, his thick-skinned forehead furrowing into dirty ridges. It was almost empty. When he finished this horse, he'd intended to do the big spooky horse. Now he'd have to make a trip into town. Bull's fat lips twisted into a grin as he realized the trip would give him a chance to spend some time in a bar.

He didn't really mind staying out here. Ryder paid him well enough. With Mitch's money on top, Bull had no inclination to talk about what he was doing and kill the goose that was laying him golden eggs. Still, Ryder complained if he so much as showed his nose anywhere else. Bull snorted. Ryder would have to stuff it. This trip was for essential supplies.

Lifting a container of liquid nitrogen, Bull brought it over to the horse and began to carefully apply it to the shaved areas.

The gelding jumped a bit. Since it was so cold, the nitrogen numbed feeling. The burn wouldn't really begin to hurt for several hours. Protruding a pale tongue between fat lips, Bull concentrated on his artwork.

In the Millers' kitchen, Amber was struck by the tremendous contrast between the Millers' homey kitchen table and the emotional coldness of the Niven's place.

"It's nice to have you here. Julie couldn't be home this weekend and three around the table seems thin for Sunday dinner," Hanna said after they'd said grace.

Amber was having a hard time eating. She took a bite of potatoes and dark, rich pot roast gravy and glanced at Gordon Miller. Could this man who seemed so kind and upright really have anything to do with the Nivens?

She watched him swallow a bite of roast and nod. "You've outdone yourself again, Hanna. This is excellent!" His weathered face looked so at peace.

The good food was like sawdust in her mouth. With a struggle Amber managed to swallow her mouthful. She was sick of pretending and had to know if she could trust these people. Impetuously she burst into speech. "Chip disappeared last night. Mitch's truck and trailer left the yard in the middle of the night."

Amber saw Ben glance quickly at his father. An intense look went between the two big men, then Gordon Miller said, "Could you have left the gate open?"

Amber's stomach hurt. All the food she had managed to eat seemed to have lumped up into a red-hot ball. Ben had looked at his father. Then Gordon had tried to make it seem like nothing bad had happened to Chip. Gordon was involved! In

Amber's panicked state there didn't seem to be any other possible explanation.

Gordon repeated his question. Amber could only shake her head mutely. She never should have said anything.

"Why on earth didn't you tell me this morning?" Ben looked stunned.

"Both of you, don't grill the girl like she's a police suspect!" Hanna said. "Can't you see that she's upset enough about her horse without you blaming it on her?" Hanna stepped closer and put her arm around Amber. "Have you looked for your horse, honey?"

Hanna's sympathy was the last straw. She had to get out of here, away from these people that she'd hoped to trust. There was no way she'd be able to use a phone in this house without being overheard.

"Excuse me." She stood and left the room. They'd probably think she was heading to the washroom. Instead Amber silently opened the back door and slipped out. She glanced into the vehicles, but there were no keys in the ignition. Ben's gray and the horse Gordon had ridden were looking at her over a corral rail. She stared at them. If she could ride out of here...She glanced back at Gordon's pickup. She'd seen a saddle and pad in the box.

In minutes she'd caught the gray and had him saddled.

As soon as Amber left the table, Ben leaned forward. "Mitch wouldn't have stolen a horse out of his own yard, would he?"

Gordon shook his head. "Ben, we don't know that Ryder and Mitch are stealing horses." He glanced down the hall after Amber. "You know, twice I've had the impression that Amber doesn't trust me."

Ben shoved his chair back as a thought hit him with absolute certainty. "She thinks we're involved with the Nivens! The first time we spent any time together I took her up to see that marsh hawk's nest I told you about. It's near their property line. I ended up pointing out Thad's Hump and babbling about how long Nivens and Millers have helped each other out." He paused, puzzled. "But I did warn her about Mitch and Ryder and even tried to get her to leave."

There was a little silence and Hanna said, "She could think you didn't want her to find out anything."

Ben turned on his father. "I don't care what you've said about not speaking against neighbors only on suspicion. I'm going to tell Amber straight that I don't trust the Nivens. Then I intend to find out just what is going on."

Gordon nodded his head. "I think you're right, Ben. I just hate giving up on anyone."

Hanna was looking down the hallway with anxious eyes. "Ben, Amber wouldn't try to run from us, would she?"

There was a back door at the end of that hallway. Amber could have slipped out with no trouble at all. In two strides, Ben was at the door. He swung it open and squinted against the bright sunlight to see Amber's red blond hair flying as she cantered over a rise.

"She's taken Smoke!" Ben yelled over his shoulder and ran toward the other horses. In seconds he was sliding a halter over the head of Denver, his father's buckskin gelding.

Gordon was on his son's heels. He pulled the gate wide. "She's heading for the Nivens' place. Must be planning to look for her horse. I'll take the pickup and try to cut her off at the gate."

Ben nodded, and in one smooth movement leapt onto the buckskin bareback. He put his heels to the beast and burst through the gate at a dead run. He could feel the buckskin's muscles bunch and shove under him as the horse accelerated. He kept his balance easily as he looked between the animal's laid-back ears at the spot where Amber had disappeared over the ridge. If she saw him following, he wouldn't have a chance. Smoke was faster than Denver and Amber was a lighter load.

Fifteen

Ben crested the ridge on the hard running horse and let out his breath in relief. Three hundred yards ahead, Amber had slowed Smoke to a trot and was heading purposefully for the Nivens' place without looking back. Ben reined Denver to the south, down the slope into a coulee that paralleled her path. Out of sight, he kept the buckskin at a hard canter.

A few minutes later Ben brought Denver up out of the coulee. The horse came in big lunging jumps as Ben asked him for speed uphill. He blasted out of a clump of poplars straight into Amber's path. Amber spun Smoke on his back legs in an attempt to escape, but Ben was quicker. Driving Denver in close he grabbed the cheek-piece of the gray's bridle.

Both horses danced wildly. Ben said, "Whoa!" and the dancing stopped. Smoke knew his voice, and Denver was a steady horse.

"Ben Miller! Let go of this horse!" Amber said, digging her heels in and tossing her head. Smoke tried to jump forward, but Ben swung Denver around, bringing the gray's head into the buckskin's sweaty shoulder.

"Amber, stop it!" Ben said in that same tone of command he'd used on the horses. "Listen to me!"

Amber leapt off the gray and ran. Ben let go of Smoke and went after her. He brought Denver alongside her and held him there at a slow lope. Amber was running in long graceful strides with her hair blowing behind her. Her beauty and panic caught at him.

"Amber, take it easy. It's okay. I'm not going to hurt you."

Amber glanced over her shoulder, her eyes wide. A branch caught her foot and she fell, tumbling downhill. In a flash Ben was off the horse. When she leapt almost convulsively to her feet, Ben caught her by the shoulders. She twisted to run, but he held fast. Ben could feel her shaking.

"Amber, the last thing I'd ever do in the world is hurt you," he said, hating the fearful look in her eyes. "Please believe me." She twisted her head so that all he could see was the rich texture of her hair. "Please listen. I'm not working with the Nivens in any way."

"So why are you stopping me?" Amber was rigid under his hands. "Are you trying to protect your father?"

"My father? You thought Dad was working with the Nivens?"

"Why did you look at him like that at dinner if he's not working with the Nivens? I saw you. It was like you both knew a secret. Please don't try to con me."

Ben let go with one hand and gently lifted her chin. "Amber, I've tried to talk to Dad before about my suspicions concerning the Nivens and he won't listen. He knows they're not good people, but he says that Christ doesn't hold out his love only to good people. He quoted Matthew at me, the part that says if you're only good to your friends you're no different from a pagan. He didn't want us to do anything about our suspicions until he had solid proof in hand. I didn't want to stand by when you could get into trouble. That's why I tried so hard to get you to leave."

Ben could see in her wide green eyes that she believed him. She dropped her head and simply leaned against his chest. Inside his arms, her lithe form felt so right.

"Thank you, God," Ben breathed. "Help me to act the way you want."

"Ben, I was so scared." She looked up at him, shut her eyes tightly, and twisted away. "I just went to church with you to try to get to a phone. I'm sorry." Her words were only a breath.

Ben watched feeling helpless as she struggled with herself. There was more wrong than the trouble at the Nivens' place, more wrong than Chip being stolen. No matter how much he wanted to, Ben knew he couldn't fix things for Amber. She had to decide to trust God. If she gave him a chance to tell it, maybe his story would help her.

Amber stood up straighter. "Ben, will you help me get Chip back, please?"

"If I can. Could you tell me a bit more about what happened?"

Ben watched her as she explained how she'd tracked Chip in the night and tried to act ignorant the next morning. His teeth clenched. Mitch Niven, the spoiled jerk! With Mitch smaller and drunk, Ben had only tried to hold him, stop him, in the fight yesterday. He should have hurt Mitch badly while he'd had the chance. If Mitch had been in the hospital, he couldn't have…

"Ben?" Amber was watching him.

Ben tried to focus. He needed to trust God, not lose his temper. That was easier said than done. He took a deep breath. "Okay, let me get this straight. You think Mitch took Chip somewhere on the ranch. That's kind of a hitch. You were keeping him on Niven property. If we call the police and Chip is still on the Nivens' place it would be pretty hard to prove theft."

"Will you come with me to look for him then? Ben, I don't care about proving anything. I just want him back safe. I intend to go and find him." She had lifted her chin and was looking very determined.

"That's what you were doing, weren't you? You were going to charge straight in there and take them all on." Ben couldn't help smiling. "You are one crazy woman, Amber Lacey, but yes, I'll come with you. I figure I can handle Ryder, and I'd positively enjoy getting my hands on Mitch again. There's just one problem. If you expect me to take on Bull Schwartz, you'd better be prepared to mop up the pieces."

"Right, I'll do that," Amber gave him her irrepressible smile. "Ben, I'm so glad you're coming!"

If he didn't keep things light Ben knew he'd never make it. He bent himself into an exaggerated bow. "Shall I catch your steed, my lady, or should I say, may I catch my steed for your use?"

"Oh! I'm sorry I took your horse, I just had to get out of there. They're doing something really weird to those horses and I want to get to Chip before it's his turn."

"Really weird?"

"I don't know how they do it, but they're turning horses into paints, changing their color by burning them somehow." She stopped looking at Denver. "Ben! You came bareback without even a bridle."

"I was in a bit of a hurry," he said dryly, then looked at her to catch her blushing. "Hey, don't worry."

"Um, the gray horse is yours, isn't he? I'd hate it if someone rode Chip without asking. I can ride the other one."

"I've watched you ride. You can take my horse anytime, even halfway through dinner. His name is Smoke." He whistled and the two horses trotted over. Ben straightened the blanket on Smoke, recinched the saddle, and handed Amber the reins.

"Thanks!" Amber mounted gracefully. He leaped onto Denver and led out at a canter.

Within minutes they'd sighted his father's truck. Ben reined in and explained their plans.

His father nodded, then said with unshakable determination that if Amber and Ben weren't back inside an hour he would bring the RCMP. "I still can't believe that Ryder Niven would turn into a horse thief."

"I don't think Ryder wanted them stolen. Mitch did that." Amber looked toward the fence. "Could we get going? I don't want Chip hurt."

Ben looked at his dad. Both of them were full of unanswered questions, but this wasn't the time to ask.

"Right." Ben led out at a trot. Once he was well onto Niven land he dropped to a walk. The horses needed a break and he needed information.

"Okay, where are we looking?"

"I don't know, but every time Bull Schwartz has turned up, Ryder has been angry with him. Also, each time Bull has had at least one paint horse with him. I think he must be staying wherever they're altering the horses."

Ben frowned, thinking hard. "There are only two places I know of where Bull could be staying. He could be in the cabins up on the forestry land, or..." he hesitated. "Maybe they've fixed up the old house behind Thad's Hump. We'll try there first."

In town, Bull Schwartz was squinting as he came out of the bar into the sunshine. It had been a good day for him. When he'd ridden his horse into the Nivens' main yard, no one was there. He'd had to reconnect a whole bunch of wires before he could drive the farm truck. That had made him swear, but as soon as he had the truck going his spirits had risen again. He'd bought Vaseline and several cases of beer to take back with him, and then headed into the bar.

Bull had drunk enough to put most men under the table, but he walked steadily back out to the truck. People who knew Bull knew to stay clear of him when he'd been drinking. The alcohol didn't seem to do much to him except to make him more ready to fight.

Getting into the vehicle, he gunned it and headed back toward the Nivens' ranch. He frowned, deepening the grime-encrusted wrinkles on his forehead. There was no way he felt like leaving this truck at the main yard and riding a horse back up to his place. Ryder could scream all he wanted; Bull intended to drive this truck straight back to the old homestead. If Ryder had a fit about that paint horse he left in the yard, that was his problem. It wasn't Ryder's biggest problem, either. Bull could hardly believe that Ryder hadn't caught on to what Mitch was doing.

Bull's mouth twisted in irritation. He didn't like Mitch's plan to take the two big bays on the cattle drive. Mitch had been a fool to pick up those three tall horses almost two months ago now. Ryder, thinking the horses were bought at auction, had told him to keep the white. He said he'd get it trained well so it would sell for decent money even if it wasn't a trendy color. Mitch had killed it instead. Not wanting a recognizable stolen horse on the place, Bull had approved. As far as he was concerned, the two bays were still trouble.

Ryder had tried them out and said that except for the fact they didn't rein worth a darn they were well broke. Ryder had complained bitterly about the excellent horses that were going for meat. Bull shook his head. He'd cornered Mitch and found out the truth. It was no wonder those horses wouldn't rein, they were stolen warm-bloods trained in the English way. Even Ryder, who spent his life hiding at the ranch, should have known horses like that would never have sold for meat.

Mitch had found a rancher with an adult daughter who did the English riding. She and her friend wanted to use the tall bays on that big cattle drive to check them out. Mitch stood to gain an extra two thousand dollars per horse over what he could get at auction. Bull had listened while Mitch talked Ryder into the scheme, emphasizing that the horses would be excellently cared for and insisting that there was little risk. Bull wasn't convinced Mitch was right about the risk.

The muscles under the grimy stubble at the corner of Bull's wide jaw clenched. It still made him mad when he thought about it. Not only was Mitch risking the whole operation to make four thousand bucks, but he was going to that awesome party of a cattle drive and leaving Bull behind. To make things worse, Mitch had bought a ticket for that twit of a woman who was working on the place now. He hadn't done a thing for Bull Schwartz, who made the whole operation work. The pink skin on the inside of Bull's lower lip showed in a pout.

Amber and Ben crested the rise on Thad's Hump. Ben had insisted they ride up there first to get a good look from a vantage point where they couldn't be seen. Amber followed as Ben led the way through a gap in the ridge. The old homestead was about a quarter of a mile away.

"They're there," Amber breathed. Down below she could see four paint horses in a corral outside the barn of Thaddeus Niven's old homestead. Chip was not in sight.

Ben nodded, looking intently, taking stock. Sensing their riders' tension, the horses froze with their ears pricked forward. To Amber's horror, Smoke saw the other horses and let out a ringing whinny. Faint on the wind, she heard the other horses answer. Ben spun the buckskin on his back legs and motioned

Amber to follow him back through the gap. On the other side he swung to the ground.

"I should have thought of that. Give me your horse. You stay low and look over the crest. See if anyone comes out to check on the noise."

Amber nodded and moved uphill. Lying on her belly on the rocky ridge crest, she flattened herself and looked. The four paints were milling around obviously excited by hearing another horse. Two of them lifted their heads and whinnied again, but the house door stayed shut.

After a few minutes, Amber slid back off the ridge and went to Ben. "There's nobody. Or if there is, they didn't come out to check."

"Hope you're right. We'll come in from behind the barn and tie the horses back in the poplars out of sight of the house."

Ben led in a long swing around the ridge and brought them in so the barn shielded them from view. Amber's heart was pounding as she tied up the gray, making the double loop of a quick release halter knot with shaking hands. They moved quietly to the barn walking through scattered rubbish. Whoever had been living here had simply flung all their household garbage on the ground behind the barn. Beer cans rolled away from Amber's feet.

Inside the barn, she wrinkled her nose. It smelled of horse and something else that reminded her of hospital wards. She bit her lip. That was the smell of seeping wounds. She'd smelled it before in the burn unit. She moved forward till she could see down the barn alley. Ben had already gone ahead. A loud thumping bang made her jump. A horse squealed, and Amber realized the bang had been the sound of a horse kicking wood.

"Amber, I don't know if you want to see this," Ben said in a flat voice.

Amber stared at the ugly bare area on the rump of the horse tied in the first stall. Enormous weeping blisters showed over an oddly shaped patch on his hindquarters. The horse squealed and kicked out again, trying to kick away the pain. He pounded with one front hoof in desperate frustration. It set her teeth on edge to think that the pain had been caused deliberately just to change the animal's appearance.

Amber's hands reached out, then she dropped them to her side in frustration. She itched to have some kind of analgesic in her hands, something she could give these animals to reduce the pain. She hated being unable to help.

Looking past the burn, Amber took in the complicated system that held the horse tied so he could hardly move. She felt more than a little sick. Around the horse's neck was some kind of rig of canvas and broom handles that kept him from biting the wound. She'd seen vets rig collars on dogs for the same purpose. Another horse with similar bald blistered areas was tied in the stall to her left. This one had the rig around its neck also. The whole place seemed like something out of a demented nightmare.

"I thought it might be something like this," Ben said, coming back. He kept clenching and unclenching his fists as if he'd like to find someone to hit.

"How do they know the burns will go white?"

"Liquid nitrogen. There's a container over there. You've heard of freeze-branding?"

Amber nodded. It was supposed to be less painful than the traditional hot brands and it left a beautiful white mark. She looked back at the first horse she'd seen. He was burned over almost half his hindquarters. A small brand didn't seem to bother the horses at all, but this!

"Ben, these horses are in pain! How can Ryder think he's rescuing horses by doing this?"

"What on earth are you talking about?"

"Something Lyle said in the truck. Ben, Ryder thinks Mitch is buying young horses at auction, horses that were going for meat. Lyle made a comment about Ryder rescuing them."

"You said Ryder isn't in on the rustling." Ben walked slowly around one of the tied horses. "I wondered about that. Horses are practically Ryder's god. Now this makes a warped kind of sense. Ryder had the horse's color changed so it would be a trendy paint horse color. A flashy paint or appy wouldn't be likely to go for meat."

"Oh, I get it." Amber stared at the burned animals. "But Ben, the fad for paints is changing."

He nodded. "The trend is moving away from spotted horses so if any of these weren't broke, some might go for meat anyway, and all the pain would be for nothing."

"I feel sorry for Ryder. Mitch is conning him, stealing horses and making money off this operation, and I think Lyle and Bull know what's happening. A couple of times I've felt like he's using rage and rudeness to keep people away because he's afraid."

"I know exactly what you mean. Still, be careful. I get the feeling that the man could be dangerously unbalanced."

The tied horse had hung his head miserably and groaned.

"We've got to stop this, Ben."

Ben's strong face was tight with anger. He nodded and strode out of sight down the central barn alley.

Sixteen

The whole time Ben and Amber were talking, a horse had been nickering, making the equine soft greeting sound. With Ben gone, the sound penetrated Amber's spinning mind and she turned to find Chip looking at her over a partition.

"Chip," she said softly, moving toward him. She stepped around the end of his stall and the breath went out of her with a whoosh of relief. He wasn't burnt yet. To reassure herself she ran her hands over his skin, but there was no mark on his shining red-gold hide. The big colt bent his head and gently lipped at her pocket.

Amber laughed shakily. "I don't have any carrots, boy. We've got to get out of here."

"Good! You found Chip," Ben said right behind her, making Amber jump. He was standing at the stall door with a fistful of scrap paper in his hand. "You're right. We've got to get out of here. I'm just going to do one thing first." He stepped toward one of the burnt horses. While Amber watched, he spit on his hand then ran it along the barn floor. Talking calmly to the horse he smeared the resultant mud thoroughly into the hair of the horse's forehead. Then he pressed one of the papers on, as if he were making a rubbing of a tomb inscription.

"Identification," Ben said over his shoulder. "Some people register their horses by cowlick print. That swirl of hair in the middle of a horse's forehead is as individual as fingerprints. If anyone has registered these, we can prove they're stolen."

"Stolen or not, what the Nivens are doing here has got to be illegal."

"Nope. If you legitimately own the horse and you're not tricking anyone, changing its appearance isn't illegal. These horses are adequately cared for and the branded areas are clean and healing. It's crazy and I think pointlessly cruel, but it's not against the law."

"But these are stolen!"

Ben stopped and looked at her. "You know that, and I know that, but we've got to prove it. I don't want this place taken apart and the evidence hidden until we can prove it."

"We can't just leave the horses here!" Amber said and then hesitated. It wouldn't do these horses any good to travel, not with big healing burns. Ben was looking at her. Amber nodded. "Right, they want these horses healthy. They won't hurt them unless they know we've been here."

Ben was rubbing at the horse's forehead with the sleeve of his shirt, getting rid of the dirt. "We have to get out of here without leaving any sign. I don't think Mitch or Bull would hesitate to kill these horses and haul them up some back coulee to destroy the evidence."

Amber's throat tightened like someone was choking her at the thought of being the cause of more death. "Ben, there is no way I'm leaving Chip in this place!"

Ben had moved on to the next horse. "I thought of that. We'll make it look like he kicked his way out, then you can lead him out of here with the gray, dally his lead shank on the saddle horn. He's loose in that box. I can rig it. There's an old fencing maul down at the end of the barn. Take him outside where I won't spook him and wait."

"What are you going to do?"

"I'll bash his stall door down as if it had been kicked apart and then make it look like Schwartz didn't shut the barn door properly."

Ben was already moving to pick up the big hammer. As Amber led Chip outside, she could hear the splintering thumps as he shattered the stall door. Once outside, Amber's eyes immediately went to the horses in the corral. One was the little mare Amber had seen before. Another looked like the horse that had been with her the day Chip got cut.

The other two were much taller and beautifully proportioned. Ruth Davis's horses? She squinted against the sun, looking more carefully. These were dramatic paints, but the background color was bay. If these were Ruth Davis's, the dead white horse had been hers, too. Amber didn't believe for a minute that the white horse had broken its leg. Mitch had killed it to get rid of recognizable evidence. Ben was right.

A sound brought Amber's head around and she was listening hard, trying to place the faint noise when Ben came out of the barn. He was pulling paper out of his pocket. "I'll just cowlick-print the paints in the corral and then we'll—"

"Ben, listen!"

In the still mountain air sound carried a long way. Both of them could hear the faint growl of a pickup truck. It was definitely getting louder. They'd joked about having to fight Bull Schwartz. Now the possibility looked horribly real.

Ben was stuffing the paper frantically back into his pocket. "Come on, Amber! Hurry! Bring Chip."

Sensing their nervousness, Chip refused to trot, shaking his head against the pull of the lead shank. He balked at the sight of the garbage, stopping completely and refusing to move. Ben went behind and clapped his hands, but Chip only spun in circles. He wasn't going to walk through the flapping plastic and glinting beer cans.

"Just a sec. I'll bring the other horses here. He'll follow them," Ben said and ran toward the poplars.

The sound of the truck was closer. They'd both get caught if Ben came back for her. Quickly Amber led Chip to a corral gate. He was dancing nervously now. Forcing her voice to be steady she calmed him, climbed up the gate, and slipped onto his high back.

Ben had ridden Denver bareback and with a halter, but Chip was an entirely different proposition. Denver was a calm and seasoned veteran who'd often been ridden bareback before. Chip was not. He shifted uneasily at the strange feel of Amber on his back without a saddle. Amber pulled on the lead shank and Chip turned in a circle. With a halter, Amber could only turn Chip one direction and she had no brakes.

She swallowed hard and tossed her head. No matter what, she wasn't staying here. "I'm riding Chip out!" She called in Ben's direction and dug in her heels. In the quiet mountain air, she was positive Ben had heard her. He'd be able to leave with the other horses.

Unsettled by the odd feel of Amber riding him bareback, Chip bolted. They flew out of the yard at an uncontrolled flat run. To Amber's horror Chip was heading straight down the vehicle track. In a few seconds she'd be in sight of the truck. She braced her knees even tighter on the colt's surging sides and pulled with both hands on the halter shank.

Chip responded by swerving off the road and heading up Thad's Hump in great leaps that threatened to unseat her. Amber grabbed for his flying mane and held on like grim death. She took one desperate look back as Chip crested the ridge. She didn't see the truck, but she wasn't sure if it wasn't there yet or if she'd just missed it.

Going down the back of Thad's Hump was worse than coming up. Each galloping leap downward ended in a thud that drove her onto the bony crest of Chip's withers and threatened to pitch her over his head. She shifted her hands. Stiff-armed, she pushed backward trying to keep her balance.

On the flat Chip really stretched out. Wind blew into Amber's eyes so hard that tears began to stream toward her ears. She'd never let Chip open up into a flat run before. It was the gait of panic and it was good to have a horse well and truly trained before one tried it. Too late for that now. Amber's legs ached with tiredness.

She swallowed convulsively in a dry mouth and began to talk. "Easy boy, take it easy, Chip. You're okay now, nobody is hurting you." She kept talking, making her voice maintain a calm, steady sound. Chip's ears flicked. He was beginning to listen, but a creek was coming up fast. Amber tried to turn the big horse. He stiffened his neck against the unfamiliar pull on his halter and kept going.

Amber realized the colt was going to jump the creek. She barely had time to set herself before he was in the air. As tired as her legs were, if he'd stumbled at all he would have unseated her, but he took the long jump with fluid ease and ran on.

A direct pull hadn't worked, so she started with quick, light jerking tugs on the halter shank, trying to get Chip to settle down enough to respond. The fence at the edge of the Nivens' land was coming up now. Amber could see Gordon's truck. Horrified at the thought of Chip trying to jump the dangerous and barely visible barbed wire, Amber intensified her efforts to turn him.

His strides began to get more relaxed and he turned. As the colt dropped into his high, floating trot Amber let out her breath in relief. The trot was full of spring and excruciatingly uncomfortable to ride bareback, but Amber didn't care. She rode Chip in three ever smaller circles before she was able to convince him to drop into a walk. The colt was quivering all over and dripping with sweat. She could feel his body rock with his breathing. After two more circles, Chip finally stood still.

Amber looked up to see Gordon Miller running toward her. "Are you okay? What happened? Where's Ben?"

Amber tried to answer but found her throat was too dry and tight to speak. Gordon stepped closer and took Chip by the halter, talking softly to the shaking horse. Amber swung around to slide off Chip's back. Her aching legs buckled, and she found herself sitting on the ground.

Gordon turned and held out a wide, solid hand. Amber got shakily to her feet. "I don't know where Ben is. We were going to lead Chip out, but he balked. I jumped on bareback and he bolted."

"Ben let you do that?"

"I didn't ask him. A truck was coming. He'd gone to bring the horses so Chip would follow but there wasn't time for that." She turned to look at the crest of the hill. "I thought he'd be right behind me."

"We'll give him another five minutes. Even if he was coming at a flat run those two cayuses of ours wouldn't be here yet. That was quite the ride. Your horse has some speed on him. I think you were airborne for thirty feet over that creek." Gordon began to walk the sweaty horse in circles around her.

Amber laughed shakily. "It didn't exactly go as planned." She wiped her numb hands on her pants and looked anxiously back at the ridge of Thad's Hump. Was Bull Schwartz beating Ben to a pulp?

"What happened back there anyway?" Gordon asked. "Obviously you found your horse."

"They're burning horses with liquid nitrogen to make them into paints," Amber said without turning around. Where was

Ben? Her legs felt as if they belonged to someone else. To add to the numb, tired feeling, her backside and the insides of her legs were wet, soaked with Chip's sweat. She spun around to face Gordon. "Look, we could tie Chip to the fence here and take your truck to get Ben. If we wait, Bull Schwartz will..."

Gordon held up a hand for silence. Faintly on the still air Amber could hear the triple beat of running horses. Chip lifted his head and whinnied. A hat came into view in the fold of a coulee and a second later she could see Ben on the gray, leading the buckskin. She let out a whoop and ran toward him. He swung to the ground and scooped her up. She hugged him tight, so glad he was okay. In a split second she realized what she was doing and pushed at him. There was no way she could afford to be in Ben's arms. Besides, his father was watching. Ben gave her another squeeze and let her go.

"Amber, that was a crazy thing to do. I thought that colt was going to bolt straight into the truck and I'd be fighting Schwartz for what was left of the two of you."

"And I thought Bull had gotten you when you took so long to turn up."

"I stayed to watch until you were over the ridge and out of sight. He never saw you, but he would have seen me if I didn't sneak out of there the back way." Ben looked at his father. "Schwartz didn't notice anything. He went straight into the house, but when he does go out and realizes Amber's horse is gone he's going to come looking. We'd better get out of here."

Gordon nodded. "Amber, you'd better let Ben lead Chip with Smoke. He can dally on the saddle horn and Smoke'll bring him along, balky or not. My Denver will give you a nice quiet ride, or if you'd rather sit in the truck, I can tie Denver behind."

Ben took Chip's halter shank.

"Wait!" Both men turned to look at Amber. "I'm not coming back with you."

"What!" Ben's eyebrows were high.

Amber shook her head stubbornly. "If we're going to catch the Nivens red-handed, I've got to go back to their place. Otherwise they'll ask questions, especially if Chip has disappeared. I don't want to be the one who makes them kill those horses!"

"No way are you going back there!" Ben said.

"Ben, listen. Ryder and Lyle left this morning for Innisfil. Ryder said they wouldn't be back until suppertime. I'm pretty sure they don't suspect me. I played stupid this morning, acted like I thought Chip had just gotten loose. I'm positive Mitch took the horse to get even with me. He yelled that everything was my fault and I'd be sorry, remember? I don't think Ryder knew he was stolen in the first place. It's not exactly something Mitch is going to tell his brother. Lyle might know when they get back, but if the escape you faked for Chip works, that won't matter anyway. If he did get loose, he would probably come home. I'll just say I found Chip down by the yard. We have to keep them from suspecting until we can prove those horses are stolen."

"Ryder actually left the farm?" Gordon asked, eyebrows up.

"I saw him leave. He's starting to suspect Mitch. He made Lyle take him to Innisfil to check for receipts. I think Lyle and Mitch have something rigged to convince Ryder the horses were bought at auction."

"Mitch always was a good liar," Ben said.

Gordon nodded. "It won't be easy for Ryder to be out of his own yard. I wouldn't count on him staying gone long."

"Look, I'll walk in, leading Chip," Amber said. "Then it won't matter if Ryder is there or not." Silence met her statement.

"It makes sense, but I still don't like it," Ben said.

"Ben, I want to do this. Please don't try to stop me."

Ben slowly handed her Chip's halter shank. "Will you take my cell phone with you for tonight and call if there's any trouble? For that matter, call if there isn't. I want to know you're okay."

"But you need that phone for work."

"I'll tell Doc Watson something. We'll work it out. I don't care!"

Gordon had been looking back and forth between the two of them. Now he nodded decisively. "You and Ben stay with the horses. I'll be back in fifteen minutes with the horse trailer and cell phone. We can have you back in the Nivens' yard in half an hour. That'll give you a better chance to get there first."

Without waiting for an answer, Gordon got into the truck and left.

"We'd better shut the gate and walk the horses down the road so we're out of sight if Schwartz comes over the hill looking." Ben handed her the lead ropes from the other two horses and moved to shut the gate. Amber watched him with her heart aching. She shook her head. Enough of that. There was a job at hand that needed to be done.

"Ben, remember Mitch made a comment to Ryder about going on the Centennial Cattle Drive."

"That's right, and Ryder said something about going himself." Ben was walking back to her. "If he does, that will be a huge step for him. I can't imagine him doing it. He's hardly been off the place in the last ten years."

"I don't know about that, but on the way home last night, Lyle and Ryder thought I was asleep. Lyle said something that makes me think they'll be selling some of the altered horses there. Listen, you're going to be there, and I want to be there, too. Mitch bought me tickets because of some bet. I'll see if Ryder lets me come with him."

Ben narrowed his eyes. "Mitch will be there too, Amber. That's crazy. Look, I'll call the RCMP tonight and bring them out to that barn. Surely there's got to be evidence of ownership for one of those horses."

Being with Ben and finding Chip had taken all of Amber's attention, but now it was over. Chip was found, and she was remembering her own problems. If Ben settled everything with the RCMP tonight, she'd be left with no buffer at all, nothing more to distract her from facing her demons.

A cloud had come over the sun. Amber pulled her arms tight against her body for warmth in the cool wind. "What if there isn't evidence, Ben? They'd get off free? You said that unless we prove the horses are stolen, they've committed no crime unless they are caught selling them, misrepresenting what they are. We have a better chance to do that at the cattle drive."

Ben had begun to argue when the noise of the truck returning brought their heads up. The gray nudged Amber impatiently in the back, knocking her forward. "Look Ben, I've got to get back. How about I call you in the night, around two o'clock and we'll plan then? Promise you won't call the police until after we talk." Even in her own ears her voice sounded nervous.

Ben reluctantly agreed and they loaded the horses, putting Chip in last. Amber climbed into the truck cab quickly. Ben's plan to clear up the whole mess this evening had made her feel as if she were looking over a precipice. She didn't want to lose Ben yet, and neither did she want to face her own empty life.

Seventeen

Ben and Gordon dropped her off just out of sight of the Nivens' yard. To Amber's relief the place was still empty. She put Chip into his corral and made sure he had food and water. She'd just begun making supper when Ryder's truck drove into the yard. He let Lyle out by his trailer and parked right by the back door.

Amber met him as he came in. "Ryder, I did find Chip. He's in his pen now." She'd carefully rehearsed the words, not wanting to lie, but still to give the impression she knew nothing. She might as well not have bothered. His face pale and stressed, Ryder walked past her and into his office as if she were invisible. Amber looked after him, her feelings a mixture of pity and fear. Did his actions just mean he was exhausted by his first day away from the ranch in years, or had he found out what Mitch had been doing?

As usual at mealtimes, Lyle would wait on the porch until Ryder waved him in. At ten minutes after five, Ryder still hadn't come out of his office. That was odd, Ryder was always rigidly on time. Should she go call him? No that would be dumb. She needed to stay as inoffensive as possible tonight. Lyle made no move to come inside but paced up and down pulling at his jacket nervously.

At quarter after, Ryder marched out of the office like an automaton and jerked open the door, motioning Lyle inside. Amber quickly put the food on the table. Ryder sat and immediately began to shovel it into his mouth. Lyle shrugged and began to eat too. Amber hesitated by the table for a second and then spoke. "Chip came back into the yard today. You were right, he must have just gotten out."

Lyle looked up, his narrow face obviously startled. "Your horse is back?"

"That's what she said, isn't it? Shut up and eat," Ryder said.

"Hey man," Lyle said. "Drake told you news that should have made you happy at Innisfil. It's not fair yelling at me."

"I said shut up and eat!" This time Ryder put down his fork and gave Lyle a murderous look out of those yellow eyes. Amber recoiled. Was the man actually insane? He finished shoveling the food into his mouth and stomped back to his office. At least he seemed unworried about Chip.

She watched Lyle leave the room. He'd been surprised Chip was back. Mitch must have told him something. She chewed on her bottom lip. She'd just have to hope that Ben's attempt to make it look like Chip had kicked his way out had worked.

As she washed up the supper dishes and tidied the house Amber was nearly asleep on her feet. She'd slept very little last night, and the day had been exhausting. The fatigue and tension gave her the same dislocated feeling she used to get working in the emergency ward in the small hours of the morning.

Up in her room, Amber stood still with her toothbrush in her hand. She stared at herself in the mirror. The verses from Isaiah came back to her as clearly as if someone were saying them aloud: *But he was pierced for my transgressions, he was crushed for my iniquities.*

Amber shook her head. This was nuts. She'd memorized those verses when she was a kid. Those verses said *our,* not *my.* Another verse she'd known as a child intruded: *Though your sins be as scarlet, they shall be white as snow.*

Amber frantically began to brush her teeth. Her sins were certainly red like scarlet. She spat as if she was trying to spit out the horror. It didn't do any good, and Amber couldn't see how God could put up with it, either. How could God just say, "Fine, that's okay"? She couldn't get rid of those verses. They reminded her that God wasn't saying it was okay. He'd made Christ pay the price so justice was done. Again Amber felt that huge bubble of love and emotion pressing at her. Her throat tightened.

"No, I can't listen to you. Not right now. There's too much happening. Leave me alone!"

She ran for her bed. Flopping onto her back, she forced herself to think about the Nivens. If those two big bays she'd seen were Ruth Davis's horses, the younger one was an imported Trakehner. He'd certainly have the Trakehner brand and possibly other marks that Bull Schwartz hadn't been able to eradicate. She could get in touch with Ruth right now and...

Amber twisted onto her belly. Contacting Ruth would tear everything wide open. Ben would find out she was a medical doctor. Maybe the cowlick prints Ben took would come up on the registry and she wouldn't need to contact Ruth Davis. She felt bad now that she had mistrusted Gordon Miller, but the fact that he was innocent reemphasized the kind of family Ben was from. There was no way he'd put up with evil in a woman he cared for.

The bed felt so good under Amber's aching body. In spite of the tension in her mind, her eyes were beginning to blur and slide shut. She dropped into a deep, exhausted sleep. The time to call Ben came and went. At 2:30 A.M. a repeated ringing sound brought her groggily awake. She bumped at the button on her alarm clock to turn it off, but the ringing went on.

Ben's phone! Amber fished wildly under her pillow. "Ben? Ben?" Amber said in a croaky, half-awake voice, fumbling for the right end of the phone to talk into.

"Amber, are you all right?"

"Uh-huh. I thought I was supposed to call you." Her voice was thick with sleep.

"But you didn't."

Amber rolled over and looked at the clock. Seeing the time, she started to apologize and explain that she'd slept through. Ben laughed. "I'm just glad you're okay. Ryder didn't suspect anything?"

"I don't think so. He was pretty stressed after being away."

"Did he find out about Mitch? If he did, I'd better call the RCMP."

Amber frowned. "No, I think that's okay, too. Lyle said something about a guy named Drake telling Ryder news that should make him happy."

"Drake rodeos with Mitch. He works at the auction mart, but I don't think he'd get involved with horse rustling."

Amber shrugged. "I don't know." Her head was beginning to clear now. Keeping her voice quiet she went on. "On the drive will we be able to get near the horses the Nivens bring to look for ID?"

There was a little pause and Ben said, "You're sure Ryder said they were bringing altered horses?"

"Yes."

Ben said slowly, "I'm signed up as one of the official vets, so even if they're not in my circle, I should be able to find some way to get a close look at the altered horses."

"You're willing to wait for the Centennial Cattle Drive then?" Amber asked.

"I don't know. Not at the cost of risking your safety. You're a very special person, Amber Lacey."

"Oh, Ben," Amber said sadly and hung up the phone. She rolled over and cried herself to sleep.

Ryder and Lyle said nothing to her at all the next morning at breakfast but simply stuffed their mouths in silence. After they'd left, Amber cleaned up the house, then went outside to check on Chip. Her stomach was full of butterflies. Ryder and Lyle had almost certainly gone up to see Bull Schwartz.

The high arch of the sky was deep blue and completely cloudless. Amber heard a truck coming before she could see it. She turned to watch the road. Were Ryder and Lyle coming back early? Had they found out about Chip? Her heart was pounding. Amber recognized Ben's truck with a rush of relief. She stood still, torn between wanting to go to him and wanting to hide. She didn't want to hurt Ben. He was too good a man for that.

Ben climbed out of the truck and came toward her. "I've only got a couple of minutes, but I wanted to stop by just to make sure you were okay. Ryder's probably gone out to see Bull, right?"

Amber nodded.

"I wish you would come back to our place. I've been thinking about it and I'd rather bring the police in now. I'd rather risk not finding evidence the horses are stolen than risk your safety."

"No, Ben. I don't know what to think about Ryder. His reasons make a kind of sense even if the scheme wouldn't work long. Mitch and the others are a different matter. Anyone who'd deliberately decide to put horses in so much pain just to make money is scum. Ben, I want to go on that drive in a way that won't make them suspicious. I want them caught."

Ben looked away, the muscles at the corner of his jaw working. She could see his chest move as he took a deep breath and turned back. "Okay, it's your call. Dad said he'd go along with my decision. You said your car isn't working. Is it anything I can fix? I'd feel a lot better if I knew you could get out of here quickly."

Amber lifted the hood of the old Chevy and showed him the torn-off wires, and he bent over the engine. His broad hands moved deftly to put things back to rights.

He spoke as he worked. "I've been thinking about the big cattle drive. If Mitch does bring those horses, we've got a good chance of stopping him cold. There'll be an RCMP officer along and brand inspectors."

"But why would Mitch ever take these horses then?"

"Mitch isn't exactly known for caution or clear thinking. Besides, there's going to be over fifteen hundred horses. Mitch knows that there's no way the officials will check very many of them. I doubt if they'll check any horses. There are very few bad apples in the Alberta ranching community. You just happened to end up with one."

He reattached a final wire, then stood up, wiping his hands. "Dad and I are going to drive down early in the day. You know the camp is divided into six colors. They call them wagon circles. Dad and I are in the purple circle. I'll be looking for you, but if I miss you, you can find us in that circle. Now let's see if this old lady will run."

The Chevy started easily. Ben switched it off and stood up. "There, at least you'll be able to get out of here if there's trouble." He paused and asked, "How are you going to explain that you're going on the drive in spite of the fact Mitch was furious with you?"

"I'll figure something out. I'll have to. Maybe just say that I really wanted to go, and that I'll pay him back." Ryder was only paying her five hundred a month, but she'd been here more than two months and spent almost nothing. She had the money coming.

"Amber, you don't have to spend your money on this. I'll pay your way."

"No, I want to do it." She glanced at Ben. If only she could let him take care of her. With all her being she wanted to let herself be enclosed by his arms. She jerked her eyes away. Very abruptly she said, "We've both got work to do. See you later."

Ben watched her graceful figure walking away from him and slammed his fist into the steering wheel. Why couldn't he get through to Amber? She was responsive to him one minute, and the next minute just about as untouchable as the snow on a distant mountain.

He drove out of the yard faster than he should have. "God, I don't know what's happening with her, but please help her to get straight with you so that we can talk." That was pretty selfish, but it was how he felt. "Keep her safe. She's crazy brave sometimes. I've been lonely so long. It would be so good if—" Ben grimaced. Sometimes it seemed God was torturing him, teasing him with something that might never come into reach. It was hard to wait and trust.

Back at the clinic, Ben was grateful for work that took his total concentration. He neutered three tomcats and removed porcupine quills from the face of an old dog that should have known better. That morning, he'd simply told Doc Watson that he wouldn't have his cell phone for a couple of days. Doc gave him a hard look. "Okay, Ben, you stay here. Take the small animal surgery. You'll be around if anything unexpected comes in I can't handle myself."

The next job, spaying a cocker spaniel, took ages. She was so obese that the yellow fat kept falling into his way.

"Your father just called," Esther said, walking into the room. "He wants to talk to you. I told him you'd get back to him when you were done."

Ben nodded and concentrated on doing a neat job of stitching. Half an hour later he carried the cocker back to her kennel and picked up the phone. "What is it, Dad?"

"I wanted to check, you're sure in your mind about not calling the police?"

Ben swallowed hard. "I know it sounds nuts, but I didn't argue much with Amber this morning. I've got this kind of confidence. I've been praying hard."

"Okay, I can go with that. Your mom was worrying. I'll tell her what you said."

"Keep praying, both of you!"

Gordon chuckled. "That you can count on."

Ben hung up and stared at the phone. What if he was wrong about not calling the police? What if Amber got hurt because of him?

That evening as Amber waited for Ryder to come back to the yard, her stomach ached with tension. Had Ben's escape scenario convinced Bull? She kept making and altering plans of how to get away from the yard quickly. More than once she wished she'd gone with Ben. The whole plan seemed goofy now.

What if the Nivens simply refused to take her along on the Centennial Cattle Drive? She paced the room and then, wanting more information, she started looking for her registration packet from the drive. She knew she'd stuck it somewhere in the kitchen. Doors and drawers banged as she searched the huge half-empty kitchen cabinets. Finally she found it in a bottom drawer. She read it through twice and started pacing again.

Apparently they'd be going through a huge area of dry grassland. People had settled there but hadn't done well. In the forties the Canadian government had bought them out to use the area for military training. Since then it had become a major training area for the British Army. Locals called it the British Block. For five days the cattle drive would meander across a vast, roadless short-grass prairie.

It sounded magnificent, but Amber's stomach still hurt. The sound of a truck coming into the yard brought her head up. She moved quickly into the kitchen and stood near the back door ready to run if there was trouble. Her car keys cut into her palm.

The men came and sat at the table without saying a word. That wasn't unusual, but it meant she couldn't stay by the back door much longer without attracting attention. She took a deep breath and carried supper to the table. Neither man so much as glanced at her. A little of the tension left Amber's body. Leaving the door open she walked back into the kitchen, but she couldn't eat.

"Lyle, get the saddles and tack loaded tonight," Ryder snapped, taking the last bite off his plate. "We're heading out at six tomorrow for the drive."

"You don't have to go," Lyle said shoving greasy hair off his forehead. "Mitch and I can..."

Ryder ignored him and shoved back his chair to leave. It was now or never. Amber walked into the dining room. "Ryder, I'm really glad Chip is back because I'd like to go on the Centennial Cattle Drive." She gestured to the information packet. "It says this trip will be the experience of a lifetime and since I'm registered..."

The little rehearsed speech she'd planned didn't sound so good in the open. She swallowed hard and went on. "Look, I know Mitch paid my way, but I'd like to pay that back."

Ryder had kept moving toward the office as she spoke. He didn't stop when he answered. "I don't care what you do, so long as you keep out of my way." The door slammed behind him.

Lyle looked at the door. He must have known Ryder would be furious if he stayed in the house, but he sidled in her direction and spoke in a hissing whisper, "Did you really find Chip loose near the yard?"

His breath was terrible. She backed away.

"Tell the truth now, woman," Lyle said more loudly.

The door burst open and Ryder bellowed, "Get out of my house and get to work, Smith." He switched his pale glare to Amber. "I expect you both to be ready to leave by five A.M."

Amber took a deep gulping breath. She was going on the Centennial Cattle Drive with the Nivens. She'd succeeded, so why was she shaking from head to foot?

Eighteen

Amber walked upstairs and packed all her belongings. Then she went outside in the late evening dusk to pack Chip's gear. When she was done, Amber spent a long time currying her horse. She traced the swirl on his forehead.

"Chip, you and I are going on the big Centennial Cattle Drive and after that...whatever happens, I'll try to make sure you're okay." Her throat closed and she said nothing more.

God's love hung over her life like a wave that threatened to engulf her. More and more clearly Amber knew that if she gave in to it, she'd have to quit running. She'd have to go back and face what had happened. She'd have to sell Chip. Amber leaned against the horse's shoulder with tears streaming down her cheeks.

When Amber finally slept that night, her dreams were full of fear. She was endlessly running from some overwhelming presence. She woke still tired. Ryder and Lyle had most of the horses loaded before she got outside. Two truck-and-trailer outfits were parked there. Amber had seen the stock trailers parked in the yard, but not in use. Before now they'd always used the one Mitch hauled. A relatively new trailer was behind Ryder's truck. Through the ventilation holes, Amber caught a glimpse of white on dark hide. The altered horses.

"You're riding with Smith. Get your horse and gear loaded on that outfit if you're coming," Ryder growled and pointed at the farm truck. He climbed into the other truck and slammed the door. Amber loaded Chip behind the two riding horses. She felt numb but not nearly as frightened as she thought she would.

As they drove out of the yard, Lyle tried to pump her about Chip.

"I already told you I found him. Why do you keep asking?"

"No reason." He gave her a sly grin. "Mitch will be happy to see you at the drive."

"Happy to see me?"

He didn't answer her incredulous question, only snickered unpleasantly and turned up the truck radio to a deafening volume. Amber remembered Mitch's bet with a sinking feeling. Mitch couldn't possibly think he'd won now, could he? She huddled close to the door and shut her eyes.

Her dreams of the night before came back to her. She sat up abruptly. It wasn't hard to figure those dreams out. In fact they were too close to reality for comfort. God was after her. Could anything be worse? She didn't have a chance. He'd made staying at the Nivens' place impossible. She couldn't keep on hiding from Ben, either.

Unbidden, a verse that she had memorized as a child came into her head: *Unless a grain of wheat falls into the ground and dies, it remains alone…* Amber frowned. Jesus had said that, talking about what it meant to follow him. If she did the right thing and told the truth to Ben, she couldn't protect herself at all. She'd be stripped bare, face-to-face with her own failure. Alone as that grain of wheat in the cold ground.

Amber stared blankly out the window. Almost anything was better than the loneliness and agony of running away. She was so tired. As they drove southeast, the land became progressively drier. The green washed out to a dusty buff. The dry grass in the ditches bent and twitched under the pressure of a hot wind. The grain in the fields grew more stunted and sparse until the cultivated fields gave way altogether to sun-dried pasture.

Three or four times Amber tried to bring her mind back to gathering evidence against Mitch Niven, but she couldn't focus. When she was in the fourth to sixth grade, her family had been in Kenya and her folks had sent her to a mission boarding school. They had Bible memory contests with prizes. Memorizing was easy for Amber and the verses had stuck with her. Now she couldn't get rid of them. Verses and fragments of verses went through her mind. The pressure of God's love was building up in her like a dam she could no longer hold back. She had no more hiding places.

Amber turned her head. Through the back window she could see her duffle sticking up from under Ryder's big western saddle. Her Bible was in that duffle. For the first time in months she wanted it in her hands. The truck turned down a small gravel road. Amber could see rooster tails of dust ahead of them marking other outfits heading for the staging area. They pulled off onto the grass in what amounted to an entire town of trucks, trailers, cattle liners, flatbeds, wagons, tents, flags, and three big pavilions.

People were unloading big semitrailer trucks of cattle into huge holding pens. Horses were everywhere. Arabs, quarter horses, massive heavy horses, parade horses, and mule teams were tied to trailers or being ridden, driven, or led back and forth through the dust.

Amber barely saw what was around her. Ryder's truck pulled up alongside as they stopped. Amber got out, and plunged her arm deep into her duffle bag. Holding her Bible in her hand, she ran away from the crowded staging area into the rolling short-grass prairie beyond. She ran hard up a long rolling rise in the ground. Amber looked back once. The wind caught her hair, whipping curling tendrils across her face. She spun around and down the far side until all the human commotion was out of sight. With a long leap, Amber gained the top of a boulder and stood facing into the wind.

"Okay, God, I give up. I'm done with running. I'm done with hiding and with hurting Ben. I quit. It's not worth it." Suddenly she was shaking from head to foot. All the grief and fear that she'd fought and hidden through the last months came pouring out. Her face twisted and she sank down, huddled on the rock.

"God, I don't get it," she gasped. "Why couldn't you have let me keep that little boy alive? Why did you allow me not to remember, not to know the right things so I could save him? Why?" She could taste salty tears in her mouth. "How could you forgive me? How can you put up with this kind of filth?" Gut-wrenching sobs tore through her and she could not stop them.

After a long time she began to calm. Her hair had come forward and was sticking to her wet, swollen face. Amber pushed it back and faced the sky. Slow tears slid steadily into the corners of her mouth.

She took a shaky breath. "God, it seemed too horrible to confess before, but I give it all to you now. I blew it. I wasn't good enough. I was too tired and I didn't know enough. Then I ran away, and I'm sure Mom and Dad are worried sick. I don't know what's going to happen to Chip and..." Amber's head sank down. Her fists were clenched. "God, the worst part is Ben. He's going to hate me."

She gave one last convulsive sob, then straightened. "Jesus, I just want to give you this whole mess. I guess I never understood what it meant to lose my life for your sake. I want to give myself up to you—Ben, Chip, everything. I'll go back and face what happened. I'll go back to medicine. I'm here in front of you stripped bare."

Amber lifted her face to the wind. A huge wave of relief washed across her as if she were suddenly pounds lighter. The cooling wind on her cheeks seemed like the touch of a loving hand. A pipit sprang up from the grass. The tiny bird spiraled high, singing in the windy blue air. Amber stood and shook her hair off her face. "It was you all the time, all the beauty, the mountains, Chip, everything." She laughed. "I thought I was so alone."

She jumped off the boulder and spun in a circle, then stopped with her arms open to the sky. "You love me!" Gradually she sank to her knees. "God, I'm still in the middle of this mess I made. Please help me get through it without doing more harm. Help me have the courage to talk to Ben."

Amber got to her feet and ran back toward the trucks. Lyle and Ryder must think she'd lost her mind. Amber grinned. It wasn't just her mind she'd lost, she'd given her whole self into God's hands and it was the best thing that had ever happened to her.

At the crest of the hill, Amber stopped, really seeing for the first time the staggering scope of the staging area. Dust and commotion blanketed an area that looked to be more than a mile across.

Semitrailer trucks for hauling cattle, flatbed trailers, wagons, motor homes, tents, horse trailers, and animals everywhere. Wow! She shook her head and started down the hill.

As she reached the flats, a man came by driving a magnificent team of gray Percherons. Sun glinted off chrome hames and made highlights in the huge team's gentle eyes. Everything seemed rich with God's love and his beauty.

A mule called, making a weird screech somewhere between a whinny and a donkey's bray. Amber jumped and then laughed as she saw the animal's skyscraper ears pointed inquiringly in her direction. It had never occurred to her before that God had a great sense of humor. As if to emphasize the point, a fat little ground squirrel popped out of the ground ten feet ahead of her, gave a sharp "eep!" of surprise, and disappeared.

She walked around the row of huge cattle trucks waiting to unload, their diesel engines rumbling as they idled. Amber wrinkled her nose at the odor of diesel fuel and cow dung and then hesitated. Mitch was heading purposefully in the same direction. When he saw her, he stopped dead.

"Amber! You came!"

Amber opened her mouth and shut it twice, trying to think of something to say. Even telling half a story to give a false impression didn't feel right to her anymore.

"Hey! Wait till I tell..." Mitch said, suddenly grinning. "Uh, look, sorry I shouted at you last time I saw you. I was pretty plastered. Lyle called me, told me your horse got out and you were worried about him. I'm glad you found him again. Come on, I'll help you get settled."

Amber stared at him incredulously. Mitch was certainly the smoothest liar she'd ever met. He must be convinced that she hadn't a clue what he'd done with Chip. He was still going to try to win that bet. Of all the self-satisfied criminal nincompoops.

Mitch grabbed her by the elbow. "Come on, I'll show you around."

Amber started to plant her feet. No, it would be stupid to fight with him now. She let herself be directed. Mitch was heading toward one of the big pavilions. "I was watching for my brother and Lyle and saw the trucks pull in. So Ryder actually came?"

Amber nodded, still too stunned to take much initiative as Mitch led her briskly across the grass.

"Ryder is going to be totally nuts with all these people." Mitch headed for the big pavilion. "You have to register and pick up your information packet in here."

"Mitch, wait. I want to pay you for the registration."

"Forget it," Mitch said.

The pavilion turned out to be a U-shaped thing with a big open area in the middle. The heavy plastic-coated fabric of the structure slatted and banged in the wind. The open area was thronged with people in western hats and denim. Huge brass-and-silver buckles glinted on nearly every belt. Mitch put his arm around her waist. His wiry arm was clamped so tightly that Amber knew she'd never twist away without making a spectacle of herself.

"Hey guys!" He yelled. "Red! Drake! Look who I've got."

Many heads turned, and two guys started toward them. Amber recognized two of the men she'd met with Mitch in that bar in Calgary.

"Talk to you guys later," Mitch called, firmly pulling Amber away from them.

Amber looked back. Those must be the people he'd made the bet with. "Mitch, let go of me."

Mitch ignored her, pulling her to the front of the registration line.

"Mitch Niven," Amber said, keeping her voice low, "if you don't let go of me this instant, I am going to make a scene."

Mitch glanced at her, then dropped his hand, letting it slide across her thighs as he did. Amber jumped away. The girl behind the table had asked her a question she hadn't even heard.

"Sorry," Amber said. "What did you say?"

"Mitch says that you're with him." The girl was pouting. She hadn't complained about Mitch cutting in line, and Amber had the distinct impression that the girl felt she belonged with Mitch.

"No, I'm not with Mitch. He did register me, but I'd like to pay my own way."

The girl smiled with obvious relief and said, "You'll have to work that out with Mitch. Here's your packet. You're in the blue circle. That means you need to camp near the blue flag. There's a picket line up for your horses." She turned away from Amber and started talking to Mitch.

Amber left the pavilion at a fast walk before Mitch could get away from the girl. Once outside she stopped to get her bearings. People, tents, trucks, and animals were scattered like confetti across the landscape. There were still trailers coming in, as well as a long line leaving. She'd read that the vehicles would be driven to Medicine Hat where the drive would end, and the drivers would take a shuttle bus back.

Her strongest impulse was to find Ben, but she needed to take care of Chip first. It took her a second to figure out just where she'd left the Nivens' rigs in all the confusion. When she got to the truck and trailer, Lyle was nowhere in sight. Ryder was in his truck but seemed almost catatonic. He ignored her when she knocked on the window. All these people must be terrifying to him.

She knocked again. "Can I help you get set up? We're at the blue circle."

This time he did turn toward her. Flinging the door open, he nearly knocked her down. "Get out of my face! I let you come along. That doesn't mean I want you whining around me."

Amber caught her balance as the truck door slammed in her face. He shoved the vehicle into gear and bumped off across the grass. She watched him go. At least he was heading toward the blue flag. Maybe Lyle and Mitch would help and he'd be okay. Amber walked to the back of the other trailer unit and unloaded Chip. He whinnied loudly at all the new horses and shied violently at the flapping tents. Twice he jerked her nearly off her feet. The walk to the blue flag seemed to take forever.

A fat hemp rope was strung waist high for a hundred yards through big holes drilled in sturdy fence posts. Along that rope, and another rope parallel to the first, dozens of horses were tied. A big pile of square bales was stacked beyond the ropes. When she looked around, Amber could see a similar setup at the two adjacent camping areas. The other three were too far away to see detail.

Amber was beginning to realize just how many horses would be coming. No wonder Mitch wasn't worried about bringing those stolen horses here. To the east of her, a purple flag was flying. Ben had said he'd be in the purple circle!

Amber squeezed her eyes shut. "God, it's going to be so hard to tell Ben. I don't want to watch him turn away from me. Please help me."

Resolutely she turned back to her horse. Once tied and fed, the colt seemed to settle a bit. Still, he kept lifting his head from the hay to whinny and look around. This big cattle drive would be good for him. By the end of the week he'd be used to flapping tents, crowds, noise, and strange horses. Amber bit her lip. He'd be a better horse for someone else.

She was going back to medicine. It wouldn't be simple, either. She'd have to live with the consequences of running away. Her medical supervisor had tried hard to get her to stay. His words echoed in her head. *"Amber, you're a very capable doctor. You must not leave. You know we can't hold your place here. A crisis of confidence isn't unusual, but you're overreacting."*

She was done with any pretensions to status. Instead of competing for prestigious residencies like the one she'd lost, maybe she'd go up north. They always needed doctors there. No matter how she went back to medicine, she'd have to sell Chip.

She patted the horse's shining neck and went to put up her tent. Once her tent was up, she found some paper and wrote a note to Ryder, asking him to give eight hundred dollars of her pay to Mitch. She left it in Ryder's truck since neither of the brothers was in view.

Calling Ruth Davis was a far easier task than facing Ben. When her tent was up, Amber set out to find a phone. She could see several semitrailer units like the type that work as offices on construction sites. Amber went up the steps of the one that said Drive Office. Five or six people were crammed into the little room. They all seemed to be talking at once.

"Excuse me. Is there a cell phone I could use?"

A harassed-looking woman nodded quickly toward a phone on the desk. "You'll need to pay for the call."

Amber nodded. After getting the number from directory assistance, she dialed. Dry-mouthed, she waited for Ruth Davis to pick up her phone. In her mind she went over words to explain why she hadn't approached her earlier. All her reasons sounded weak and selfish.

The phone rang and rang but no one answered. With a mixture of relief and frustration Amber put down some money for the calls and walked back out into the wind. She stood for a second gathering her courage, then started out to find Ben at the purple flag.

Trying to call Ruth Davis had made Amber realize just how self-absorbed she'd become. She'd been deaf to other people's needs. Ben had wanted to tell her about his life and she'd cut him off. With a tight chest, Amber asked God to forgive her.

Two preteen kids cantered by on chunky quarter horses, dust spurting from under their hooves. A young man went by at a smart trot, his horse dragging a bale he had roped and dallied to the saddle horn. In the confusion of tents and activity Amber could see no sign of Ben or his father. She walked forward through the commotion around the purple flag. Amber could feel her heart beating. Finally she saw Gordon Miller visiting with a group of people near a wagon.

"Amber! You're here. Is everything all right?" Gordon's eyes were intent and concerned.

"More all right than it's been for a long time."

Gordon gave her a puzzled look, then turned to introduce her to his friends. The names of the six or seven people didn't stay in Amber's head. She barely noticed their firm handshakes and warm smiles, though she did make an effort to smile back.

"I imagine you're looking for Ben?" Gordon said. "He's at an organizational meeting for the official vets. He should be back in an hour or so."

"We might not be as handsome," a paunchy older man said, grinning, "but you're welcome to sit and visit with us for a bit."

"Would you like something?" A kind-eyed middle-aged woman pointed at an array of food and drink on the wagon's tailgate.

"Thanks a lot, but I'd better get going." Amber hoped she didn't sound rude. She'd never be able to make polite conversation when she was so keyed up to talk to Ben.

"I'll tell Ben you're here safely and that you came looking for him," Gordon said.

"Thanks." Amber started back toward the blue flag.

Nineteen

As Amber walked back toward her tent, she clenched and unclenched her hands. She'd been so keyed up to talk to Ben that it was hard to have to wait again. She wanted the tension over, yet she also felt relief. For a little while she'd been reprieved. A crowd of horses and people around a fifteen-foot-high metal tank drew Amber's eye. Through the confusion of legs, heads, and manes, she caught glimpses of white plastic watering tubs. At least she could make sure Chip wasn't thirsty.

Chip snorted at the other horses and shied from the strange tanks. Amber hung back, giving him time to look the situation over. Across the tank, a teenage girl had brought in a team of Belgian horses. White blazes showed through their thick blond forelocks as they dipped their muzzles into the water. One of them started to play, blowing and splashing. He lifted his head and plunged it back in, sending a fountain of water across the tank and splashing a woman with her back to Amber.

With a start, Amber recognized the woman as Ruth Davis. On second thought, why shouldn't Ruth be here? It seemed most of the horse people in Alberta were along. Amber swallowed hard and prayed for courage. Chip had smelled the water now and tugged forward. She held him back until Ruth turned and led her horse away from the water tank.

"Excuse me," Amber said stepping forward. "Um, I..." Under Ruth's sharp gaze, Amber hesitated. Chip was bobbing his head impatiently.

"Don't I know you?" Ruth asked.

"Yes, I mean, we met back east, and you wanted to buy my

horse at the Glenmore high point show. I need to talk to you."

Chip suddenly took matters into his own hands. Impatient for a drink he started for the water trough, dragging Amber along.

"Come over to my place when you've finished watering your horse," Ruth called in her British accent. "I'm in the green circle."

Fifteen minutes later, Amber was sitting in the grass in front of Ruth Davis's tent explaining that she thought she knew what had become of Ruth's stolen horses. Her heart was in her mouth. Ruth was of the old school that brooked no nonsense. Her horses were her life. Amber didn't think she'd be very tolerant, and she quickly found out she was right.

"You mean you had some idea of where my horses were at that high point show and didn't tell me?" Ruth's voice was sharp.

"I didn't know for sure then."

"I don't understand you. I know you were pursuing a medical career. You left that to be a maid? Then when you found your employers were breaking the law in this despicable manner, you stayed with them and said nothing? You must be out of your mind."

"I'm speaking out now." Amber tried to keep her voice steady. "The thing is, I don't know for sure if they're your horses."

"I've got cowlick prints of all three with the registry, and of course Ramiro and Cappuccino have the Trakehner brand. Where are they? Have you called the police?"

"If I'm right and Mitch stole your horses, the horses are here on the drive."

"He actually has Ramiro, Cappuccino, and Lavade here, on the Centennial Cattle Drive?" Ruth was on her feet. "Where are they? Show me!"

"Wait! We can't just charge in. The horses aren't the same

color they used to be. They're paints now. It would just be Mitch's word against ours. He rodeos and lots of people know him. While people argued, he could take the horses and leave. I thought if we waited until we were out on the trail and there were no horse trailers around to hide or move horses..."

Ruth's narrow nostrils were pinched and white with fury. She visibly took a deep breath. "You're right. If this slimy toad of a man has made my horses into paints, we will need identification." Ruth frowned. "Lavade is so light a gray as to be basically white. How could they turn him into a paint?"

Amber shook her head. "They didn't. I think Lavade is dead."

Ruth turned her head away abruptly. When she lifted it and spoke her voice was rough. "We will bring these people to justice! I'll look for you tomorrow night at nine P.M. by the green flag."

Amber watched Ruth Davis stride away, a wealthy, powerful woman who had made horses the center of her life. Amber bit her lip. Ruth Davis had been horrified at Amber's actions, and she didn't even know why Amber had run. How would Ben react? Firmly she reminded herself that she was forgiven; Christ had paid for her sin. He loved her no matter how anyone else reacted.

She wanted the reassurance of God's Word, the feel of a Bible in her hands, but there were things to do first. She went back across camp and checked on Chip, who seemed to be settling down nicely. Should she check to see if Ryder was okay? He'd seemed so stressed. Amber walked down the line of tents until she could see Ryder's truck and trailer. There were a couple of tents up. Lyle was working on one. Things looked okay. She moved away before they saw her, crawled into her tent, and dug out her Bible.

The tent rustled in the steady wind. Amber stretched out on her sleeping bag and began to read. The twenty-third Psalm was like balm on an open wound. "Even though I walk through the valley of the shadow of death, I will fear no evil, for you are with me."

A deep peace flooded her. God was with her no matter what she had done, and he would help her through. Again she gave God the whole situation. She prayed for Ben, then Ryder, and finally after hesitating even for Lyle and Mitch.

Lying there, watching the tent material flap in the wind, Amber slowly realized something. All her life she'd been pushing herself hard, trying to be the perfect person, the perfect doctor. That was why she hadn't been able to accept the fact that she hadn't been all-knowing. Amber sighed and relaxed. She wasn't perfect and God loved her anyway.

Amber laid her head down to think about what to say to Ben, and what she should do about going back to medicine. Instead she fell asleep, the most restful sleep she'd had for months. She missed supper and slept through the night.

Amber woke very early the next morning with a feeling of newness. She stretched and went out, pulling on a jacket against the morning chill. Already, a few people were moving in the horse lines. The sunrise was a blazing orange stripe along the east side of the earth. The land rolled in long, flat, sun-gilded waves, touching the sky in a nearly flat horizon. The wind had dropped so that pale gold grasses, backlit by the dawn, stood still in the cool air.

Looking at the dawn, Amber's being was full of praise. The words of the doxology swirled through her head as she stood and brushed out her hair in long sweeping strokes. *Praise God from whom all blessings flow.*

The song didn't cease as she fed and curried Chip. He

nuzzled her pocket for oats as the song went on, *Praise him, all creatures here below.* She felt that both she and the horse were God's creatures held in the hollow of his hand. As a child she'd thought that meant nothing bad could happen to her. Now she knew differently. God didn't keep his people in bell jars. The fallen world was a harsh place where people got hurt. His peace and security ran deeper than that. The apostle Paul's words came into her mind: *I consider everything loss compared to the surpassing greatness of knowing Christ Jesus my Lord.*

Since yesterday so many verses she'd memorized as a child made sense in a deeper way. That verse was right; her medical career, Chip, and even Ben weren't anywhere near worth the surpassing greatness of knowing Christ as her Lord.

Amber looked in the direction of Ben's tent. Sin hurt people. When Ben found out, it would hurt him too, not just what she'd done, but the way she'd deceived him. Oh, she hadn't actually lied with words, but she'd not told the truth, and now there would be pain. Maybe Ben would forgive her and accept her. He was a good guy. He might forgive her, but he wouldn't care for her the same way. Ben deserved someone better.

Picking up her Bible, Amber headed out of camp. She crested a ridge and, out of sight of the camp, opened her Bible. The words spoke to her more vividly than they ever had in her life. Engrossed, she didn't notice the steady rhythm of a trotting horse until it was very close. She jerked up her head to see a rider, silhouetted against the sky.

"Ben?" she said, standing up.

"You're up early." He reined in his horse beside her. "I looked for you for hours last night, then came over this morning to see if I could catch you by Chip, just in time to see you walk over this ridge."

"I came out to read my Bible. Oh, Ben..." Her throat closed.

"Reading your Bible?" He swung off his horse and lifted her chin with one gentle finger. "Amber, are things all right between you and God now? Did you get whatever it was straightened out?"

She nodded and he swept her into a warm embrace. With her heart aching, Amber stood still, using all her willpower not to respond. Ben let go and stepped back. "What is it? Have the Nivens caught on? Are you in danger?"

Amber could only shake her head.

"Look, if you're worried about the Nivens, we'll work that out. I've got some plans. I found out that Mitch leased the altered horses to a couple of women in the green circle. What were you going to tell me about them?"

Relieved to be able to put off the dreaded moment of truth a little longer, Amber said, "Look for a Trakehner brand."

Ben raised his eyebrows high. "Trakehner!"

"Remember that woman I was kind of hiding from at that high point show, Ruth Davis?"

"These are her horses, the ones that were stolen?"

Amber nodded, then told him she was meeting Ruth that evening. As she talked, she was nerving herself to explain why she'd hidden from Ruth Davis, but Ben cut in.

"You're meeting her at nine this evening? I'll be there." He glanced at his watch. "Speaking of the time, I've got to get back. Come with me?"

He swung onto Smoke, took his foot out of the stirrup, and reached down. He looked so hopeful. Besides, she still needed to talk to him. Amber handed him her Bible and put her foot into the empty stirrup. Taking his warm, strong hand, Amber swung up behind him. He laughed. "I am so glad you got things straight with God. I've been praying " He whooped and kicked Smoke into a canter.

Amber squealed and grabbed him around the waist to keep her balance. She couldn't help laughing with him as they tore back to camp. Ben was fun! If only…

Ben pulled Smoke into a smooth sliding stop. "I believe this is your exit, madam." He jumped off to help her down.

"Ben, I've got to talk to you. It's not about the Nivens, it's about me."

Ben sobered. "There's nothing I'd like better, Amber, but I can't talk now. I should have left for the cow herd fifteen minutes ago, but I didn't want to go without finding you. Look, if you come over there after you pack up, we might get a chance to talk."

"Where? I haven't seen any cattle since they were unloading them yesterday."

"They're keeping them a good couple of miles from the main camp. It'd be quite a wreck if a couple thousand Longhorns stampeded through the tents and horse lines."

Amber's eyes went wide at the thought. "So who's watching the cattle?"

"There's a cow boss and drovers, mostly young guys from ranches. They asked me to help gather today. They'll need extra experienced hands because the animals don't know each other or the routine yet. When we get going each day, they'll let a third of the riders from here come along. Just sign up with your wagon boss and go over there for the briefing. I really do have to go." Ben swung onto Smoke and called over his shoulder, "I'll be looking for you."

With Ben gone, Amber looked around and realized hers was almost the only tent standing. All around her, people were finishing packing their gear and saddling horses. Quickly Amber folded her tent. She lugged her kit to the blue flag and threw it on the huge heap already there. Apparently a truck would pick it up and haul it to the next camp. Amber sighed; so much for an authentic cattle drive. She ran for the catering tent. She didn't have time for breakfast, but she grabbed her sack lunch and ran back to get Chip saddled.

The whole huge camp was in commotion. Teamsters were hitching heavy horses and mules. Thirty or forty wagons were lined up on the west side of the camp and some were already heading out. Riders and horses were everywhere. Kids on beautifully trained ranch horses cantered around in little groups, showing off.

As Amber was saddling Chip, she saw an older man in chaps mount a horse which ducked its head and started a stiff-legged buck. His friends laughed and cheered as he swore and jerked the horse into a tight circle. It quit bucking, stood stiffly for a minute, and started to lie down.

"Real broke horse, George," one of his friends yelled, laughing as the man climbed off. The horse stood up and the man got back on, this time with no hitches.

Amber found she had been standing with Chip's bridle in midair watching. She quickly put it on him and mounted. Like the rancher's horse, Chip was excited by all the activity. He snorted and pranced. Amber took him away from the crowd at a brisk trot. Other riders were doing the same thing to calm their horses. There was noise of hooves close behind her. A horse swept past at a run, and for a few seconds Amber had her hands full as Chip tried to bolt after it.

She looked up to see the same horse and rider turning to come past her again. It was Mitch on his bulldogging horse. "Quit it!" Amber yelled, fighting Chip as Mitch swept by again, then circled back.

Mitch brought his horse to a beautiful sliding stop beside her. "Hey, don't be so uptight. I've gone through the whole bunch of people from the blue area looking for you. Candace, that girl at registration, wanted to ride with me, but I told her I was already booked. You and me are going to have a great day."

"Mitch, Ben asked me to meet him. I'm going to find our circle boss and tell him I'm going with the cow herd."

Mitch laughed. "You're kind of late for that. The boss didn't get as many riders as he could have sent, but the ones that did go left half an hour ago."

"Mitch!" a voice called, bringing both their heads around. It was Lyle Smith managing to look weedy even in his best western duds. "You better get back. Ryder just about had a hernia when you took off. Unless you want lots of attention when he totally flips out, we'd better stick with him and keep him away from most of the people."

"Come with us," Mitch said.

"Ryder doesn't want the girl." Lyle brought his horse over. "It'll just make him worse if you bring her. Come on, Mitch. There's six days left of the drive. You can chase skirts later."

"Do I care what Ryder wants? Amber is coming with me." Mitch sidestepped his horse, cutting in front of Chip and herding him toward the camp. Amber spun Chip on his hind legs and dodged. Mitch swore and cracked Chip on the butt. Chip bolted up the rolling hillside. By the time she had the big colt calmed down she was a good half mile out. She trotted to the top of a rise and looked back. Mitch wasn't coming after her.

Amber let out her breath in relief. Her eyes widened as they took in the scene below. A long line of wagons was trailing out to the south, dust blowing behind them in rolls like translucent cotton wool. Riders peppered the hills and grassland, thicker around the wagon trail and thinning out to each side. Dust farther to the west caught her eye. Amber looked and realized she was seeing the cow herd. They were on the move too, going southwest down a different fold in the land than the main cavalcade.

Fast movement brought her eyes back to the main camp in time to see a mule team bolt. Riders swept out to intercept them and bring the team back under control. Amber swallowed. She could never pull that stunt riding Chip.

Again she looked out to the cattle herd. Mitch had said the blue flag could have sent more riders. That meant it wouldn't matter if she went with the cattle. Amber lifted Chip into his springy trot and headed for the cattle. No matter how much it hurt, she really did need to talk to Ben.

That dusty, sunny day made a memory that would stay with Amber for a long time. There were miles of open grassland between her and the cattle. Riders were spread out across the land. Amber rode alone, yet she was less alone than ever before. She felt like one glad thread in a tapestry of praise. The huge arch of blue sky overhead, the rolling grassland, tiny birds, and the strong young horse under her, all singing with her in a wild silent psalm of joy. Several times in bowls in the prairie she was out of sight of any human being.

Before noon she found the tracks of the herd. Two thousand cattle left a braided trail of trampled grass. It was not narrow but seemed so in the tremendous expanse. Once Amber came upon a group of three pronghorn antelope. They were looking toward some other riders and didn't see her immediately. Amber had time to look at their oddly painted bodies. The hair on their hindquarters was puffed out, making big white chrysanthemums of alarm. They saw her and moved off in a fluid, stretched-out trot. Amber laughed and set Chip after them. They stretched out further, easily outdistancing the horse.

When the land folded the right way, she could see the cattle.

About half were old-fashioned Longhorns. Their horns glinted in the sun above the dark, dusty braid of the herd. She could see riders spread out ahead, behind, and to the sides.

It wasn't until almost four o'clock that she rode over a final rise and saw them up close. The riders had gathered the cattle in a wide bowl of land with a big slough in the bottom. The little lake, maybe a quarter of a mile across, lay glinting like silver in the curve of the land. Cattle made a dark necklace around the edge. Already the drovers had begun to set up camp. She could see them unharnessing three chuck wagons in a dip to the east.

Slowly she rode Chip around the rim of the bowl, drinking in the scene. Riders were posted on the crest of the ridge all the way around the bowl. The one nearest her waved, then turned his attention back to the cattle. She could hear the feet of the cattle splash in the water.

Chip pulled anxiously toward the lake. He was thirsty. She took him down, moving slowly. The big horse hesitated at the soft edge of the slough, then stepped forward. A huge spotted steer with an almost six-foot span of horns looked at them, then went back to the serious business of grazing.

After he drank, Chip wanted to lunge back out of the muck at the edge. Amber held him back to a walk, not wanting to spook the cattle. Movement on the rise above caught her eye and Amber saw Ben on his gray coming toward her. Her heart lurched. His very shape was familiar and beloved to her, as if it were burned in her mind. Just seeing him made her glad, but it also meant she'd have to talk to him. She swallowed hard and turned to face him. It hurt her that Ben looked so pleased to see her.

Twenty

Amber!" Ben said with a glad smile. "I saw you go down to the water. I've been looking for you all day."

"I started late and cut cross-country. Ben, it was the most beautiful ride! I saw pronghorns."

"You know your face looks lit from the inside. Come on, let's go up on the ridge and talk. That way we can watch the drovers setting up camp. This is where the authentic cattle drive is happening. There's no semitrailers or catered meals here. It's something special you probably won't see again."

He spun the gray and set off at a rocking canter. She stopped beside Ben at the top of a hill. In the drovers' camp, smoke was already rising from the little wood-burning stoves that sat on racks behind the chuck wagons. Two men seemed to be making a rope corral with crossed poles they'd taken off the sides of the wagons.

"Here comes the jingle string," Ben said, pointing.

Amber looked and sucked in her breath at the beauty. Thirty or forty loose horses were sweeping around the far side of the rise, manes and tails flowing in the wind. Golden dust half obscured their outline so that they looked like some abstract ideal of wild horses. As they came closer, Amber could see that five riders were with the loose horses. Two of the five put on a spurt of speed, going to the front and slowing the running horses.

High, ringing whinnies filled the air as the horses in camp greeted the newcomers. Chip took a deep breath and added his voice to the rest, shaking Amber in her saddle with the intensity of his whinny. The loose horses swirled in a circle and then filed easily into the corral where several men were pouring out piles of oats.

Amber let out her breath. "That was beautiful! But what on earth is a jingle string?"

"They're the drover's remounts. A lot of those guys will be riding night herd and they'll need fresh horses. I guess they're called the jingle string because old-time cowhands used to keep bells on a few of the loose horses so they could hear them at night. The man who rode herd on the remounts while they were grazing was called the jingler or wrangler." Ben was watching the drovers camp with an intent look on his face. He turned back to Amber with a big grin. "Isn't this great?!"

His eyes were so happy. Amber bit her lip. "Ben, I need to tell you something."

"I'm listening." Ben instantly sobered, his hazel eyes intent on her.

"I haven't told you the truth about myself." She swallowed hard, looking down. "Ben, I've been dreading this. It's only in the last two days that I've been able to accept God's forgiveness." The words stuck in her throat.

Ben reached out and took her hand. "Amber, I know you'll tell me when you're ready; meanwhile, if God has forgiven you, how could I not do so? Amber Lacey, you are very special to me."

Wild hope rose in Amber. Firmly she shoved it down. Ben didn't know what she'd done; how could he accept her? She had to get the words out.

Someone coughed just behind them, making Amber jump. She turned to find one of the drovers not ten feet away. Embarrassed, Amber tried to drop Ben's hand, but he held on and gave it a little squeeze before he let go.

"Uh, I hate to interrupt this lovely scene, but they sent me up to ask if you wouldn't look at a saddle gall on one of the horses before you go back to the main camp." The man grinned. "I guess they didn't realize you were otherwise engaged."

"No problem, Jake," Ben said. "I'll be right down."

Jake tactfully cantered off. Ben turned back to Amber. "I'd better go down there. It's my job. I may be a while because they're sure to have other animals that need care. I do want to hear what you have to say if you need to tell me. There are things I need to tell you as well. You could come down into the drovers' camp and wait for me?"

There was no way she could stand to go down in the drovers' camp and watch Ben work. They'd be teasing him about her and..."I'd better go back."

"I'm sorry I can't come with you," Ben said. "I'll try to get there to be with you when you meet with Ruth Davis. If I'm not at your tent by nine, I'll look for you by the altered horses in the green line."

Amber forced words through her tight throat. "Ben, it's okay. I know it's your job. I'll look for you tonight."

Ben touched her cheek. "Chin up, Amber Lacey. God loves you, and you know what? I think I do too."

He turned Smoke and trotted into the drovers' camp, leaving Amber sitting there with her heart pounding. Driven by the whirl of emotions in her head, Amber stuck her heels into Chip and headed off toward the main camp perilously close to a dead run.

The main camp looked huge as Amber came over the rise above it. It lay spread out on the land like a colorful anthill. She slowed Chip, and they came in at a walk. The horse lines, dark with tied horses, made a huge interrupted circle on the grassland. Just inside them, like dots of bright confetti, tents were going up. In the center, the big catering pavilions were already up.

At the blue camp Amber tied Chip to the horse line and unsaddled him. Amber had never felt more in need of a shower in her life. She was hot and covered with dust and horsehair.

As soon as she had her tent up, she put on shorts and a T-shirt. It felt incredibly good to get her riding boots off. She stretched her cramped, dirty feet and wiggled her bare toes in the wind. Being barefoot felt so good that she didn't bother with shoes.

Stepping carefully around prickly pear cactuses in the grass, she went to take Chip to water. As he drank, she realized the colt might like to be washed off as much as she would. A bucket was sitting by the water tank. The first time she poured water on his back, Chip flinched, then he stood with his eyes half shut in bliss as she soaked him all over. As she scooped and poured, cool water splashed on her feet and ran down her arms, feeling incredibly good.

Other people and horses were coming and going to the watering tank. Several had followed her lead and were splashing water on their horses. One man with a team of Clydesdales was taking extra care to soak their necks where the horses' skin had been under the hot, heavy collars all day.

Amber was dipping her bucket in the tank when a splash of cold water hit her hard in the small of the back. She spun around to face Mitch's handsome, laughing face. Mitch threw the rest of the water. Chip shied, jerking Amber away from the tank. Amber danced backward, trying to hang on to the frightened horse. Her hair flung out and stuck to her wet face. She got Chip stopped and faced Mitch, just as Chip shook, splattering her with filthy water. Amber jumped and put her foot on a cactus.

"Ouch! Mitch Niven, you are such a pain!"

Mitch laughed. "Hey, even mad and muddy, you'd win the wet T-shirt contest any day in my books. I came to invite you to a party. A bunch of my buddies, Red and Drake and them, the ones you met at the bar in Calgary, well, we're going to fill some of the big horse watering tanks with hot water from the shower truck and have a hot tub party. Clothes are optional."

"Sorry, Mitch, I have something else booked tonight." She turned to go.

"No," Mitch said loudly. "Wait."

Amber kept walking but Mitch followed. "Look, I'll pay you two hundred dollars if you come. It's a bet I have with some guys. You come and we both win."

Amber shook her head. With his determination and athletic ability Mitch could have accomplished so much. Instead he was doing horrible damage to the horses he stole, to his brother, and, to a lesser extent, to others. Still, since she understood forgiveness, she'd found it hard to really hate anyone.

"Mitch, I really can't come." Amber tried to ignore her sore foot and the muddy water dripping off her hair into her face. "Even if I could, I wouldn't."

Mitch swore and spun on his heel. "You've been nothing but filthy bad luck. First I waste eight hundred bucks paying for you to come along, and now this."

"I asked Ryder to give you my wages for that," Amber called after his retreating back.

If Mitch thought she was bad luck now…Amber shook her head and bent to pull the cactus off her foot. Luckily all the spines came out. Limping slightly, she set out to find the shower truck.

Twenty people at a time were filing into a semitrailer container box. It had been rigged with shower heads partitioned by curtains. One had a minute to get in and get undressed, then someone outside threw open a big valve that gave everyone three minutes of hot water. There was a lot of good-natured teasing going on. Amber laughed with the others. She left feeling wonderfully clean and much more cheerful, but she couldn't stop thinking about Ben.

At supper, Amber saw Mitch and his friends at a distance. She walked in the opposite direction with her plate of food. At least if Mitch was at a party he wouldn't likely be around the altered horses at nine o'clock tonight.

Ben worked as fast as he could, but he didn't manage to get back to the main camp until the last people were going through the supper line. He grabbed a meal and ate it standing, keeping an eye out for Amber. If only Jake hadn't come to fetch him until after Amber had finished what she was going to say.

Ben swallowed the last bite of steak and glanced at his watch. He should be at an organizers' meeting in ten minutes and after that was the veterinarians' meeting. He shoved his paper plate into the garbage and stood there torn. He ought to go to the meetings. They were part of his responsibility as an official vet and Amber wasn't expecting him till later. Still, more than anything he wanted to go look for Amber.

"Hey, Ben." Stan Potter, one of the other vets, bowlegged, potbellied, and perpetually smiling, was heading over with a stack of dirty plates. "Come on, can't be late."

Ben sighed and went with him.

After supper, Amber watched the show for a while. Anyone could go pick up the mike. Two groups of people had pulled together excellent country western bands. Others joined them on everything from banjos to spoons. A couple of people got up and recited goofy cowboy poetry. Through it all, Amber kept glancing in the direction of the green line. As it got closer to nine o'clock, she got more and more nervous.

Ben wasn't waiting for her at her tent at nine. Amber swallowed hard and went to find Ruth Davis. In the green line they could easily see the big paints, their white spots showing clearly in the summer dusk. As they came closer, Ruth sped up, a kind of headlong determination in her walk. Amber thought she saw someone move on the far side of the horses, but when she looked closely she saw nothing. The nearer of the two tall horses turned his head, flicked his ears forward. He nickered a greeting.

"Cappuccino!" Ruth rubbed the horse's neck. "Oh, my boy, what have they done to you?" The other horse nickered too, reaching for Ruth. "And you too, Ramiro."

Ruth stepped between the horses, running her hands across their skin, feeling the great blotches of white. "I could kill the man who did this. These burns are still healing. You can see these are my horses. I'm going to get the police right now!"

"I'll come with you," Amber said.

"And have that jerk come and move the horses while we're gone? No, you stay here. I'll be right back." She strode away toward the drive office before Amber even had a chance to protest.

Amber moved a few steps away from the horses and sat on the stack of bales between the lines. Ben had said he'd meet her here. If only he would come, she'd feel much safer. A light wind had come up, making her glad she'd worn her jacket. Again she thought she saw movement in the horse line. Shivering a little, she stood up to look but could see nothing.

Later, looking down between the horse lines, Amber

thought she saw Ben's figure in the distance. She walked a few paces to see better. Hard hands suddenly grabbed her elbows, jerking them painfully behind her. A wave of beer breath nearly choked her as a rough face shoved against her ear from behind. "What are you doing here, Amber?"

"Mitch, let go of me!" Amber yelled furiously. She twisted, violently kicking backward.

Mitch swore as her heels connected with his shins. She felt herself jerked upward by her elbows until she was afraid Mitch would dislocate her shoulders.

"You humiliate me in front of my friends, then I come to check and find you here by these horses. I think it would be better if you just disappeared in the night. There's plenty of coyotes to clean up the mess."

Mitch started to haul Amber through the horse lines to the dark encircling night. Kicking and twisting, Amber fought silently until she remembered that she'd been taught to scream if she was attacked. She took a deep breath and screamed with all her might. Mitch swore and clamped a wiry arm across her face. She bit down hard, he jerked his arms away, and she screamed again. With a vicious twist, Mitch threw her to the ground. His hand was on the back of her head, fingers digging into her scalp. Amber's mouth was full of dirt. A knee dug in between her shoulder blades. She twisted violently only to catch a glimpse of the gleam of a knife coming at her.

There was a thud and the weight went off her back. She had the impression of two powerful bodies locked just above her. As she rolled out of the way to keep from being trampled, she could hear Ben yelling.

"Mitch Niven, you leave her alone!"

Dizzily Amber scrambled to her feet and tried to focus. Mitch and Ben were circling each other. Mitch held the knife angled upward. The horse lines were chaos as the animals spooked at the commotion. A dark form launched itself through the horse lines in their direction.

"Watch out!" Amber screamed. "It's Ryder."

Ben turned and Mitch jumped at him. Ryder's uncontrolled rush tumbled all three men to the ground. Drawn by Amber's screams, people were shouting and running toward them. Someone grabbed Mitch. Others got hold of Ryder and Ben. Amber saw Mitch move the knife between his body and arm, hiding it. Ben and Mitch stood still, but Ryder fought like a mad thing.

Amber dodged backward to keep clear of the men trying to hold Ryder. She had assumed Ryder was after Ben, but he was screaming at Mitch as he fought the men holding him. "You stole those horses. I was watching and saw them greet their owner. You made me burn horses that had no need of the pain and you killed that good white horse. My own brother..." His voice rose into incoherent rage.

Movement caught Amber's eye. She looked up to see Ruth Davis, two RCMP officers, and several other men coming at a run. "Horse thieves. Stop the horse thieves!" Ruth Davis yelled in a penetrating voice. "They stole my horses and I can prove it."

Suddenly loose, Ryder leapt past Amber. He was snarling like an animal as he jumped Mitch. There was a flash of steel in Mitch's hand and Ryder went down in a heap. Mitch took two strides and slashed Cappuccino's lead shank. He was halfway through an athletic leap onto the horse's back when Ben's fist brought him crashing to the ground. Cappuccino bolted into the dark as Mitch rolled onto his feet. The sharp crack of a gunshot stopped them in place.

"Drop the knife or the next shot won't be into the air." Amber let out her breath in relief when she heard the authoritative voice of the RCMP officer.

Mitch dropped the knife with a snarl, but Amber wasn't paying attention anymore. A man was down with a knife wound and Amber at heart was still a medical doctor. She moved to Ryder Niven's side. She was bruised, filthy, and shaking all over with reaction to the violence, but as she unbuttoned Ryder's shirt her hands steadied.

Ryder was lying limp with his eyes tightly shut. He didn't respond to her voice. Amber had the impression that he wasn't unconscious from the wound. Already unbalanced, he'd folded mentally, completely withdrawing from an intolerable situation.

The wound was in the upper part of his chest, just under the collarbone. It was a sucking wound. Amber knew that the more air that went into that wound when he inhaled, the more quickly Ryder's lung would collapse. She put her hand over the opening, sealing it off. Several people around her were shouting, "Medic!"

The general commotion around them suddenly rose to a crescendo. "I don't care if I killed him!" Mitch was screaming. "He's crazy anyway. He's the one that was burning horses. Don't blame any of it on me. He's the one. The woman with him is a troublemaking idiot!"

The knot of men holding Mitch surged forward as he tried to get at his brother and Amber. Amber glanced up to see Ben standing solidly between her and danger. Regret shot though her like a jolt from a painful tooth. If only things could be good between Ben and her. Determinedly she turned back to Ryder.

"Medic." A man put down a large first-aid box and crouched beside Ryder.

"I'm a medical doctor," Amber said quickly. "I need to put on an occlusive dressing."

As the medic flipped the box open, Amber looked up. Ben's

hazel eyes were wide with shock. "You're what?"

Before she had time to answer, Ruth Davis marched toward them, closely followed by one policeman. "This woman, Amber Lacey, was working for the Nivens. She told me my horses were here. She knows what they did to my animals, how they had them freeze-branded into paints."

Ben quietly blocked Ruth Davis. "As you can see, Amber can't help you right now, but perhaps I can." Amber watched them walk away. She swallowed hard. This wasn't the way she'd wanted him to find out she was a doctor. With an effort she brought her mind back to her work and applied the dressing.

Twenty-One

Red and blue lights flashed across the grass. Amber hadn't realized it, but an ambulance was also following the cattle drive. It moved with the trucks, out of sight of the main drive but always accessible. Now it came bumping forward. In a few seconds she was talking to one of the official doctors along on the cattle drive. She explained what had happened and what she'd done. "This man may also be unstable mentally. The Millers know his history if you need that later."

"There's a helicopter waiting that belongs to the British military. We'll take him out on that," the gray-haired doctor said quickly as two men moved Ryder onto a stretcher and slid him into the ambulance. They thanked her and took over so competently that she had no qualms about leaving Ryder in their hands. She needed to find Ben and try to explain.

After the ambulance had bumped away, Amber couldn't see Ben anywhere. Ruth Davis wasn't in sight, either. Clumps of people stood around talking excitedly. Several tried to talk to her, trying to confirm details. Amber hardly heard them. She smiled at them blankly and kept walking, searching for Ben in the silver moonlight.

She headed for the trailer that served as the cattle drive office. It was packed with excited people who all seemed to be talking at once. Amber couldn't see Ben, but Ruth Davis was there.

"Excuse me," Amber said. Only the man nearest to her turned to look.

"You're Amber Lacey, aren't you?" He spun around. "Hey guys, here's someone who should be able to give us some answers."

Suddenly every eye in the room was on her. People called out questions. With a shaking hand Amber pushed her hair out of her face.

"Give the lady some room. She's white as a ghost," one of the men said.

Kind hands were helping her into a chair. Someone pushed a cup of something into her hand. They crowded around talking at her. She took a swallow of hot, strong coffee and closed her eyes tight trying to shut out the commotion.

Suddenly Ruth Davis was beside her. The woman's strong penetrating voice easily overrode the others. "Can't you see she needs some quiet?"

The trailer was soon silent except for the sound of boots shuffling on the floor. One man started to apologize. Amber shook her head. "I was looking for Ben Miller. Do any of you know where he is?"

Ruth Davis's eyebrows went up. "He flew out with his father and the suspects on that military helicopter. They were needed to show the RCMP the way. The man who was injured had a cell phone and no one knew if he'd called out. They wanted to get there before the operation was taken apart. We thought you were with them until you turned up here with a face like a ghost."

The room spun dizzily. Gripping her chair for support, Amber got to her feet and walked unsteadily out the door. Ben was gone. He'd left without bothering to talk to her. Numbly Amber headed for her tent. She was hardly aware of Ruth Davis beside her. Twice the woman tried to head her toward the first-aid trailer, but Amber's exhausted head had room for only one idea. She kept going toward her own tent.

Inside the tent, she fell onto the bed. Her battered mind and body dropped into the haven of sleep as if falling into a deep pool.

~

Ben didn't realize that Amber wasn't inside the big military helicopter attending Ryder Niven until he was actually climbing in the door. As soon as he saw she wasn't there he began to back out. Carl Jack, the RCMP officer, held on to his arm.

"We'll come back for the girl, but we need you as a witness now."

"Carl, you know me. I'll find Amber and come." Both men were shouting to be heard over the noise of the rotors.

Carl stared into Ben's eyes for a long minute. "I have your word on that?"

"You do."

"Just a minute."

As he stood impatiently on the helicopter skid, his hair and clothes tossed in the wind from the rotors, Ben could see Carl and the pilot conferring and then talking on the radio. Carl nodded decisively.

"Okay, Ben. We'll have a helicopter here to pick you and the girl up at eight A.M. tomorrow."

"Thanks, Carl," Ben said with relief. He'd arrived back at the drive office not long after Amber had left. He headed for her tent only to meet Ruth Davis coming out.

"You!" Ruth said. "When she came to the office, I told Amber you'd left on the helicopter and the girl looked like she was going to faint. She came back over here looking pale and stunned." Ben started to push past her.

"Wait, she's asleep now," Ruth said.

"We need to talk. If she thinks I left..."

"Leave her be. Let her get a bit of rest before she faces more emotional trauma."

Ben hesitated and finally nodded. Ruth Davis was right. It couldn't hurt to let Amber get some rest. She'd been through a lot. Tomorrow morning would be soon enough to talk. He walked away slowly.

The discomfort of sleeping in her clothes woke Amber very early the next morning. Dawn was only a faint band of gray on the eastern horizon. She stretched, finding aching muscles all over her body, and rolled out of bed. Her arms above the elbow were bruised deep into the muscle where Mitch had grabbed her. She ached with a pain that was deeper than the physical trauma. Ben had turned away from her. It hurt even worse than she'd thought it would.

The seams on her jeans had bit into her legs. She rubbed the sore places as she pulled on clean clothes. She'd leave today and go back to finish her medical training. No matter how Ben had responded, she would have had to do it anyway at the end of the drive. She'd hoped they could have stayed in touch, been friends.

"God, I couldn't have stood this without your love. Please help me." Amber bowed her head as a feeling of peace washed over her.

Outside the tent a light wind was sweeping across the grassland. Through the gaps in the high overcast sky, the last few stars gleamed. Swallowing hard, she lifted her chin and walked toward the horse lines. Ben wouldn't be her only loss today.

Chip nickered in greeting and reached out his nose toward her. "Hey, boy, how would you like to belong to Ruth Davis? She'll take good care of you." She rubbed the big horse's neck. "I've got to go back to medicine. Last night working on Ryder, I knew that for sure." She sighed and leaned on the horse's shoulder. "I was too proud. No one even blamed me for that little boy's death. I'll be more careful now and certainly more humble."

Chip turned his head and blew gently on Amber's arm, then jerked his head impatiently. "Okay, I'll get you some food."

Carrying the prickly hay, Amber looked down the horse lines and saw the Nivens' horses. Mitch and Ryder weren't going to be feeding them today. Lyle Smith had likely been picked up by the police. Not liking to see any animal go hungry, Amber fed them too.

By the time she was finished, the clouds were showing pink on the underside. Maybe this whole mess would help Ryder get the attention he needed to heal. Maybe Ben would help. He was such a kind man. Amber looked down the horse line, her sight blurred by tears. She set out to find Ruth Davis. It was very early, but Amber wasn't going to wait.

Amber planned to get Chip safely sold to Ruth Davis and then see if one of the caterers or someone else was leaving with a supply truck. She'd get a ride out, and the earlier the better as far as she was concerned.

Ben Miller was awake and pacing the horse lines in the purple camp. He wanted to go to Amber, but it wasn't even five in the morning. Ruth Davis had been right to let Amber sleep. It would be stupid to wake her up so ridiculously early.

He hadn't slept much. Over and over in the night he'd gone through the reasons Amber might have run from her medical career. The fact that Ruth Davis had said she'd looked so shocked when she found out he was gone gave him hope, but it also made him want to go to her, to reassure her. She couldn't really think he'd abandon her, could she? He walked determinedly toward the blue line but stopped himself once more. He'd wait half an hour and then go find her. It would still be early, but people would be moving by then.

"Ruth. Ruth Davis," Amber called softly outside Ruth's tent.

There was a shuffling noise. "Yes, what is it?"

"This is Amber Lacey. Sorry to bother you so early, but I need to talk to you."

"Amber Lacey? Give me a second. I'll be right out."

True to her word, Ruth emerged in very little time, her face still swollen with sleep. Immediately Amber began to apologize again for waking her.

Ruth shook her head impatiently. "You got two of my horses back. You can wake me anytime. Now what is it?"

Suddenly remembering, Amber said, "One of them bolted into the night when Mitch got caught. Cappuccino, wasn't it?"

"He's fine, if you consider being covered with unsightly white patches all right. Paints are supposed to be all the rage. I suppose I'll get used to their new look. You surely didn't wake me to ask about the horses."

"No, actually, I need to leave the Centennial Cattle Drive right away and fly back east. I wondered if you'd still buy Chip from me. I know you've got two horses back, but I can't take him with me and I was hoping—"

"Yes, I'll buy him."

Amber looked at Ruth, startled at the suddenness of her answer.

"If you want to sell him," Ruth enunciated as if speaking to a slow four-year-old, "I'd be happy to buy the colt. He's a beautiful horse." She named a price that was more than fair. "Will that do?"

The sudden reality of losing Chip made her throat tight. Amber swallowed hard and lifted her chin. "Yes, that's good. Would you take ownership now? I want to leave this morning. I've decided I'm going back to medicine. I want to get going while I still have the nerve."

"Good," Ruth said emphatically. "A woman of your potential should be doing something worthwhile."

Amber shook her head. "It's not that. It's just that I'm sure now that's where God wants me."

"God, is it? Never had much time for that nonsense myself."

"It's not nonsense, you know. The Bible says that 'In God's presence is fullness of joy.' It's true. That joy has been like an anchor for me in the last few days, a safe place no matter what."

"They did teach the Psalms in the English school system, not that it sank in much. Maybe it would be worth my time to rethink that. But enough of religion now; we've got business to do. Wait a second while I write you a check." She dug out her checkbook. While she was writing she said, "Leave the horse where he is. I'll talk to the drive organizers and arrange something."

Twenty-Two

At five-thirty, Ben went to the blue circle. The whole camp was waking now. As he got closer Ben started to jog. Dawn light was laying long shadows beside every tent. Amber's was quiet.

"Amber, wake up."

There was no response. He tried again, then realized the tent door was open. She was already up. He ran for the horse lines. Chip had been fed and Amber was nowhere in sight. She must have gone out to read her Bible again. In seconds he was on Smoke and heading onto the open grassland at a canter. He had to find her!

Amber was walking to the catering tent. With all the food that was being eaten each day, it wasn't hard to figure out that the caterers would have trucks coming and going to some population center each day. When she asked who was in charge, the woman serving breakfast nodded toward the kitchen. "Look for a fat man with a bald head, only don't tell him I said that. George is a good guy."

He was too. When she told him she had strong personal reasons to leave the drive, he looked at her troubled face and then nodded.

"Okay, there's a truck leaving in half an hour."

Wind lifted Amber's hair as she stepped outside. The grass was blowing in long waving ripples across the hills. People were feeding horses and folding tents as Amber headed for the blue line.

The circle boss gave her a sharp look when she told him she'd be leaving. "You won't get any money back, you know," he said. "Besides, there's no way you can get your horse out."

Feeling numb and detached, Amber explained that she'd sold Chip to Ruth Davis and that she didn't care if she got any money back. She packed up her gear, carried it over behind the catering tent, and sat beside it, cross-legged on the grass, to write to Ben. No matter how he'd reacted, Amber felt she owed him an explanation.

She could hear the streams of people coming in for breakfast. She was out of sight behind the tent and had no inclination to eat. The words came slowly. Gritting her teeth, she forced herself to think back so that she could tell him exactly the mistakes she'd made. Before she was done, silent tears were running down her cheeks making cool streaks in the wind.

"Ben," she wrote at the end, "you helped me tremendously in this hard time, reminding me of my Savior's love and forgiveness. I knew the verses at the end of Romans 8, but until this summer, I've never really understood them. You're a solid, healthy man, strong in God's love. You deserve someone better than me, someone as unscarred and healthy as you are."

She thought for a second about telling him just how much she cared for him. But what good would that do? Writing the words would just hurt both of them.

"I'm sure God wants me to go back to medicine, so that's what I'm doing. I'll look for another residency, maybe up north. Thanks for your help." Quickly she wrote one more sentence. "If you want to find me, Capi Cloud, Shane Cloud's sister will know where I am." She wrote out the address in quick neat letters and then added, "If you don't contact me, I'll understand. I'm sorry if I hurt you. Resting in God's love, Amber Lacey."

She folded the paper, put it in an envelope, and wrote Ben's name on the outside. Amber stroked his name once with her finger and stood up. A chunky man with graying blond hair was walking toward the truck. She took a deep breath, wiped her eyes, and stood.

"Hi, George said you'd be able to give me a ride out."

He nodded, switched his coffee cup to his other hand, and reached to shake hands. "I'm Chris Masters, be glad to."

In minutes they'd stowed Amber's gear and were bumping away from the camp. After fifteen miles of rough roads, the truck was on the pavement. Masters was a taciturn man who made no attempt to talk to her. Amber watched the grassland scroll away behind her. It was better this way. If Ben wanted to find her, he could. She wouldn't have to watch him struggle to tell her he wasn't interested. Tears stung Amber's eyes as she said softly, "God go with you, Ben Miller, just as he is with me."

The catering truck dropped Amber in the small city of Medicine Hat. By the time Amber had found a bank and cashed Ruth Davis's check, it was afternoon. Half an hour on a pay phone had her booked on a bus to Calgary, a night in the airport hotel, and a flight back east the next morning.

Back at the Centennial Cattle Drive, Ben had been nearly frantic. He'd circled the entire camp twice on Smoke and returned to find Amber's tent gone. He couldn't find it in the heap left for the semitrailer, and she wasn't in the horse lines with Chip. Seeing Drew Orner, he'd questioned the man.

"Don't blame me. I told her she wouldn't get any money back, but yeah, she's the broad who told me she'd sold her horse and was leaving."

"How? When? Why?"

"I didn't ask. None of my business," he said and turned his

back on Ben to finish saddling his horse.

Ben stood rooted in place, staring at the man's back. Could Amber be running so she wouldn't have to give a statement to the police? Was there something she didn't want them to know about herself? She had said twice there was something she was ready to tell him. The pleading look she'd given him when she saw his shocked expression at finding out she was a medical doctor wouldn't leave his mind. More than he wanted anything in his life before, Ben Miller wanted to find Amber Lacey.

"Who'd she sell her horse to?" Ben demanded.

The circle boss turned around slowly. "She told me. Said it was some woman; I don't remember her name."

Ruth Davis had wanted to buy Chip. Ben set out to find Ruth. The high clouds of early morning had gotten thicker and lower. A fine rain was falling. It gave the riders a chance to get out their fancy slickers. Quite a few people had put plastic covers over their Stetsons. Ben's was uncovered and dripped water from the edges as he strode across the camp. He didn't have much time before the helicopter came. Then he'd have some real explaining to do.

Ben saw Ruth at a distance and broke into a run. Taking long strides over the wet grass, he dodged through the people in line for breakfast.

"Ruth! Ruth Davis!"

She stopped and watched him approach.

"Do you know where I can find Amber?"

"I saw her this morning. She sold me her horse and I didn't think to ask if you'd found her."

"Why did she sell Chip? Did she say what she was doing?"

"Just how well do you know Amber?"

"I feel like I know who she is." Ben looked away, "But I know almost nothing about her background. All she would say was that something had made it hard for her to trust God."

Ruth looked at him thoughtfully. "I knew Amber very casually back east. She was just finishing her medical residency. She told me this morning that she was going back to medicine."

"Where?" Ben said.

"I'm sorry, I don't know. Her residency was in Toronto, but I doubt if she could go back to the same position."

Ben swallowed hard and voiced his fears. "Did you have the impression that she was trying to avoid talking to the police? Did she seem afraid of them?"

"No, I didn't. In fact, I'm sure she wasn't thinking of that at all. She seemed to be upset and nerving herself to sell Chip and leave. I doubt if the fact she might need to testify in court even occurred to her. If she's not still on the cattle drive site, you might catch her at the Calgary airport. She said something about catching a flight."

The sound of a helicopter brought Ben's head up. He glanced at his watch. Eight o'clock and he still hadn't found Amber. With a quick thank-you to Ruth, he sprinted toward the copter.

Carl Jack climbed out of the helicopter and listened to Ben's explanation and plea for time.

"This woman has sold her horse and might have left the drive. Ben, I don't like it. She was working for the Nivens. Are you sure she wasn't involved in the rustling herself?"

"I'm sure about that. Look, there are other things happening between her and me. She may be on the site yet. Help me find her."

"I have every intention of finding her," Carl said. "We picked up Bull Schwartz last night. I saw the horses in that barn. What they were doing is disgusting."

"Amber had nothing to do with that. I was with her when

she saw those horses. She was just as appalled as you are."

Carl gave Ben a sharp look. "You were there?"

"I was. I'll give you a statement, but first let's find Amber."

It didn't take long to find out Amber had left on the catering truck. Carl sent out a message on the radio. The Medicine Hat police picked the truck up at the first supplier, but Chris Masters had already dropped Amber off. Since they hadn't talked, Masters had no idea of where she'd be going.

Ben ran for the drive office. Ruth had said Amber was flying out. He'd catch her at the airport. It took him only minutes to tell the organizers he had to leave. They even agreed to let him take one of the pickup trucks that followed the drive in case it was needed. Ben couldn't find his father and left a message for him. Gordon hadn't been up when he went to find Amber. He was probably in the crowd eating breakfast, but Ben and he had prayed together the night before. Ben knew his father's prayers were with him.

Coming back to tell Carl what he was doing, Ben struggled with himself. Should he tell the police that Amber might be flying out? He wanted to be the one to find her, but he didn't have the access to passenger lists that the RCMP did.

Carl looked up. "Ben, don't look so hollow-eyed. We're not going to call a full manhunt on your Amber. I didn't like it that she ran, but I think you're right. She doesn't seem to be implicated with the horse rustling."

"I appreciate that. Amber said something to Ruth Davis about flying out. Could you check and see if she's booked out of Calgary anytime soon? Carl, I have to find her."

The pause that followed as Carl thought that through seemed to Ben to last for weeks. Finally he nodded. "Yeah, okay. We do want her statement. I'll get back to you at your place tonight."

"No, I'll be at the airport with my cell phone."

Carl laughed. "You really have got it bad." He took the number and went to get on the radio.

Twenty-Three

Alberta was a huge province and Ben had a lot of miles to cover. It was two in the morning before Ben was at the Calgary airport. Tense and very tired, he paced under the bright artificial lights. At least Calgary's airport was small. It had only one big departure area, but that was several hundred yards long. Two flights left before dawn, but Amber was on neither of them. Ben stopped in front of one of the information terminals. Three flights were leaving just after six. If he wasn't careful, he could miss her in the press. Why hadn't Carl called?

After an uneasy night, Amber was up early to get ready for her seven o'clock flight. She also needed to find a stamp and envelope somewhere to mail her letter to Ben. The shop in the hotel foyer wasn't open yet. Maybe the woman at the desk would sell her a stamp. Amber ran her hand through her hair nervously. "I really do have to get a letter mailed before I leave. Isn't there anywhere I can get a stamp and envelope?"

"I think there's a machine that dispenses stamped envelopes over at the airport. It's after you go through security though."

"Thanks!" Amber hurried through the walkway. It was more than an hour until her flight left. She had intended to eat first, but getting the letter mailed to Ben was more important. She wanted that off her mind. Amber glanced down the concourse. There was quite a press of people at the other end where the passengers for three earlier flights were checking in. She hesitated. Was that Ben down there? Amber shook her head impatiently.

She'd only seen the man for an instant and he was a long way away. Her imagination was definitely getting out of hand.

Ben was focused on making sure he didn't miss Amber in the crush. He wasn't wasting energy scanning the slack areas. Moving to a new vantage point, he stepped up on one of the seats and scanned the crowd again. He jumped when his cell phone rang, then answered with a quick jerk.

"Carl, is that you?"

"Yup. Ben, your girl is booked on the seven o'clock United flight." He gave the flight number.

"Thanks, man," Ben said, and sprinted for the United stations down in the quiet area. Only one station was open and that clerk was dealing with someone else. Ben shifted from one foot to the other and finally cut in. "Excuse me. I need to find someone urgently and she's booked on your seven o'clock flight. Has Amber Lacey checked in?"

The clerk held up her hand and continued to deal with the customer, who seemed to have a complicated problem to do with rebooking flights. The customer, a well-padded businessman, glanced over at Ben and then really looked at him.

"For pity's sake," he said, turning to the clerk. "Help the man now. He's desperate and what I'm doing can wait."

"I need to know if an Amber Lacey has checked in."

"That's privileged information, sir."

Ben clenched his fists. "I know she's booked. Please, just tell me if she's come through."

"I can't do that."

Ben's shoulders slumped. He turned slowly to find somewhere to watch from. It was early. She probably hadn't checked in yet.

“What does she look like? There was a woman who checked in just ahead of me.” It was the businessman.

Ben spun around. “Red-blond curly hair, freckles, slight with big green eyes. Did you see her?”

The man was nodding. “Yeah, it was her. She just headed for security. Run, man!”

“Thanks!” Ben called over his shoulder. He sprinted for the security check and arrived just in time to catch a glimpse of red-gold hair far down the hall on the opposite side. He ducked through the metal detector door at a run, dodging an old lady and the guard on the far side. Alarms went off. People shouted and Amber turned. Her mouth fell open and she dropped her duffel. Then he had his arms around her. He held her tightly, saying her name over and over.

Amber clung to him for a second. “Ben? How did you find me?” She pushed at him. “Stop it. You still don’t know—”

The cavalry arrived in the shape of running security guards. Over Amber’s head Ben saw one drawing a gun.

“Take it easy.” He stepped back with his hands raised. “I needed to catch Amber. That’s all.”

That didn’t seem to help. He heard Amber protest as they shoved him against the wall and frisked him. Two RCMP officers arrived, a man and a woman. They started to escort him off to a secure room.

“Amber, don’t leave until we talk. Please! Rebook your flight. I’ll pay.”

She stared after him for a second, and then ran to catch up. “I’m coming with you.” They tried to shut Amber out of the room. Ben heard her say defiantly, “How do you know he didn’t hand me a bomb or something? You saw us make contact.”

One of the security guards laughed. “That I did, close contact, I’d say.” He let her in. With his laughter the tension dropped. Still, they had a female security guard search Amber before they sat them both down for a statement. To Ben's relief, Amber wasn't the least bit shy about giving her name to the police.

While they were talking to the female officer, the other officer called Carl Jack at Ben's request. Ben heard him laugh, then say, "No, I don't imagine you figured he'd blast through the security check. Okay, I'll take her statement about the rustling incident."

It took some time to get that done. When Amber got to the part when she'd first suspected that Mitch had picked up Ruth Davis's horses, she looked at Ben apologetically. "I should have said something, but I wasn't sure and Ruth knew I was..."

Ben waved her off.

"Wait a second," the male officer said. "I want to hear what the lady has to say."

"I'd had some contact with Ruth Davis back in Ontario. She knew I was a medical doctor. But I didn't want anyone out here to know that." Amber's face was pale and she wouldn't look at Ben.

"Had you done anything illegal?" The policeman was leaning forward.

"No, nothing like that. It was just something I was having a hard time dealing with personally."

Ben's heart turned over at the tension in her voice. He reached to take her hand. She pulled away and continued her statement, telling how Chip had disappeared and how she and Ben had found the burnt horses.

"You should have come to us immediately," the female officer said.

Ben nodded. "Carl has already raked me over the coals for that. We wanted to catch them doing something that would get more than a token hand slap. Altering the color of horses you own isn't illegal. I checked."

"Surely those jumping horses were identifiable."

"I didn't know that." Ben said.

"I did but..." Amber shook her head and went on to complete her statement. At the end she said, "I'm positive Ryder Niven had nothing to do with the rustling. His plan was to buy healthy young horses that otherwise would have gone for meat and alter them to a popular color. He jumped Mitch when he found out what his brother had been doing."

Without comment the officer finished writing, had Amber read and sign her statement, then asked for an address to contact her if she was needed to testify. Glancing at Ben, Amber gave them Capi Cloud's address. "I won't be there but I'll keep Capi current about where I am."

The officer nodded and let them go with a warning. As they went to walk out of the room, the security guard motioned to Amber. "Better hurry if you still want to catch your flight."

Ben put a hand on her shoulder. "Amber, please stay."

Slowly she nodded. Everybody in the room cheered.

As soon as they were by themselves, Amber turned to Ben. "I've got full fare tickets, and Ben, after we talk I still need to leave."

He made a noise of protest.

Amber clasped her arms tightly across her body. "I have to, Ben."

"Okay, you do what you need to do, but first let's talk. We'll go out to Nose Hill Park. There's lots of room to walk without being bothered."

Neither of them said anything during the drive there.

Amber was torn. She'd been incredibly glad to see Ben, but she almost felt as if God were being mean. Why was he making her tell Ben what she'd done face-to-face? Silently she prayed for help. It would take every iota of courage she possessed to face Ben's rejection.

Nose Hill turned out to be sweeping knolls of prairie grassland rising above the city. It was a clear day. Wind swept in gusts, rolling through the grass like a hand patting cat's fur.

As soon as the vehicle stopped, Amber said, "Ben, I'm sorry. You think you care for me, but you don't. I'm not a very nice person at all. Before, I used to think I was okay. I had friends. I was good at things. I liked healing people. I didn't know how proud I was and I didn't understand grace at all. Then I made a mistake that caused a child's death."

Amber had been staring straight ahead, trying to get the horrible task over as quickly as she could. Now she turned. "Ben, I ran away. I made things way worse. I've hurt you and I didn't talk to Ruth Davis when I should have. If I had, maybe her horses wouldn't have been burnt. I'm sure my folks have been worried sick."

"But you said you'd gotten things straight with God."

"I did. It's amazing, but I know Christ has forgiven me. I understand that now, though I can't figure out why he would want to. That doesn't change things between us, though. You're not like me. You're sound and healthy and just plain good. Ben, I caused a child's death! You deserve someone better, more basically sound, than I am."

Amber ducked her head and silently fought her tears.

"No, Amber!" Ben said.

"Yes! I don't know why God didn't just let me leave. I wrote a letter telling you all about it and mailed it, but he made me tell you face-to-face." Now she was really crying.

Ben got out of the car and walked around to her door. Opening it, he held out his hand for hers and said, "Come, let's walk. There are some things I have to tell you, too. If you'd let me tell you before, maybe we could have avoided a lot of pain."

As they walked, he explained to Amber how for a while he'd turned away from his faith. "I didn't really rebel, but I had no deep personal commitment to Christ. Then one summer I met Jasmine Muddle and did I fall hard." Ben's voice was quiet, but Amber could tell it was costing him to tell her this.

"I think every other guy in three townships knew Jasmine had, to say the least, loose morals. But I'd been away at vet school. Maybe she liked me, or maybe she was just playing me for the fool I was. Anyway, she took care to keep me in the dark. She was into the party scene, so I came right along. Mitch and his friends were a big part of that scene. This went on for maybe a month, and I was beginning to wonder about Jasmine but not letting myself admit it. One night, partly because of that, I was drinking harder than usual, and I found her in my car in, as you might say, a compromising situation with another male."

Ben sighed. "It was only God's grace that there were people around to break up the fight. It took five of them to pull me off that guy. With the drink and the beating, I was pretty shook up. Trevor Birch, a really decent guy at heart, offered to drive me home. He'd been drinking too. On the way he plowed into a telephone pole. He died. I ended up in the hospital with a lot to think about."

When Ben finished his story, he turned to face her. "So where's the sound, healthy person who's too good for you,

Amber Lacey?" His voice was rough with emotion.

"Ben, Trevor Birch chose to drive when he'd had too much to drink. You didn't kill anyone."

"Did you kill deliberately?" Ben asked unbelievingly.

"No!"

"Were you blamed for the death by the other doctors?"

"No, they didn't blame me, but I blame myself. There was a big pileup on the interstate. I got called in in the middle of the night. There were people running, gurnies everywhere. The triage staff put me into a cubicle to deal with this cute, red-haired five-year-old, told me he had a broken leg. They'd missed an internal bleed and so did I. Ben, I didn't check the way I should have. I was treating a broken leg while Danny was bleeding to death. When I caught it, it was too late. He died on the operating table."

She turned her head away from Ben into the clean wind. For a long moment she stood fighting for composure and watching the wind sweep across the grass. Still facing away from him she said, "I couldn't stand myself. I couldn't face Danny's parents, or mine, or my friends. I was afraid to be a doctor. I ran, and you know the rest."

Ben gently turned her to face him. "Amber Lacey, God has forgiven you. How could I do less?"

"Just because you've forgiven me doesn't mean you want to be around me."

"Don't you want me?"

"Oh, Ben!" Amber gasped. "How could you think that? I love you so much it aches."

Ben tipped Amber's head gently so he could look into her eyes. "Amber Lacey, I love you with all my heart. Will you be my wife?"

Amber stepped back, tripped on the grass, and nearly fell.

She gasped. "That's nuts, Ben, you don't know anything about me. You don't know my family. You don't know where I grew up, or why I want to be a doctor. You can't mean it."

"I know enough. I know you're a woman who knows God's love and forgiveness. I know you're beautiful and brave and totally amazing, Amber Lacey. I'd be proud to be married to a medical doctor. Will you make your life with me?"

Ben theatrically got to his knees. Amber laughed breathlessly at his antics and tried to tease back. "Do they need a family doctor where you come from, sir?" she asked in a voice that was unsteady with tears.

"I do," Ben said solemnly as if he were at the marriage service already.

"Ben, all teasing aside, I've still got to go back and get into a residency. I can't stay here."

"I'm not teasing," Ben said, getting to his feet and taking her hands. "I know you have to go take care of things. That makes sense, but they need rural doctors in Alberta desperately. You could check into doing your residency near here."

"I don't know. I promised I'd do what God wants now, no matter what."

"That's what I want too, more than anything and for both of us. I know we have a lot of learning and talking to do. I'd love to meet your family. In all seriousness, I think both of us working together could make a real impact for God in this community or any other where he chooses to send us. Amber Lacey, at the proper time, will you be my wife?"

Through the tremendous surge of happiness that swept through Amber she managed to whisper, "Yes, Ben, with great joy."

This time when he took her into his arms, Amber responded

with all her heart. There was nothing left to fear. Together, with God's help, she and Ben would face the future.

Dear Reader,

Last winter was a dark time for me. Nothing terrible happened, but somehow I felt very alone. I began to doubt God's goodness and to trust him less. Like Amber, I questioned his love for me.

In searching God's Word, the eighth chapter of Romans came to mean a lot to me. It starts with the pain of the consequences of sin, then goes on to promise that God won't abandon us. He'll use whatever happens for the good of those who love him. The chapter ends with the tremendous reassurance that nothing can separate us from God's love.

Chip, Amber's horse in this book, is based on a real animal I trained last summer. The things I'm learning about trusting God reminded me of Chip. At first he was frightened of everything. As he began to trust me, he would hesitantly let me ride him past flapping flags or over unfamiliar jumps. By the end of the summer, he was moving into unfamiliar situations with confidence.

For me, books are fun, a way to escape and enjoy another world for a while. I hope this book leaves you refreshed and encouraged to trust God no matter what circumstances you're going through.

Write to Karen Rispin
c/o Palisades
P.O. Box 1720
Sisters, Oregon 97759

THE PALISADES LINE

Look for these new releases at your local bookstore. If the title you seek is not in stock, the store may order you a copy using the ISBN listed.

***Dalton's Dilemma*, Lynn Bulock**
ISBN 1-57673-238-X
Lacey Robbins, single mother of her sister's four children, is seeking adventure. But she never expected to find it by running into—literally!—handsome Jack Dalton at the roller rink. And she never expected the attraction between them to change her life forever....

***Heartland Skies*, Melody Carlson**
ISBN 1-57673-264-9
Jayne Morgan moves to the small town of Paradise with the prospect of marriage, a new job, and plenty of horses to ride. But when her fiancé dumps her, she's left with loose ends. Then she wins a horse in a raffle, and the handsome rancher who boards her horse makes things look decidedly better.

***Shades of Light*, Melody Carlson**
ISBN 1-57673-283-5
When widow Gwen Sullivan's daughter leaves for college, she discovers she can't bear her empty nest and takes a job at an interior decorating firm. But tedious work and a fussy boss leave her wondering if she's made the right move. Then Oliver Black, a prominent businessman, solicits her services and changes her mind....

***Memories,* Peggy Darty**

ISBN 1-57673-171-5

In this sequel to *Promises,* Elizabeth Calloway is left with amnesia after witnessing a hit-and-run accident. Her husband, Michael, takes her on a vacation to Cancún so that she can relax and recover her memory. What they don't realize is that a killer is following them, hoping to wipe out Elizabeth's memory permanently....

***Spirits,* Peggy Darty (October 1998)**

ISBN 1-57673-304-1

Picking up where *Memories* left off, the Calloways take a vacation to Angel Valley to find a missing woman. They enlist the help of a local writer who is an expert in Smoky Mountain legend and uncover a strange web of folklore and spirits.

***Remembering the Roses,* Marion Duckworth**

ISBN 1-57673-236-3

Sammie Sternberg is trying to escape her memories of the man who betrayed her and ends up in a small town on the Olympic Peninsula in Washington. There she opens her dream business—an antique shop in an old Victorian—and meets a reclusive watercolor artist who helps to heal her broken heart.

***Waterfalls,* Robin Jones Gunn**

ISBN 1-57673-221-5

In a visit to Glenbrooke, Oregon, Meredith Graham meets movie star Jacob Wilde and is sure he's the one. But when Meri puts her foot in her mouth, things fall apart. Is isn't until the two of them get thrown together working on a book-and-movie project that Jacob realizes his true feelings, and this time he's the one who's starstruck.

***China Doll*, Barbara Jean Hicks**

ISBN 1-57673-262-2

Bronson Bailey is having a mid-life crisis: after years of globe-trotting in his journalism career, he's feeling restless. Georgine Nichols has also reached a turning point: after years of longing for a child, she's decided to adopt. The problem is, now she's fallen in love with Bronson, and he doesn't want a child.

***Angel in the Senate*, Kristen Johnson Ingram**

ISBN 1-57673-263-0

Newly elected senator Megan Likely heads to Washington with high hopes for making a difference in government. But accusations of election fraud, two shocking murders, and threats on her life make the Senate take a back seat. She needs to find answers, but she's not sure who she can trust anymore.

***Irish Rogue*, Annie Jones**

ISBN 1-57673-189-8

Michael Shaughnessy has paid the price for stealing a pot of gold, and now he's ready to make amends to the people he's hurt. Fiona O'Dea is number one on his list. The problem is, Fiona doesn't want to let Michael near enough to hurt her again. But before she knows it, he's taken his Irish charm and worked his way back into her life...and her heart.

***Beloved*, Debra Kastner**

ISBN 1-57673-331-9

Wanted: A part-time pastor with a full-time heart for a wedding ministry. When wedding coordinator Kate Logan places the ad for a pastor, she doesn't expect a man like Todd Jensen to apply. But she quickly learns that he's perfect for the job—and perfect for her heart.

***On Assignment*, Marilyn Kok**
ISBN 1-57673-279-7
When photographer Tessa Brooks arrives in Singapore for an assignment, she's both excited and nervous about seeing her ex-fiancé, banker Michael Lawton. Michael has mixed feelings, too: he knows he still loves Tessa, but will he ever convince her that they can get past the obstacle of their careers and make their relationship work?

***Forgotten*, Lorena McCourtney**
ISBN 1-57673-222-3
A woman wakes up in an Oregon hospital with no memory of who she is. When she's identified as Kat Cavanaugh, she returns to her home in California. As Kat struggles to recover her memory, she meets a fiancé she doesn't trust and an attractive neighbor who can't believe how she's changed. She begins to wonder if she's really Kat Cavanaugh, but if she isn't, what happened to the real Kat?

***Canyon*, Lorena McCourtney**
ISBN 1-57673-287-8
Kit Holloway and Tyler McCord are wildly in love, planning their wedding, and looking forward to a summer of whitewater rafting through the Grand Canyon. Then the actions of two people they love rip apart their relationship. Can their love survive, or will their differences prove to be too much?

***Rustlers*, Karen Rispin**
ISBN 1-57673-292-4
Amber Lacey is on the run—from her home, from her career, and from God. She ends up working on a ranch in western

Alberta and trying to keep the secrets of her past from the man she's falling in love with. But then sinister dealings on the ranch force Amber to confront the mistakes she's made—and turn back to the God who never gave up on her.

***The Key,* Gayle Roper**
ISBN 1-57673-223-1
On Kristie Matthews's first day living on an Amish farm, she gets bitten by a dog and is rushed to the emergency room by a handsome stranger. In the ER, an elderly man in the throes of a heart attack hands her a key and tells her to keep it safe. Suddenly odd accidents begin to happen to her, but no one's giving her any answers.

***The Document,* Gayle Roper (October 1998)**
ISBN 1-57673-295-9
While Cara Bentley is sorting through things after the death of her grandfather, she stumbles upon evidence that he was adopted. Determined to find her roots, she heads to Lancaster County and settles in at an Amish farm. She wants to find out who she is, but she can't help wondering: if it weren't for the money in John Bentley's will, would anyone else care about her identity?

ANTHOLOGIES

***Fools for Love,* Ball, Brooks, Jones**
ISBN 1-57673-235-5
By Karen Ball: Kitty starts pet-sitting, but when her clients turn out to be more than she can handle, she enlists help from a handsome handyman.

By Jennifer Brooks: Caleb Murphy tries to acquire a book collection from a widow, but she has one condition: he must marry her granddaughter first.

By Annie Jones: A college professor who has been burned by love vows not to be fooled twice, until her ex-fiancé shows up and ruins her plans!

***Heart's Delight*, Ball, Hicks, Noble**

ISBN 1-57673-220-7

By Karen Ball: Corie receives a Valentine's Day date from her sisters and thinks she's finally found the one…until she learns she went out with the wrong man.

By Barbara Jean Hicks: Carina and Reid are determined to break up their parents' romance, but when it looks like things are working, they have a change of heart.

By Diane Noble: Two elderly bird-watchers set aside their differences to try to save a park from disaster, but learn they've bitten off more than they can chew.

Be sure to look for any of the 1997 titles you may have missed:

***Surrender*, Lynn Bulock** (ISBN 1-57673-104-9)

Single mom Cassie Neel accepts a blind date from her children for her birthday.

***Wise Man's House*, Melody Carlson** (ISBN 1-57673-070-0)

A young widow buys her childhood dream house, and a mysterious stranger moves into her caretaker's cottage.

***Moonglow*, Peggy Darty** (ISBN 1-57673-112-X)

Tracy Kosell comes back to Moonglow, Georgia, and investigates a case with a former schoolmate, who's now a detective.

***Promises,* Peggy Darty** (ISBN 1-57673-149-9)
A Christian psychologist asks her detective husband to help her find a dangerous woman.

***Texas Tender,* Sharon Gillenwater** (ISBN 1-57673-111-1)
Shelby Nolan inherits a watermelon farm and asks the sheriff for help when two elderly men begin digging holes in her fields.

***Clouds,* Robin Jones Gunn** (ISBN 1-57673-113-8)
Flight attendant Shelly Graham runs into her old boyfriend, Jonathan Renfield, and learns he's engaged.

***Sunsets,* Robin Jones Gunn** (ISBN 1-57673-103-0)
Alissa Benson has a run-in at work with Brad Phillips, and is more than a little upset when she finds out he's her neighbor!

***Snow Swan,* Barbara Jean Hicks** (ISBN 1-57673-107-3)
Toni, an unwed mother and a recovering alcoholic, falls in love for the first time. But if Clark finds out the truth about her past, will he still love her?

***Irish Eyes,* Annie Jones** (ISBN 1-57673-108-1)
Julia Reed gets drawn into a crime involving a pot of gold and has her life turned upside-down by Interpol agent Cameron O'Dea.

***Father by Faith,* Annie Jones** (ISBN 1-57673-117-0)
Nina Jackson buys a dude ranch and hires cowboy Clint Cooper as her foreman, but her son, Alex, thinks Clint is his new daddy!

Stardust, **Shari MacDonald** (ISBN 1-57673-109-X)
Gillian Spencer gets her dream assignment but is shocked to learn she must work with Maxwell Bishop, who once broke her heart.

Kingdom Come, **Amanda MacLean** (ISBN 1-57673-120-0)
Ivy Rose Clayborne, M.D., pairs up with the grandson of the coal baron to fight the mining company that is ravaging her town.

Dear Silver, **Lorena McCourtney** (ISBN 1-57673-110-3)
When Silver Sinclair receives a letter from Chris Bentley ending their relationship, she's shocked, since she's never met the man!

Enough! **Gayle Roper** (ISBN 1-57673-185-5)
When Molly Gregory gets fed up with her three teenaged children, she announces that she's going on strike.

A Mother's Love, **Bergren, Colson, MacLean**
(ISBN 1-57673-106-5)
Three heartwarming stories share the joy of a mother's love.

Silver Bells, **Bergren, Krause, MacDonald**
(ISBN 1-57673-119-7)
Three novellas focus on romance during Christmastime.